SHIFT

Also by Jeri Smith-Ready

Shade

SHIFT

JERI SMITH-READY

SIMON AND SCHUSTER

A simon pulse book

First published in Great Britain in 2011 by Simon & Schuster UK Ltd,
1st Floor, 222 Gray's Inn Road, London WC1X 8HB
A CBS COMPANY

Published in the USA in 2011 by Simon Pulse,
an imprint of Simon & Schuster Children's Division, New York.

Simon Pulse, and colophon are registered trademarks of
Simon & Schuster UK Ltd.

A CIP catalogue record for this book is available from the British Library

ISBN 978-0-85707-186-6

10 9 8 7 6 5 4 3 2 1

This book is a work of fiction. Names, characters, places and incidents
are either a product of the author's imagination or are used fictitiously.
Any resemblance to actual people living or dead,
events or locales is entirely coincidental.

Printed in the UK by CPI Cox & Wyman, Reading, Berkshire RG1 8EX

To those who make music.
Many books—many lives—would be impossible
without you.

Acknowledgments

First, as always, a giant thanks to my eternally patient and supportive family and friends. By now it must feel like I live on Mars, we see each other so seldom. I miss you!

To my "first readers": Patrice Michelle, Jana Oliver, Cecilia Ready, and Rob Staeger, whose insights helped me find *Shift*'s story buried in the rubble of a rough draft.

To my "second readers": Sya Bruce, who helped me groom Zachary into a proper Scotsman (and taught me my new favorite word); and Terri Prizzi, for helping me groom Logan into a proper, um, non-jerk.

To my Street Team, especially Street Team leader Stacey Cross, for spreading the *Shade* love. To all the readers who wrote to me about *Shade*, especially Karen Alderman, Carrie Clevenger, and Jennzah Cresswell for their music suggestions. Inspiration goes both ways.

To the staggeringly fabulous folks at Simon Pulse—Bethany Buck, Mara Anastas, Jennifer Klonsky, Katherine Devendorf, Anna McKean, Paul Crichton, Lucille Rettino, Carolyn Swerdloff, Cara Petrus, Mary Marotta, Christina Pecorale, Jim Conlin, Victor Iannone,

Teresa Brumm, Mary Faria, Venessa Williams, and Laura Antonacci; plus a shout across the pond to Kathryn McKenna and Lydia Barram in the Pulse UK office. Having this talented and enthusiastic team at my back has made my job a joy.

To my intrepid agent, Ginger Clark, for clearing my brain of the messy business gunk so I can focus on writing. As years go by, I feel prouder and luckier (not to mention smarter) for having her on my side.

To the hardest-working YA editor on the planet, Annette Pollert, for humoring and even embracing my belief that perfectionism is not a disease (because then it would be called "perfectionitis"). Her daily heroics would exhaust Han Solo *and* Indiana Jones.

Thanks most of all to my husband, Christian, for his love and patience, and for giving me the Big Answer that one day during lunch. You believe in me enough for both of us.

The course of true love never did run smooth; . . .

The jaws of darkness do devour it up:

So quick bright things come to confusion.

—Shakespeare, *A Midsummer Night's Dream*

Chapter One

I held my breath as it began, the last verse of the last song. Logan's last playlist.

He'd left behind four years' worth of musical messages. Like the ballad mix, *Missing the Shit out of You*, the punk/hip-hop compilation, *Songs for Breaking Stuff*, and the geek-rock study aid, *How to Not Hate Calculus*.

Some lived in the CDs stacked on my bookshelf, blue plastic jewel cases perfectly aligned. Others lived in the MP3 player crooning softly on my nightstand.

The one Logan created after he died, *Sucks to Be a Ghost (Sometimes)*, was ending now, with a hushed acoustic tune. One voice, one guitar, the way he'd played for me so many times. The song was a bonus track—an afterthought for the artist, but a thread of hope for us.

I'd played all of Logan's mixes, one each night for the last ten weeks. Waiting here at my open window, I'd listened to every note. Called his name. Watched my breath turn to steam in the bitter winter air.

They said he'd never come back. Once a soul transforms from a bright violet ghost—with all the thoughts and hopes of a living person—into a dark, raging shade, it's over.

No hanging out with humans, except to make them sick and dizzy.

No settling scores or righting wrongs.

No passing on and finding peace. Ever.

Shading is a one-way trip to hell.

But what "they" didn't know was this: Logan had already made that round-trip—from ghost to shade and back to ghost—right there in my front yard.

If he'd done it once, he could do it again. I just had to believe. And wait.

It was easy at first, when he'd been gone a day, a week, a month. I held on to the memories of his ghostly light: Logan in the confession booth, telling me how it felt to die. Logan on the witness stand, saying all he'd ever wanted was me. Logan in my bed, his violet glow illuminating my bare skin.

But as the icy winter slouched toward a slushy spring, the nightmarish memories took over. Logan sulking over my friendship with Zachary. Logan raving when I broke up with him. Logan turning shade when he tried to pass on to eternal peace.

My chest ached even now, remembering that night in the Green Derby pub. He'd said good-bye to those he loved—first with words, and then with music, singing "The Parting Glass" while his brother and sister played guitar and fiddle. The perfect finale before leaving this world forever.

But just as the golden-white light of peace pulsed within him, something went wrong. Darkness devoured Logan's form, turning him into a shade before our eyes. He fled in shame and sorrow. No one had seen him since.

I tightened my grip on the windowsill as the singer whispered his last plea, striking a final soft chord. The silence was filled by the sounds of Baltimore at midnight—the hiss of a flickering streetlight, the rustle of a breeze in the trees, the wail of a distant siren.

I had no more music to lure him. Only words.

"Logan, where are you?" I ran my thumb over the spot under the sill where he'd carved our initials. It gave me the strength to steady my voice. "I know you don't want to be like this. I know you want to come back. So please come back."

Doubt and fear began to choke me. What if he didn't want to come back, not even for me? I had to know for sure, no matter how much it hurt.

"Are you happy this way? Do you want to stay a shade? If you want me to give up on you, just say so. Show me a sign." I closed my eyes, ready to wait one last time.

A soul-shredding shriek filled my brain. I wanted to cover my ears, but couldn't pull my hands off the windowsill. I needed an anchor to keep from falling, keep my body and mind from flying apart in the face of Logan's desperate wrath.

He surged through my window—surged through *me*—in a burst

of black energy that stole my strength. I collapsed on the floor, quaking and retching.

"AURA!! I TOLD YOU NOT TO WAIT!!"

"I don't—listen—to shades." I forced out the words while I could still remember how to speak.

He screamed again, turning my world into a runaway roller coaster hurtling off its tracks. I clung to the edge of my bedroom rug, fighting to stay conscious.

As Logan keened, my mind seized on an image of him as he was five months ago, performing with his band hours before he died: his bleached-blond hair glowing in the stage lights, his sky blue eyes full of fire. My shooting star.

"You can't fool me," I spat through gritted teeth. "You burn too bright for this."

Silence fell, as if a shroud had been dropped over the entire world.

He was gone.

I squeezed my eyes shut tighter, dreading the sight of my empty room. The whirl of vertigo and the weight of sorrow pinned me to the floor. I wanted to stay there forever.

But then a glow appeared, so bright I could see it through my lids. I gasped and opened my eyes.

"Wow."

Logan's soft whisper halted my heart. I looked up, past his high-top Vans, gleaming violet in the dark.

Up past his shirt, hanging open like on the night he died.

Up into his astonished face.

"Aura, it worked!" Logan examined his violet arm like he'd never seen it before, then looked down at me. "Oh my God, are you okay?" He dropped to his knees, then reached for me the way he had a hundred times, in and after life. "Did I hurt you? Did you hit your head? Should I get help?"

I shook my head and sat up, fighting the fading dizziness. My mouth opened, but tears thickened my throat so that I couldn't say his name.

"Hey, hey, don't do that." Logan caressed my cheek with a hand only my heart could feel. "You know I hate to see you cry."

My eyes raked his ghostly form. He was back the way I remembered him—the voice, the smile, the shimmer that seemed brighter than any other ghost's.

It was really, really Logan.

My breath burst out, mixing a sob with a laugh. "I thought I'd never see you again."

"You didn't think that for a second. You believed in me." He spoke in a soft, awed whisper. "I love you."

"I love you, too." I wiped the tears soaking my face, even as new ones flowed.

"I can't believe I'm here. Let me look at you." Logan's hands shook as they carved out the space around me, as if making sure I was here, too. When his gaze returned to my face, his forehead crinkled in concern. "Aura, have you been sleeping enough?"

I rubbed my eyes, aware of the dark circles underneath. "I've been so worried." I whispered so I wouldn't wake Aunt Gina in the next room. "What happened to you?"

He let out a groan and dragged his palms over his temples.

"I don't even know where to start. My head still feels like a hurricane."

"Take your time." I patted the floor, for some reason fearing that if he didn't stay put, he'd disappear again. "Start at the beginning. Why did you turn shade?"

He sat cross-legged in front of me, shoulders sagging as if from exhaustion. "I was going to pass on that night after the trial. That was the whole point of it, right?"

"Supposedly." My aunt's law firm specializes in wrongful death cases, on the "peace through justice" theory that winning a lawsuit helps a ghost leave this world, content and satisfied.

"I felt phenomenal after we won." Logan smoothed the legs of his cargo shorts. "At peace, you know? Like I'd said everything I needed to say." He clenched the pocket seams. "But by the time we were at the Green Derby for our farewell concert, I wasn't so sure."

"Dylan told me you felt tainted." I cringed at the memory of the guilt on Logan's younger brother's face. "He blames himself for letting you try to pass on."

"No! It was my fault. I *was* tainted, from that other time I shaded, even though it was just for a few seconds. And from all the crazy shit I was still feeling—about dying, about my family's court case putting you through all that pain." He looked away. "About losing you."

I twisted a lock of my dark, wavy hair around my finger, fighting that familiar guilt. "But you seemed so happy when we said good-bye."

"I *wanted* to be happy. I wanted to let go of you and my whole life here. I guess I wasn't ready."

It hurt that he had been able to share his doubts with Dylan and not with me. Logan must have known how much I wanted to move on myself.

"If you weren't ready, why not wait?"

"I couldn't let everyone down. That huge crowd had come out to watch me find peace. And my family—I'd hurt them so bad by dying. Passing on was the only way to make it better." He put his face in his hands, fingertips creasing his cheeks. "Instead I made it worse."

I felt sick watching him relive those moments. But I had to know. "What happened?"

Logan dropped his hands and seared me with his mournful gaze. "I was almost there, Aura. I could see heaven. The door was open, the light was on, there was music so gorgeous you'd die just to hear it. And then—*bam!*" He punched a soundless fist into his palm. "The door slammed in my face. Having that light ripped away from me was like dying a hundred times in one second." He ran both hands through his hair, gripping the pale spikes. "I freaked. Ricocheted into shading, I guess. I'm so sorry."

"You're a ghost again now, that's all that matters." I fidgeted with the bottom button of my purple silk nightshirt, longing to soothe his agony with a touch. But that was still impossible. "What happened after you turned shade? Where were you all this time?"

"All what time?" He jerked his head to look around my room. "What day is it?"

"March twentieth." I checked the clock on my nightstand, which glowed 12:08 in pale blue digits. "March twenty-first."

"Holy shit, almost three months." He took a moment to absorb this. "I couldn't see day or night. All I knew was I had to stay away from the living." He pulled his bare knees to his chest, folding in on himself. "I didn't want to cause any more pain."

Logan had shown more restraint than most shades. The mere presence of those bitter spirits can debilitate anyone who sees ghosts, which includes me and everyone younger.

Even though shades were still rare—I'd seen four in my life, including Logan—they were becoming more common. And after three kids died a few years ago from a shade-induced fall from a balcony, the Department of Metaphysical Purity created a special forces unit—the Obsidian Corps. While the rest of the DMP focuses on research and technology (supposedly), the Obsidians have one mission: eradicating shades.

But since shades can't be captured or contained, the Obsidians try to prevent them by detaining "at-risk" ghosts who seem on the verge of shading. Unfortunately, detainment involves a one-way trip inside a little black box lined with obsidian to prevent the ghost's escape. A lot of innocent ghosts get captured in the process—ghosts who need help, not punishment. Not a fate I wanted for Logan.

"How did you turn back into a ghost?"

"You called me, I came," he said as if it were obvious. "You made it happen, Aura."

I squinted at him, confused. "But I've been calling you every night since you shaded."

"I couldn't hear you until a few minutes ago. There was so much noise." He put his hands to his ears. "It sounded like feedback from a million amps."

"God, it must have been torture."

"It was." His voice shook. "Hell is real, Aura. I was there, and I'm never going back."

"I won't let you." I swept my hand through his, wishing again that I could hold him close and keep him with me in this world. But he couldn't stay forever. "Can you pass on now?"

"I don't think so, not yet." He massaged the hollow of his throat. "Too many shady vibes. I've gotta make some changes. I spent my whole two and a half months as a ghost either feeling sorry for myself or trying to get attention."

"News flash—all ghosts are like that. And no wonder. You can't go anywhere you never went when you were alive. You can't even see other dead people." The extreme suckage of being a ghost is why most of them pass on right away, unless they have something—or some*one*—to stick around for. "So what else could you do?"

"I can do lots of things. Get this." Logan dropped his knees into a cross-legged position again, scooting closer in excitement. "When I was a shade, I held on to three hopes to keep my soul from ripping apart." He extended his thumb. "Number one. Remember when I said I wanted to make a difference? I can make the hugest difference, now that I've turned from a shade back to a ghost. This has never happened before, right?"

"As far as people know."

"Tons of witnesses saw me shade out at the Green Derby that night. If the world finds out it's not permanent, maybe the Obsidians will stop locking up shady ghosts and find some way to help them." He gestured between us with his thumb. "Maybe together we can figure out how."

"Sure." My stomach fluttered at the thought of another media circus. But it was time to stop forgetting the world—and time to start changing it. "By the way, they don't call them 'shady' ghosts anymore. They call them at-risk ghosts. ARGs for short."

"Since when?"

"Since you. The press totally skewered those Obsidian agents who tried to capture you."

"Good. Especially after the way they roughed up you and Dylan. Were you hurt?"

"Just some bruises." I rubbed my wrist, which had already been sprained before I'd hurled myself at the agent.

Logan cocked his head. "So I'm famous now?"

He looked way too pleased with himself, so I changed the subject. "What was your second hope?"

Logan's face lit up, literally glowing brighter. "I want to make music again."

"But Mickey and Siobhan are too old to hear ghosts." His brother and sister were eighteen—twins, in fact—born before the Shift.

"I'll sing with post-Shifters. It'll be easier to rehearse if I can communicate with my bandmates."

"What about the audience?"

"You'll hear me, and so will everyone younger than you." He grinned. "Prime market, right? We'll be the first band that was made for you guys. The labels'll be lining up to sign us."

I stared at him in disbelief. The promise of a recording label contract was what got Logan killed in the first place. To woo him into signing, the A and R rep from Warrant Records had given him cocaine, which, mixed with copious amounts of alcohol, had stopped his heart forever.

The old Logan was back, and only a little wiser. I hoped a little was enough.

"I've been writing more songs in my head," he said, "about being a ghost and a shade." His face turned smooth and solemn. "How I'd die all over again just to touch you."

He swept his ethereal hand over my solid one, and I thought I felt the motion of air against my skin. But it was just my imagination, juiced up by wishful thinking.

"Aura, you were my third reason. The only one that matters."

My lungs tightened. Logan had come back for me, but was I still in the same place? The night he shaded, I'd pressed the pause button on my life.

But with the spring thaw, I'd lurched into slow-mo: a night out clubbing with my best friend, Megan, a shopping trip with Aunt Gina. An afternoon at Zachary's intramural soccer game (I hated watching soccer, but I liked watching him, more than I wanted to admit).

Now that Logan was here again, I could hit the play button, move at the speed of life. But in which direction?

"I don't know if I can do this."

"Do what?" He kept smiling, but his voice cracked a little.

"Be with you that way." The words seemed to shred my throat on their way out. "Like before."

His smile vanished. His lips parted, then closed, then parted again. "Aura, I—" Logan stood up fast, radiating nervous energy. "I came back for *you*."

"Not just for me. You had to save yourself."

"You saved me." He pointed at me. "You had the power."

"We don't know that. Besides, you told me not to wait for you, remember?"

"Well—yeah. But that was when I was a shade. And now I'm not."

"We said good-bye before you ever shaded."

"And all this time you've been trying to get me back." He lifted his palms. "Doesn't that mean something?"

"I didn't call for you so you could be my boyfriend. I did it because you were suffering. I did it because I love you."

"But if you love me—" He took a step back, then another. "Is there someone else now? Are you with that Scottish guy?"

"I'm not with anyone. But yeah, I care about Zachary." I noticed I looked away when I said his name, just as I had once been unable to meet Zachary's eyes when I spoke the word "Logan."

"'Care about'? You care about music, you care about football, you care about freaking awesome cookies." Logan quieted. "What does that mean when it comes to him?"

"We're friends." A cold breeze swept my bare arms. My window was still open.

"And?"

"And we're going out tomorrow night." I rose on shaky legs and went to the window. "There's an ancient-astronomy exhibit opening at the Maryland Science Center."

"So it's for school," he said with relief. "That paper you're doing?"

"Our adviser got us into this special preview reception. It's kind of a big deal." I slid the window shut, my fingers almost slipping. "We're going out to dinner first."

"With your adviser."

I fastened the latch. "No."

Behind me, Logan fell so silent, I would've thought he'd disappeared if it weren't for his violet reflection in the window.

"Who's taking you to the prom?" he said finally.

"No one's asked." No one I liked, at least.

"I asked you the day after Homecoming, remember?" He came to stand beside me. "Let's go together."

The idea should've made me laugh, but instead I wanted to cry at the memory of Homecoming. We thought we had all the time in the world together. Less than a week later, he was dead.

"Ghosts can't get into my school." I turned to face him. "Ridgewood is totally BlackBoxed."

"Then we'll dance together outside. It'll be warm enough by May. Everyone'll join us, and it'll be a big—"

"Logan, you're dead."

He jerked back as if I'd slapped him. Then his face twisted into jagged lines. "You didn't mind before. You didn't mind me lying in your bed every night. You didn't mind me whispering in your ear while you touched yourself."

My breath froze in my lungs. Logan slowly covered his mouth, his eyes turning round and wide.

He staggered back. "Oh God. Aura, I'm so sorry. I can't believe I said that."

I covered my burning face with my hands. The old Logan would've never been so harsh. What had shading done to him? "That was as much for you as it was for me."

"I know, and I loved it. I loved you. I still love you so much." He stepped forward, his glow shining through the cracks between my fingers. "I know we can't have the future we wanted, but we can have now, right?"

"I can't do this anymore." My hands muffled my words. "Promise me we'll just be friends, or leave me forever."

"Fine. Friends. Whatever you want." His voice shook with fear. "You know I mean it. Ghosts can't lie. Aura, look at me."

I lowered my hands. Logan was leaning over, eyes level with mine. With his shirt fallen open, I could see the planes of his violet chest— and my name tattooed over his heart. It would be there forever.

"Promise me," I said.

"Better yet." He lifted his left hand, palm down, fingers spread. "Spider-swear."

I finally laughed. We'd invented the secret handshake, as serious as a blood oath, when we were six years old. Spider-swear had never been broken.

I spread my own fingers and slid them between his. We folded our palms down, extended our thumbs for the spider's antennas, and wiggled our fingers for the eight legs.

"Spider-swear," we said together, eyes locked, as solemnly as when we were kids.

A sudden heat gripped my hand. I ripped my gaze from his face, to the place where we had joined.

Logan's whisper cut the shocked silence. "Whoa."

My mouth opened but no sound came out. *Impossible.*

I could feel him.

A warm palm pressed against mine, the webbing of our fingers locked together. It couldn't be real.

"Don't move," he breathed, softer than ever. Logan slowly wrapped his fingers around my hand.

Tears spilled down my cheeks as I realized it had to be a dream. Logan hadn't come back to me. He was still a shade, roaming the world alone, poisoning post-Shifters with his bitterness.

He was still in hell.

I closed my eyes. "I don't want to wake up. Please, God, don't make me wake up."

A gentle hand touched my face. I flinched away, expecting Aunt Gina, who would shake me out of sleep and offer comfort food.

The hand touched my cheek again. It wasn't soft and cool like Gina's. It was warm, with calloused fingertips like those of . . .

. . . a guitar player.

"Aura," Logan whispered, "it's not a dream."

I opened my eyes. He was touching my face.

Logan. Touching.

My other hand brushed aside the edge of his soft cotton shirt and met the smooth flesh of his chest. Flesh that was no longer violet, but instead looked as it had when he was alive.

My heart pounded when its counterpart thumped beneath his skin. "How?"

"I don't care," he said, and kissed me.

Chapter Two

I kept praying.

I prayed while Logan locked the door and marveled that he could touch a solid object.

I prayed while he picked me up and carried me to the bed, like he had before he died.

I prayed while he kissed and touched me, urgent but deliberate, as if memorizing my taste and feel, as if *I* were the one who could disappear any moment.

I prayed this wasn't some massive cosmic joke.

As I peeled off his shirt, Logan gave a nervous laugh. "I've been wearing that thing for five months."

"And it doesn't even smell bad." He, on the other hand, smelled amazing. One inhale against his bare chest brought me back to October eighteenth, the night I'd last touched him. "Logan, you're alive."

"Definitely feels like it." He grabbed my hand as it reached his waistband. "Hang on."

I froze. Was he going to call me on the fact that I was pawing him like a nympho two minutes after breaking up with him?

"We don't know how long you'll be like this." My fingertips dug into the lean muscles of his lower back.

"But—did you go on the Pill while I was gone?"

I stared up at him. "Are you kidding me?"

"Look, if I'm really alive, even if it's temporary, what if I get you pregnant?"

"That's impossible."

"Ten minutes ago I turned from a shade to a ghost, which is also impossible. Then I turned from a ghost to . . . whatever I am now—and that's even more impossible. And if you get pregnant and I'm not really alive, what would the baby be? Half-ghost? Half-dead?"

I clenched my fingers around his arm. Logan, of all people, was thinking about consequences. Shading had changed him more than I thought.

"I'm not on the Pill. I don't have anything."

The corner of his mouth quirked. "I'm kinda glad you didn't need it."

"Hey, it's not like I was saving myself for the day you had a body again, so don't get excited."

"Too late." He curved his fingers around my jaw and kissed me, hard enough to turn my limbs to liquid fire.

It was easier then, just to make out. Like old times, before the do-we-or-don't-we question. Before I worried I wasn't enough for Logan. Before I worried about losing him to his groupies.

I waited for my old anxieties to come crashing in. Now that he was back—and solid—wouldn't other girls be all over him again?

Maybe. But he'd proclaimed his love for me under oath. He'd clung to thoughts of me while he was a shade. And there was that tattoo. So I wasn't worried anymore.

Not about *his* feelings.

He pulled away, just an inch. "This changes everything, right?"

Lying beside him, I soaked up the sight of his face in full color, the way I thought I'd never see it again outside of photographs.

"I never stopped loving you, Logan. I never will."

His thumb traced the edge of my lip. "Even if I become a ghost again? Or a shade?"

"I meant what I said."

"But you didn't say that you changed your mind about breaking up with me."

I pressed my palm to his stubbled cheek, wishing I could freeze time. The future meant nothing compared to this.

"Aura, I don't need an answer this second. Whatever happens . . . right now, I'm happy."

A single tear slipped out of my eye, rolling over my temple like hot wax down a candlestick. Logan caught it.

"Hey, look." He held up his wet fingertip. "I finally wiped away your tear."

I smiled despite my doubt. "Thank you."

"It's the least I can do, considering I cause most of them."

The sadness in his eyes stabbed at my heart. The twitch in his jaw twisted the knife.

I pushed him onto his back and kissed him hard, my hair falling in dark curtains around his face.

Groaning deep in his throat, Logan slid his hands down my back and over my hips—hands that were strong and solid for the first time in five months.

"Don't make us stop," I pleaded. "I don't care what happens later. I want to be with you now."

"Now," he echoed.

When our clothes were gone, Logan coaxed me back on top of him. "It'll hurt less this way. I wish I'd known that the first time. Then—"

He cut himself off, and as we stared into each other's eyes, we silently filled in the rest.

If it had hurt less the first time, then I wouldn't have made him stop. Then on his birthday he wouldn't have been so nervous and gotten so drunk, and then I wouldn't have yelled at him for almost passing out, and then he wouldn't have taken that cocaine to wake himself up for sex.

And then he never would have died.

I closed my eyes. "It doesn't matter now."

"Yeah. Let's pretend we believe that."

I kissed him softly, ready for this at last.

Suddenly my face hit the pillow, crushing my nose against the warm sheet. I turned my head and opened my eyes.

I was surrounded by violet.

I shoved myself up and saw Logan lying beneath me, but he might as well have been invisible.

"Aura, what happened?" He grasped for my arm, but his hand went right through me. He gaped at his body, which was clothed again in his baggy shorts and open shirt. "Oh God. No."

"Logan?" I clawed at him. "Logan, come back."

"I don't know how!"

I stuck out my trembling hand. "Spider-swear, like before."

He slid his fingers between mine.

"Spider-swear," we said together, but our hands passed through each other like they were made of air.

Like Logan was made of air.

"No . . ." I jammed my hands against my eyes. "Why?"

"I don't know." He rolled off the bed. "Goddamn it! God-fucking-damn it!" As he paced, the edges of his form started to darken and ripple.

"Logan!" I rushed to block his path, not that I could stop him. "Calm down or you'll shade again."

He clutched his hair. "I was alive, Aura." His voice crackled with static. "And God, you look so beautiful." He reached for me, then recoiled. His hand was shot through with black lightning.

"Logan, look at me." I waved my arms, though his shady energy made me dizzy. "Look at me!"

"I can't look at you!" He turned away and hunched over, covering his face. "I want you so much, it makes it worse."

I stood helpless as he tried to contain himself. The black streaks zipped over his body, following the lines of his muscles and bones, as if a thousand invisible knives were carving him up.

"Logan, you can fight this. Stay with me. Please."

For a moment the black lightning zoomed faster, stronger. Then, just when I thought he would disintegrate, the streaks slowed and faded until he was all violet again.

A knock came at my door. "Aura, are you all right?" Aunt Gina called. "I heard you yelling."

"Shit." Logan straightened up. "I've gotta get out of here."

"No!" I grabbed my nightshirt from the floor. "If someone else sees you, they might report you to the DMP. Then the Obsidians will trap you in one of their little boxes forever."

Aunt Gina rattled the doorknob. "Are you on the phone at this hour? Why is your door locked?"

"Just a second!" I called to her as I slipped on my nightshirt, then turned to Logan. "I'll only tell her you're a ghost again, none of that other stuff."

He looked at me from the corner of his eye. "Put on some pants."

I did as he asked, for his sake as much as my aunt's. Then I opened the door.

Gina stood with her hands on her hips, her short blond waves flat on one side from bed-head.

I smoothed my own hair, hoping it wasn't too tousled.

"Logan's back."

Chapter Three

"They call them the loudest band in New York!" Megan shouted over the gut-bending bass and distorted guitars as she accelerated toward another yellow light. "Which makes them the loudest band in the world, right?"

The car hit the intersection a split second before the light turned red. "Yes!" Megan hissed, bobbing her head and pumping her fist. The section of dark red hair not pulled back into her tombstone barrette swung against her cheek.

We weren't late for school. Megan tended to drive to the tempo of her music—which was always fast. This morning it was her latest discovery, A Place to Bury Strangers. I'd laughed at the name, until I heard ten seconds of the first song and fell in love.

I closed my eyes and let the drum machine's driving beat and the singer's dreamy monotone soak my brain. They were loud, for sure, but not angry. Frustrated, maybe, even defeated.

"I'm definitely getting a copy." They seemed like the kind of band I'd listen to alone, letting the earbuds trap the noise inside my head. I'd crank up the volume until I couldn't hear my own thoughts.

"They're Mickey's new favorite band." A slow, ponderous song began, thumping out of the speakers and turning the sunny morning's mood as gray as fog. Megan lowered the volume with a few taps of her green-lacquered nails, then pulled a stick of gum from the pack on the dashboard shelf. "But I'm not sure he should be listening to this stuff right now. He's broody enough as it is. You saw him last Saturday at Black Weeds, just sitting at the bar, not dancing, barely looking at the band. Definitely not looking at me." Her voice curdled with hurt, reciting the details of their latest fight.

I frowned as I checked my makeup in the visor mirror, and not just because of the puffiness under my dark brown eyes. Megan's words reminded me of the pain Logan had brought his family. More than any of us, his older brother, Mickey, blamed himself for Logan's death, which had dumped him into a giant vat of self-hatred that threatened to drown Megan, too.

Then after Logan shaded and disappeared, it got worse for all the Keeleys. Not only had their son and brother fallen into what they considered hell—which, according to Logan, turned out to be correct—the entire tragedy had happened in public.

Megan interrupted herself to ask me, "You're coming to the gig tomorrow night, aren't you?"

"Of course." So she wouldn't see my smile, I looked out the passenger window at a hawk perched on our school's wrought-iron fence.

I was dying to blurt out the news that would turn everyone's life right side up again: Logan was back.

But until Aunt Gina made sure Logan was safe, I couldn't tell Megan, because she'd tell Mickey, whose sudden happiness would make everyone suspicious. The Keeleys would find out tomorrow night anyway, after Mickey and Siobhan's acoustic show at the Green Derby.

Gina was probably at the courthouse right now, asking a judge for Logan's order of protection against the Department of Metaphysical Purity. That way, the DMP agents—or "dumpers" as we often called them—couldn't touch him unless he was close to shading, and even then they'd have to get a warrant.

Megan took a sip from her Lollapalooza water bottle as we pulled into a parking space. "Listen to me, I'm practically hoarse from bitching about Mickey. You must be sick of it."

I gave her a sympathetic look. "Probably not as sick of it as you are."

I started to get out of the car, but a horn blasted before my door was open an inch.

"Bitch alert," I said as a sleek black BMW convertible glided into the space beside us. Becca Goldman glared past me from the driver's seat.

A surge of loathing gave me the courage to get out of the car instead of cowering like I wanted to.

"Put a leash on your friend, McConnell," Becca snapped at Megan, ignoring me. "Next time I won't honk, and you'll be missing a door."

"Try it, and you'll be missing a tooth." Megan cracked her gum in Becca's direction.

"Hmph." Becca tossed her long sable hair in a motion straight out of a shampoo commercial. Then she strutted down the walkway toward the school, followed by her three minions, Hailey Fletcher, Chelsea Barton, and Rachel Howard (Megan and I joked that Becca required her friends to have names with the same number of syllables as hers).

Maybe two minions was more accurate, I thought, as Rachel hung back instead of following the other girls. She was a senior, like them, but we'd been friends since I moved to our Charles Village neighborhood when I was two.

"Hey," she said, falling into stride with Megan and me. "I heard you and Zach are going out tonight."

"That's the plan."

"Do us all a huge favor and hook up with him? Becca thinks she still has a shot. Maybe she'll find another obsession if you mark your territory." When Megan and I laughed, she said, "Okay, that sounds totally vile. But you know what I mean."

I nodded, but the thought of having dinner with Zachary, much less, um, *marking* him, made me too nervous to answer.

Besides, I had to figure out how I felt about Logan. My gut clenched at the memory of his hands, his body—his real, solid *weight*—against me. This morning when I woke I'd almost thought it was a dream, until I found Logan pacing my living room like a stray tomcat.

We approached the Ridgewood front courtyard, where the sunlight bounced off the water burbling in the fountain. The area was full, as usual, since our school was totally BlackBoxed to keep out ghosts.

Unfortunately, the thin layers of charged obsidian in the walls also blocked cell phone signals.

At the courtyard, Rachel returned to Becca's entourage, and Megan and I went to join our friends near the fountain.

Zachary stood facing away from us at the center of the small crowd, which seemed to be passing an object around as he told them a story. As usual, he was curbing his native Glasgow accent enough to be understood. But not enough to curb the hotness.

"I stayed on the right side the entire way this time," he said. "It was a bloody miracle." His remark was met with laughter and a round of what looked like mock applause.

Jenna Michaels spotted us as we approached. "Aura, Zach has a surprise for you."

He started at the sound of my name, then grabbed a small card out of Christopher's hand and slid it into the back pocket of his own jeans.

Zachary turned to me, green eyes clouded with worry, a frown erasing his usual dimples. "Let's talk for a second, aye?" He led me to the side of the courtyard, where we sat at one end of the slate-topped stone wall.

I wondered what was wrong, and if it involved the DMP again. The agency had followed me ever since they'd figured out I was the first person born after the Shift. And Zachary? He was the last person born before.

But it was no coincidence we'd found each other. Zachary's dad, Ian, was an agent for the DMP's British counterpart, MI-X. Exactly a year before our winter solstice births, Ian and my mother each visited

Ireland's Newgrange passage tomb (an ancient megalith like Stonehenge, but older and cooler). Something cosmically huge happened the morning they were there, something that led to the Shift itself a year later. Zachary and I swore we'd be the first to know what it was.

He curled one leg onto the wall to face me straight on. "You know how you were going to fetch me at six to have dinner before the reception?" He scratched the back of his neck and the soft dark waves of hair that brushed it. "There's a bit of a change in plans."

I should have been relieved. Now that Logan was back in my life, I needed time to sort out my feelings for him and Zachary. Still, my stomach sank with disappointment.

Zachary placed a white laminated card on the wall between us. "Instead, I'll fetch *you* at six."

I grabbed his driver's license. "You passed?"

"No, I gave up and had a false one made. See, it says I'm twenty-five, so I'll save on car insurance, too."

I examined the birthday on the license—same date and year as mine. I laughed at his joke anyway. "Congratulations!"

"And our dinner destination is now a surprise, since I am in total control of our travels."

"Ooh. What should I wear?"

"I dunno." He regarded me from under long, dark lashes. "Something stunning?"

I twisted the strap of my book bag with sweaty fingers. "So is this a real date now?"

His face turned serious. "Do you want it to be?"

As I met his gaze of cautious hope, my own desire and fear

arm-wrestled for my answer. It ended in a draw, so I waffled.

"Didn't your dad say the DMP would freak out?" The First and the Last, the agency called me and Zachary. They tried to keep us apart so we couldn't—I don't know, rupture the space-time continuum or whatever. MI-X was a lot less paranoid.

"Since when do you care what the DMP thinks?" Zachary asked.

"I care if they start chasing us again like they did back in December on our first date. Our last date."

"Our only date." He took his license back and slipped it into his wallet. "It wasn't all bad, was it?"

My face heated at the memory of our one long kiss. "No. It wasn't."

"Besides, my father's doing a good job keeping them out of our lives. We'll be fine, so long as we don't do anything reckless, like dance naked in the street."

The heat spread to my neck, which I started rubbing. How could I go out with Zachary after all that had happened last night? Then again, he'd be leaving when school was out in June. He'd waited patiently for almost three months while I mourned Logan's shading, and now, just when I'd been ready to move on with my life, Logan had reappeared. Did that mean I had to keep denying my chance to be with Zachary?

"If anything," he said, "I think the DMP is losing interest in you, since there's been no sign of—you know."

I knew who he meant. "Actually," I whispered, unable to look at him, "Logan's back."

Zachary's breath caught, and he leaned closer. "As a shade or a ghost?"

"A ghost."

He went completely still and silent. I imagined the scientist in him thinking, *This is bloody incredible / it's never been done before / must theorize and investigate and solve this mystery.*

Meanwhile, the guy in him was thinking, *That fucking bastard.*

"Why now?" he said with a mix of amazement and annoyance.

"I don't know. Logan said that last night was the first time he could hear my voice." I picked at a loose slate chip on the wall beside my knee. "He said it was torture."

"Who knows about this?"

"Aunt Gina. I don't trust anyone else yet."

His voice softened. "But you trust me?"

I wanted to tell him the rest, but definitely not while we sat here in front of our friends and enemies.

"I thought together we could figure this out. Any ghost weirdness might have something to do with the Shift."

"Especially if you're involved." He nudged my knee with the toe of his sneaker. "And if you're involved, I'm involved."

A grateful smile warmed my face. I couldn't tell if he meant we were linked because of our births, our research project, or something much more. Whatever the connection, he was on my side, despite Logan's reappearance.

But would he still feel that way after he knew the whole, impossible truth? I hoped I had the guts to find out.

Chapter Four

Zachary came to my house at 5:59.

Peeking through the blinds of my bedroom window, I watched him stride down the sidewalk, his steps swift and fluid with athletic grace. He twirled his key ring around his fingers, consciously unselfconscious. Maybe he knew I was watching him.

I turned to Logan. "I gotta go."

He was sitting on my bed, arms crossed tight over his chest, as if he were literally trying to contain himself. "Thanks for not asking me to zip you up."

This was a whole new realm of awkward. I clicked on my MP3 player, nestled in its docking station. "My pre-exam playlist. Four hours of de-stress songs." A haunting acoustic tune trickled out of the speakers.

Logan breathed in deep through his nose—not that he needed to breathe, but the simulation seemed to calm him.

I tucked my phone into my tiny black silk purse. "Aunt Gina says she'll come up and say the rosary a few times."

"That's nice of her."

Gina and Logan were a lot more Catholic than I was. I didn't know any post-Shifters who followed organized religion faithfully. We knew too much about death and the afterlife to fit into any set of unchanging, centuries-old belief systems.

From the living room below, I heard Gina exclaim, "Well, look at you!" I couldn't hear Zachary's response, since unlike my aunt, he was using his inside voice.

I quickly put on my necklace, a garnet pendant my grandmom had given me that once belonged to my mother. As the silver chain slithered over my neck, I realized I had worn it for Homecoming—my last big date with Logan before he died.

I opened the bedroom door, then paused. "I'll be home by midnight."

"Whatever. I'm not your dad." Logan cringed a little. "Sorry, I didn't mean—you know what I mean."

"It's okay." I wasn't sensitive about losing my father, since I'd never known him. Only my mother knew who he was, and she'd taken that knowledge to the grave when I was three.

As I crossed the threshold, Logan said, "Who is this playing?"

"Great Lake Swimmers. You like it?"

"It's pretty." He smiled at me. "Have a good time."

"Thank you." The music was definitely working, I thought as I started to shut the door.

"Don't get laid," he added.

I pretended not to hear.

When I arrived downstairs, Zachary was standing in the living room, sporting an ivory dress shirt and a dark green tie with light green flecks that brought out his eyes.

Eyes that devoured my approach like I was a Popsicle on a hot summer day. Damn.

"Special occasion?" Aunt Gina asked him, smiling so hard I thought her jaw would cramp. "You two are awfully dressed up for a trip to the museum."

"Aura agreed to a date," Zachary said, "so that makes it special. Unusual, at least."

"Well, with any luck, it won't be special for long." She cleared her throat and swept aside her blond bangs. "Unusual, I mean. It won't be unusual for long." She grabbed my wrap off the dining room chair. "Maybe you should go before I make more of an idiot of myself."

"Oh, you couldn't do that." I kissed her cheek. "Bye!"

I was at the door before realizing Zachary wasn't right behind me. I turned, then followed his incredulous gaze into the dining room.

On the end of the buffet, in a bud vase, sat a dried rose, one of six red roses Zachary had given me in December. The only one I hadn't given back. Evidence of how much he meant to me, even after all these weeks of waiting for Logan.

I hoped the feeling was still mutual. Now that my vigil was over, I was ready to think about moving on. Slowly.

Outside on my row home's covered porch, I tried to put on my wrap against the chilly breeze, but it got tangled around my arm and the strap of my purse.

"Here." Zachary rescued the wrap, then, facing me straight on, draped it over my shoulders. His fingers brushed my upper arms as he drew it forward. "Is this right?"

I gazed up at his face, golden on one side from the porch light, and silver on the other from the fading dusk. "Uh-huh," I stammered, then remembered to close my mouth.

"You, er . . ." Zachary let go of the wrap and took half a step back. "You look pure gorgeous." Then he leaned in and softly kissed my cheek.

Before I could mumble a feeble, "Thanks, you too," he offered me his arm. As we descended the porch stairs, I held the railing with my other hand to steady myself. *Maybe it's too cold—and my head's too swimmy—for these strappy heels.* But the shoes were a perfect match for my black-and-white knee-length crinkle dress, the one I'd been saving for—well, this.

As we moved toward the low iron gate separating our front path from the sidewalk, I resisted the urge to look back at my bedroom window. Just imagining Logan's violet glow behind the closed blinds was bad enough.

Zachary had found a primo spot on my street only half a block up, and his parallel parking job wasn't too tragic. Not that parking a Mini Cooper took a lot of finesse.

"Cute car," I said.

"It's no' cute, it's cool." He opened the hunter green door. "My dad says it makes him feel like James Bond."

"It does kind of look like—oh!" I yelped when the front seat turned out to be lower than I'd expected. Hiding my grimace of embarrassment, I pulled my wrap out of the way so Zachary could close the door.

As he rounded the front, I fastened my seat belt, noting the oversize speedometer and backlit armrests.

To my surprise, Zachary's long legs had no trouble fitting under the dash. He flashed me a quick smile as he put on his own seat belt.

"Definitely cute," I said under my breath.

"Sorry?"

"Nothing. Just admiring the"—I flailed my hand in his general direction—"the dials."

"Don't look." He shielded the screen of the GPS with his right hand as he thumbed in the address. "It's a surprise."

A female computerized voice came from the GPS speaker. *"Empiece al sur en St. Paul Street."*

"You realize it's set on Spanish," I told him.

"Sí." He checked his side-view mirror, then the rearview, then the side-view again, before pulling onto the street.

"Isn't it hard enough to drive without translating?"

"It works opposite sides of my brain."

I slammed my hand on the dash. "Red means stop!"

"Right." He stomped on the brake pedal, barely halting before the intersection. "That's universal."

Since he seemed to have trouble simultaneously speaking and driving, I kept quiet until the GPS voice told him to *"Vire a la izquierda."*

At the next stoplight I said, "Megan uses the English guy's voice for her GPS. She says it has more authority."

Zachary snorted. "The last thing this Scotsman wants is some stuffy old Sassenach telling him where to go. You Yanks have too much love for your former oppressors."

"It's because of Monty Python. And probably the world wars."

His only response was a grunt, so I shut up again. He seemed nervous enough for both of us, so I felt calm as a sleeping cat.

Until we reached our destination in Little Italy.

"Chiapparelli's?" I ran my fingers over the chain of my garnet necklace and looked at the blue awnings flapping in the breeze.

"You were supposed to have your birthday dinner here, remember?" He put the car in park and waited for the valet. "Before the DMP ruined everything."

"It's my favorite restaurant." Which was why Logan brought me here before the Homecoming dance. Not that Zachary would know that.

He examined my face, his eyes dark and serious in the amber dashboard light. "Would you rather go somewhere else?"

The young valet was jogging toward the car. I had to decide in the next few seconds: Would I let the past keep screwing up my present and my future?

"No, it's sweet." I let go of my necklace and gave Zachary a quick kiss on the cheek. He beamed like a little boy with a carnival prize.

The valet opened my door, and I stepped onto the sidewalk. A ghost stood in the middle of the street, about fifty feet away, but before I could see whether it was a man or a woman, its violet glow winked out.

Because Zachary was out of the car. Something about him made ghosts flee on sight. Logan used to call him "Mr. Red" because to him, Zachary looked like he was wearing clothes of that color. Ghosts hate red, maybe because it's the color of life, or maybe because it's at the opposite end of the light spectrum from their own violet hue. Red isn't a foolproof repellent like the BlackBox technology's obsidian, but it helps.

No one knew about Zachary's power besides him and me, and some friend of his back in Scotland who'd been the first to notice. It's why he hung out almost exclusively with members of our school's senior class, who couldn't see ghosts and therefore wouldn't notice he was scaring them off.

The hostess showed us to a candlelit table for two by the window. When she left us, I told Zachary in a low voice, "At least with you I don't have to sit in the back room where it's all bright and non-ghosty."

He leaned in closer. "I hope someday you realize, that's no' the best part of being around me."

The memory of the best part stole my speech as my gaze lingered on his lips. If I were his girlfriend, I could kiss him right now. Brush his mouth with mine and make him sigh my name, make our finger-tips tingle in anticipation of being alone together.

But how could what happened with Logan last night not change how I felt with Zachary?

Megan might say it was because what I had with Zachary was real, not just a lost dream. I couldn't deny that something lived between us. Something that had been simmering for months.

Zachary cleared his throat. "So Logan's back."

I opened my mouth to explain, then shut it again. After thinking about it all day, I still didn't know where to start.

"Aura, I'm your friend first, so you can tell me everything." He drummed his fingertips on the menu. "But hurry up and get it over with, aye?"

"I'll try." I slowly unrolled the cloth napkin from around my silverware. "I'd been calling for him every night since he shaded. I played all the mix CDs and playlists he made. Last night I ran out of music, so I just called. That's when he came."

"As a ghost?"

"No. He zorched through the window as a shade." I rubbed my forehead, remembering how my brain seemed to slosh out my ears. "Then I guess I talked him down, and there he was, all violet again."

"Amazing." Zachary was listening close, chin on his hand. For now, the fascinated scientist was in charge. "So you think it was the music keeping him away?"

"I don't know what made last night different. Except—I told Logan to give me a sign if he wanted to stay that way. I thought maybe he was happier being a shade, and if he was, I was ready to let go. Maybe he was trying to prove me wrong."

Zachary's brows lowered. "Or maybe he knew you were slipping away from him. I mean, if you were."

"I was." *Maybe I still am.* Being with Zachary, even just as friends and research partners, made me feel at home in the world. Like I might not be crazy for wanting to dig deeper, find bigger truths. About the Shift, about life and death. About us.

"Where is he now?"

I swiped my hand over my neck, adjusting the garnet pendant. "At my house."

Zachary sat up straight. "Was he—when I came in—"

"He was upstairs. Sulking."

"In your room." When I nodded, he added, "And he'll be there when you get home."

"Our house was the only safe place for him to hide while Gina got his order of protection. Out in the world someone might recognize him. He can't go to his family, because they moved somewhere he's never been, and besides, their house is totally BlackBoxed." They'd needed it, since shades can go anywhere, and they could afford it, after winning the lawsuit against Warrant Records. "It's just for one more day. Tomorrow we're going public, and then he'll be safe from the DMP."

"So where will he sleep tonight?"

"Ghosts don't sleep. You know that."

"Where will he be while *you* sleep?"

"Downstairs again. Zach, you said I could tell you anything."

"Right. Right." He rubbed the side of his face, as if to wipe away evidence of his feelings. "Maybe we should eat first. Dole out the truth in wee digestible bits." He lifted the menu. "So what's good here?"

Zachary ordered one of the homemade pasta dishes I recommended, something Logan never did. Not that I was comparing them. Even when Zachary spent most of the dinner conversation asking about me instead of talking about himself, I didn't compare them.

And when I went to the ladies' room, it was the hot pepper in the penne arrabiata that made me sniffle and need to blow my nose with toilet paper. Not memories of Homecoming dinner. Not seeing "our" table, the one Logan had reserved because it sat under a light bright enough to blot out ghosts. Not remembering how Logan's hair had gleamed in that golden light.

I returned to the table, dry eyed and dry nosed. Zachary stood to push in my chair, wearing an excited smile.

"What's up?" I sat and picked up my fork, then realized I had no appetite for the rest of my pasta.

"I was sitting here thinking." He returned to his own seat, smoothing his tie to keep it out of his food. "What could be the same about last night and that other night—you said Logan had become a shade once before but turned right back to a ghost."

"On my birthday." Logan's jealousy—combined with an obsidian necklace my aunt had given me and the red sheets she'd put on my bed—had driven him over the edge.

"*Our* birthday," Zachary corrected. "The first day of winter. The solstice."

"Usually." Memories of that night would always haunt me. Logan's shady energy had made me so dizzy, I fell off the roof of my porch, where I'd been sitting while we argued. Right before I blacked out, Logan came to my side, as a ghost again, brought back by his love for me and fear for my life.

"Aura, listen." Zachary's urgent voice caught my attention. "Last night was the beginning of spring. The equinox."

I gaped at him. "So Logan un-shaded on both the solstice and the equinox. That can't be a coincidence. How come I didn't think of that before?"

"You were probably a bit distracted by his return. So was I, until you left the room and I could think straight about it."

Maybe we were finally getting closer to the truth. I smacked the edge of the table. "Zach, this totally fits with our research, all the stuff about Newgrange."

He pulled out his phone and started a web browser. "We can check the exact times of the last solstice and equinox right now. Should we tell Professor Harris when we see her tonight?"

"Not yet. Listen, there's something else." I paused, wishing I could lock up the words before they escaped. "Remember you wouldn't let me tell you everything until we ate?"

He slowly set down his phone. "What did I miss?" His voice dripped with dread.

"Last night was different from December twenty-first in one major way." I looked down at my lap, dismayed to see a splotch of tomato sauce on my dress. "Logan didn't just turn back to a ghost."

"Would you like this wrapped up?"

I started at the sound of the waiter's voice. "Um, yeah. Thanks."

"Dessert or coffee for either of you?"

I shook my head.

"Just the bill, please," Zachary said.

"Right away, sir." As the waiter reached for my plate, Zachary's eyes widened.

"No!" he said. "Just bring the box."

"He's here. Might as well let him take it." I lifted the plate to the waiter, then gasped.

On the table lay a note, slipped under my plate while I was in the restroom: *Want to go to the prom? (With me?)*

The waiter chuckled. "I think that's my cue to bring the check."

"No hurry." Zachary watched the waiter depart, then turned back to me. "Well, that could have been better timing. What were you about to say?"

I lifted the note. "I was about to say yes."

"Really?"

I mirrored his grin. "Is that so hard to believe?"

"Some days, yeah." He grabbed his phone. "Where do you want to go for dinner? We should make reservations right now. Should we come back here or try somewhere new? No, we should try somewhere new. This probably isn't formal enough, is it? What do you think?"

I stammered in the face of his sudden enthusiasm. Zachary had always played it so cool. Cool didn't scare me. I was cool with cool.

"I know where we'll go," he said, before I could reply. "The restaurant on top of that hotel. You know which one I mean? On Charles Street?" He thumbed through a listing on his phone. "Or is it Mount Vernon Place?"

"Wait, slow down."

"The view must be stunning," he said, his words trampling mine. "And after, I thought a late-night cruise along the Chesapeake Bay. I hear it's—"

"Zach, time-out. We don't have to make all our plans this second."

"Of course we do. If we want the best places, we have to reserve early. Everyone says so."

"But—" I wiped my forehead, suddenly hot. My mind was still spinning from our talk of Logan and the equinox. Compared to that, the prom seemed distant and insignificant. "I can't think that far ahead right now. Can we just—"

"You don't have to think. I'll take care of it all. It'll be a surprise."

A surprise, like bringing me to the restaurant I last ate at with my dead boyfriend.

Backed into a corner, I blurted, "Does it have to be just the two of us?"

Zachary gave me a blank look. "Isn't that the way it's done?"

"Sometimes." As I spoke, I folded his note lengthwise, then lengthwise again. "I thought maybe we'd all go as a group. Megan and Mickey, Siobhan and Connor."

"You want me to go to the prom with the Keeleys." He said it as a statement, which made it sound ridiculous.

"They're my friends. Megan's your friend."

Zachary went completely still. He stared at the note, which I'd folded into a thin strip. "What were you going to tell me before the waiter came? Something about Logan?"

"The prom issue has nothing to do with him."

"Doesn't it?" His voice was low and vulnerable, and it ripped my heart in half.

"Last night, he didn't just change from a shade to a ghost. He changed from a ghost to a—an I-don't-know-what." I looked Zachary in the eye—I owed him that much. "He was human again. In full color. Solid. For at least fifteen minutes."

Zachary's face froze. "Solid."

"Yeah."

"He was—he was solid. Solid." Zachary seemed to be testing the word, as if it were in a foreign language.

"Solid, like a person."

His face stayed rigid even as he started to blink rapidly. "Solid."

"You don't believe me?"

"You must have been dreaming."

"No, this was real. Logan remembers it, too."

"Then *he* was dreaming, or he was lying to you."

My voice rose. "Ghosts can't lie."

"You know what else they can't do?" he hissed. "Become solid."

I felt a surge of indignation. "Since you know everything, then explain how my lips got sore. How did I get stubble burn on my face and my—" I stopped when I saw his eyes, then covered my mouth. "I'm sorry. I'm so sorry." I dropped my hand. "But I need you to believe me."

Zachary sat back in his chair. Then he pressed the bowl of his spoon, making the handle flip up again and again as he gathered his thoughts.

"What were you doing when he changed?" His voice had chilled, like a police interrogator's.

"Spider-swear," I said.

He looked up from the spoon. "Spider-swear?"

"It's a thing we did when we were kids, to promise something." I folded my hands to demonstrate. "Our fingers make the legs, and our thumbs are the antennas."

"The what?"

"Antennas. Antennae, whatever. The things that stick out of their heads." I wiggled my thumbs.

Zachary opened his mouth, then shut it again.

I remembered the most important detail. "Oh! I was making Logan promise to just be my friend."

Zachary's left eyebrow twitched. "But then he became solid, and then your lips got sore. So clearly he didn't keep the promise."

"No." I let my hands fall apart. "I didn't call him on it at the time."

"Because everything changed, once he had a body."

Did it? That was the billion-dollar question. If in another three months I could touch Logan again, if only for a short time, would I let that possibility keep me from getting serious with Zachary?

I had no billion-dollar answer. Not yet.

"At that moment," I said carefully, "yes, it did change everything."

Zachary slid his fingers over the crease in the tablecloth, flattening it again and again. "What were you doing when he changed back to a ghost?"

I laid my hands on the table, wishing I could crawl under it. "We were about to make love."

"Here's your—oh, dear." The waiter, who had apparently overheard my last sentence, slid my leftovers and the check onto the table and started to slink away.

"Wait." Zachary stood, dug four twenties from his wallet, and tossed them on the bill tray. "Cheers. Keep the change."

Zachary and I didn't speak in the car. He'd reprogrammed the GPS, and when the Spanish robot lady told us to turn north toward my house instead of south toward the Science Center, I knew our night was ending early.

As I twisted Zachary's prom invitation into a pretzel-shaped knot, I searched for words that wouldn't make him feel worse. For both our sakes, I didn't want to upset him while he was driving.

My street had no parking spaces, as usual. "You could try the next block," I said, hoping we could sit and talk this out.

"I'll just let you off." He slowed as he neared my house. "I'll ring

Professor Harris and tell her we'll miss the reception."

I gathered my wrap and purse, flustered by the night's abrupt conclusion. I had to say *something*.

"How about this?" I said. "As a compromise, we could go to dinner just the two of us and then party afterward as a group."

He stopped the car with a sudden brake, jolting my body forward against the seat belt. Then he looked at me, turning only his head, not his body. "Sorry?"

"For the prom."

He spoke evenly. "Aura, I'm no' taking you to the prom."

My stomach somersaulted. "But you asked me. You can't un-ask me."

"I just did." Zachary set his wrists atop the steering wheel, fists clenched, arms rigid. "All the way home I've been thinking about this game we've been playing."

"Game?"

"Becca chases me. I chase you. I'm starting to wonder, am I running in the wrong direction?"

My chest tightened. He had to be bluffing. "Are you . . . you're going to ask Becca to the prom?"

"It's none of your business."

I fumbled for a reply, my tongue suddenly parched. "She'll say no. You're a junior."

"It's a junior-senior prom, aye?"

"Yeah, but she wants to be prom queen. Only seniors can be prom king and queen. You can't be king."

His voice flattened. "Then I'll be her prince consort."

He wasn't bluffing. He'd had enough.

"And by the way?" he said. "Spiders don't have antennae. The bits sticking out of their heads are the chelicerae."

"The what?"

"They use them to stab their prey with poison." He spat out the last word.

"No, they're antennas, because they—" I thought of the Harry Potter movie with the giant spider, imagining the ferocious pincers next to its mouth. "Crap, you're right. Now I feel stupid. Happy?"

He stared out the windshield. "Not at all."

The chill in his voice filled me with panic. "Zach, we'll do it your way. We'll go to the prom alone. You've been so good to me, you deserve it."

"I *deserve* it?" He leaned across me and opened the passenger door. "Get out."

"But—"

"I'm not a dog to throw bones to."

"I didn't mean it that way!"

"Yes. You did." The louder his voice got, the more it shook. "I've sat in the corner, being a good boy, waiting for my master to notice me."

"It's not like that."

"You're bloody right it's not like that." He turned to face the front again. "Not anymore."

A horn honked behind us. I climbed out of the seat. "I'll call you."

Zachary zoomed off, the car's momentum slamming the passenger door shut. The woman driving behind him glared at me as she sped past. I looked away, my conscience too shattered to give her any attitude in return.

My feet felt like lead as I climbed the front stairs. Halfway up, I realized I'd left my leftover penne in Zachary's car. I wondered if he'd eat it or hurl it into his apartment building's trash chute.

"Excuse me," said a voice to my right.

I turned to see a young woman's ghost loitering on our next-door neighbor's porch. She wore what looked like a thigh-length wedding gown with a veil that fell only to her shoulders. Ghosts' appearances are captured in the happiest moment of their lives, so there was no telling how old she'd been when she died. But the 1960s had clearly been her high point.

"Looking for someone?" I asked her.

"My husband. We lived here until 1978. He passed away in '99." She peered through my neighbor's living room window. "I died just last week. My name's Alice, by the way."

"Hi. I'm sorry, but ghosts can't see each other." She should know that, but pre-Shifters never listened to us.

"I thought we'd be the exception," ex-Alice said. "We were soul mates."

I forced a tight smile. Must be nice to believe in such things. "I've never seen a ghost at this house. How do you know your husband hasn't passed on?"

"My granddaughter saw him last month again, at our cabin at Deep Creek Lake."

I stepped up to the painted blue railing separating the two porches. "Maybe if you pass on, he'll follow you. Maybe he's been waiting for you to join him."

"Oh." She brushed her veil off her cheek. "You could be right. I'll just check a few more places."

"You can't see him in this world."

"I have to try." She started to turn away, then stopped. "Thank you for your help. You seem like a nice girl." Ex-Alice vanished.

"No," I told the empty space she left behind. "I'm an asshole."

I knocked softly on my bedroom door, which made me feel like a stranger.

"Come in," Logan and Gina said.

I opened the door to find them kneeling in front of my aunt's Saint Peter's altar, which she'd moved from downstairs. All three pillar candles were lit, and a rosary dangled from her hand.

"Hi, hon." Aunt Gina beamed up at me. "You're home early."

"Hot date turn cold?" Logan said.

I set down my purse. "How are you guys doing?"

"He's here? Thank God." Gina crossed herself as she got up, her knees cracking. "Glad I wasn't wasting my breath." She glanced at the ceiling. "Not that prayer is ever a waste."

I pointed to Logan. "He was right next to you."

Instead of freaking out like most pre-Shifters would, she gave a satisfied smile. Before the Shift, Gina was one of the rare people who could see ghosts. I had a feeling she missed those days sometimes.

"I'm going to get some cereal and catch up on paperwork." She kissed my cheek. "Logan can stay for a few minutes, but then he goes downstairs—*before* you change your clothes."

Grimacing, I shut the door behind her, then went to my dresser.

"What's wrong?" Logan said.

I opened my blue star-shaped keepsake box and placed Zachary's knotted prom invitation inside. "I don't want to talk about it." I replaced the glass lid, which now sat askew.

"If it has to do with Bagpipes, I don't want to talk about it either."

I sat on my bed, exhausted from the fight with Zachary. "He might be able to help us."

Logan sat beside me. "How?"

He seemed so calm. I wondered if his demeanor was from the praying or just having Gina with him. Knowing someone cared. Guilt tugged at me for leaving to go on a date.

He listened, eyes bugging now and then, as I explained Zachary's theory about the solstice and equinox.

"But if that's right," he said, "why hasn't it happened before? You'd think someone would have noticed by now that ghosts were popping in and out of shadedom on those days, or getting their bodies again." He laid his hand over mine. "Hey, maybe we're a special case because of our connection."

I returned his hopeful smile. "Maybe. But there's a lot that people don't know about ghosts. Maybe this happened before but wasn't reported, or no one believed it."

"Or someone kept it secret, like the DMP." Logan looked at the *Starry Night* poster on my wall. "That's new. Where'd you get it?"

I figured one more truth couldn't make this night any worse. "Zachary gave it to me. His dad took him to New York to see the Van Gogh exhibit." I didn't mention that Zachary apparently had a matching poster in his own bedroom, which I'd never seen.

"Ah." Logan clenched his hands together in his lap. "Good colors, at least."

"That's why it's there." The painting's violets, blues, and blacks were the most soothing for a ghost. I'd rid my room of red while Logan was a shade, to make it easier for him to return.

"Speaking of stars," I said, "our research project might help us figure out your solstice-equinox issue."

"The stargazing thing?"

"That's the busywork part." I held back a groan as I realized Zachary and I had our next sky-mapping session on Wednesday. At least we'd finish our work fast, since we wouldn't be wasting time flirting—or talking, for that matter.

I started to explain the rest of our project, but Logan wasn't listening. He had that same look he had when he was getting an idea for a song. As if something was speaking to him from another world, and if he held absolutely still for another second, the right words or tune would reveal themselves.

I waited for him to notice I'd stopped talking.

"Aura," he said slowly. "Do you realize what this means? If I can change on the solstice and equinox, then maybe in three more months, I could have a body again."

"Maybe." I wasn't sure if I wanted that for him. To be corporeal for a mere fifteen minutes almost seemed worse than not at all.

"And oh my God, think about it!" Logan leaped to his feet and paced, trembling. "I changed from shade to ghost last night, and the ghostness stuck. What if next time, I turn solid and it sticks?" He stopped and turned to me. "Aura . . . I could come back to life."

The world tilted for the hundredth time in the last twenty-four hours. "Logan, that's impossible."

"We thought a lot of things were impossible." He spread his arms. "Maybe nothing is impossible."

"That's crazy talk. Dead people don't come back to life."

"There are a million examples in the Bible. Jesus, Lazarus, that dude in the chariot."

"That's not a million. Who was in a chariot?"

"Old Testament guy." He snapped his fingers without sound. "Elijah. He brought a kid back to life, I think. The point is, miracles happen. If freaky shit went on with your mom at Newgrange, then maybe there's something special about you." He angled his chin. "I mean, besides being hot and smart and generally amazing."

I rolled my eyes at his flattery. "I'm not Jesus, and neither are you."

"We don't have to be Jesus. We just have to be us."

I had a sudden urge to flip on the light, so I wouldn't see that manic hope in his eyes.

"One thing at a time." I stood and moved back to my dresser, unclasping my necklace. Luckily, he hadn't noticed it was the same one I'd worn to Homecoming. "Since I'm home early, we should talk to Gina about what to say to your family tomorrow." I opened the door of my cabinet-style jewelry box. "When they come over after Mickey and Siobhan's gig?" I prompted when he didn't answer.

I looked over my shoulder to see him facing me, the altar's candle-light shining through him from the other side.

"And then what?" He gestured to the bed. "Do you want me to stay with you tonight?"

"You were cool with staying downstairs last night."

"Last night I was a shady wreck. Now I'm totally together."

True, I hadn't seen his form crackle or shadow the entire day. But that wasn't the point.

"I can handle anything," he said, "even—you know." He slid his gaze down my body. "If you want."

I turned away, cheeks burning, gripping the edge of the dresser for support.

"Gina won't know I'm in your room." Logan's voice was closer, behind my shoulder. "Somehow you always stayed quiet." He laid his hands beside each of mine, so that if he'd been solid, I would've been pinned between his body and the dresser. "Remember?"

I closed my eyes. I'd never forget our nights of soft cries and whispered urgings. After touching Logan for real again, part of me wanted to relive those moments more than ever. At least it would be something more than nothing.

"I love you, Aura," Logan whispered. "Body or not, as long as I'm in this world, I want to be with you."

I opened my eyes to see our faces reflected in the jewelry box mirror. Mine was barely visible through the forest of necklaces, but Logan's glow shone around their edges, bright as the moon on a clear winter night.

I slid off my wrap, then reached back to unzip my dress.

My gaze fell on the overstuffed keepsake box, where Zachary's note peeked out from under the lid. Buried in the note's twists and folds was a hope for the future.

To win Zachary back would take a fight—a fight that maybe I deserved to lose. And no matter what, in three months he'd be gone across the ocean. But I had to try.

I dropped my hands. "I can't, Logan. I'm sorry. Please go downstairs."

After the span of a breath, he stepped away, gingerly, as if his violet form might shatter if he made a sudden move.

"I'll be waiting," he said, and disappeared.

Chapter Five

The last Jamaican ginger ale." I slid the green bottle ahead of me as I sat in the booth beside Dylan. "You're welcome."

Logan's younger brother intercepted the soda before it crashed into the Green Derby's appetizer menu. He made a face at the bottle's label. "They didn't have extra spicy?"

"Picky little princess," Megan sang across the table, wielding her red plastic straw like a conductor's baton before plunging it into her Coke. "Why do you guys always face away from the stage? Don't you want to see Mickey and Siobhan sing?"

Dylan and I exchanged a look. Like me, he could barely stand to be in the same room where Logan had shaded out, much less stare at the exact spot. I could only imagine what it was like for Mickey and Siobhan to play in the midst of such memories.

But their pain would end tonight. The Keeleys had agreed to

come back to our house for dessert after the show, where Gina would gently break the good news about Logan's return. Then Logan would come downstairs, so that at least Dylan, who was sixteen, could witness him in all his ghostly glory. I couldn't wait to see their faces when they realized his shady torment was over.

The pub in downtown Towson was crowded, even for a Saturday night. Mickey and Siobhan were making a name for themselves with their acoustic Irish folk act, the Keeleys (not to be confused with the Keeley Brothers, the punk band they'd shared with Logan and two friends).

"Here they come. Yay!" Megan slammed down her glass and stood to applaud twice as loud as anyone else.

I turned to see Mickey and Siobhan mount the small platform at the far end of the bar. The twins' understated entrance was a funeral march compared to the way the Keeley Brothers would explode onstage with Logan as their front man.

Siobhan gave the hooting crowd a nod and a shy wave. But Mickey might as well have been alone in the room.

They took their seats before the microphones and did a quick tuning. I looked at their parents, who sat at a nearby table with my aunt Gina. Mr. and Mrs. Keeley clutched hands across the table, white-knuckle tight, as if fearing they'd lose two more children on that stage.

Mickey pulled the mic to his lips and regarded the quieting room. The brim of his cap shadowed his eyes and pressed a wave of brown hair over his right brow. His stillness held as much power as Logan's hyperanimation.

"Good evening. We're the Keeleys, and this first one, as always, is for Logan."

Mickey closed his eyes and began to sing a cappella, clear and soft and incomprehensible, the Gaelic syllables rolling off his tongue. Siobhan joined in on the chorus, her own voice high and sweet, with a keening edge that reminded me of how she'd wailed when Logan died.

I rubbed the spot in the center of my chest that ached whenever I thought of that night. The joy of Logan's return from shade could never erase the pain of his death. I didn't dare hope, like Logan did, that the summer solstice would bring him back to life. Some things couldn't be overturned by love or hope or the blindest of faith.

On the second verse, Mickey softly strummed his guitar, and Siobhan's fiddle began to croon. The mournful strains sliced my gut. Irish ballads had a way of dredging up everything I'd ever been sad about—my parents, Logan, and now Zachary—and shoving it to the front of my mind for maximum brooding.

Across the table, Megan watched Mickey with glistening eyes. Beside me, Dylan shifted his ginger ale in an imaginary square, the cardboard coaster stuck to the bottle. A clump of straight brown hair swooped over his temple, obscuring his eyes. I stirred the ice in my Diet Coke and wished for a stronger drink.

Though the mood of the music changed as the show went on, Dylan and I stayed put—not watching, not dancing, despite Megan's pleas. I knew I could wipe away the gloom on Dylan's face with one sentence—"Your brother's a ghost again"—but it would spoil the careful plan that Logan, Gina, and I had created. I kept checking my watch and counting down the minutes until we could leave.

Siobhan and Mickey ended with "The Parting Glass," the song Logan had performed on that stage before shading. Everyone stood to toast and sing—everyone but Dylan and me.

"I wish they wouldn't play this every time," he said as he scratched the last shred of label from his ginger ale bottle.

"It's how they deal."

"They only deal with Logan through the music." He pushed the label tatters into a pile, using the side of his hand like a snowplow. "They never talk about him, not even with me."

I looked up at Megan, standing beside our booth. A corner of her mouth angled down. "Me neither," she said. "Maybe we should take up the guitar."

He smirked. "I was thinking didgeridoo."

I laughed at the image, which eased the pain of the song's last chorus. Hearing anyone but Logan sing "Good night and joy be with you all" sent an imaginary shard of glass through me.

"Oh my God," Megan squeaked. Her eyes went round as Ping-Pong balls.

I turned to the stage to see Logan sitting in the back corner, behind his brother and sister, applauding without sound.

My heart leaped at the sight of him, then sank when I realized the shit storm that was about to strike, in *three* . . .

"What's wrong?" Dylan craned his neck to look over the back of the booth.

Two . . .

"Holy fuck!" He shoved at my arm. "Aura, move. It's Logan!"

One.

Mrs. Keeley's shriek pierced the room like a microphone's feed-back. "Logan?! Where?"

"Mom, he's a ghost again!" Dylan pushed past me as I slipped out of the seat, rubbing my ears. "Logan!"

Mr. and Mrs. Keeley's chairs clattered as they lurched from their table toward the stage. They followed close behind Dylan, who was parting the crowd like a running back, elbows splayed.

The dozens of pre-Shifters started to catch on. Everyone spoke at once, louder and louder, murmuring words like "shade" and "ghost" and "impossible."

It wasn't just the wall of noise that made me want to flee the pub. Logan had thrown our entire world—*my* entire world—into chaos.

I pushed past a pair of confused onlookers to get to Gina's table.

She glared up at me. "Did you know he would show up here?"

"No, I swear! I would've tried to talk him out of it." Not that it would've worked. "How could he do this to us?"

"Us? Think about his family. He'll give his father another heart attack."

"That was the whole point of waiting until later, so they wouldn't freak out. Now everyone is freaking out."

We watched Logan give Megan and Dylan virtual high fives, while Mickey stood against the back wall, Siobhan clinging to his shirtsleeve. The eyes of the older Keeley siblings raked the stage for the brother they would never see.

"What do we do now?" I asked Gina.

She scanned the pub, worry lines creasing her forehead. "I think that you, Megan, and Dylan are the only post-Shifters here. That means we can control the message."

"Message?"

"The media are bound to arrive any minute, like they did when Logan shaded. This is an even bigger story."

"Oh God." Not more reporters. I had a lot more secrets now than I'd had at the trial. After all, I'd witnessed, maybe enabled, the world's first shade-to-ghost transformation.

Way to go, Logan. Fury rose in my throat. *If you weren't dead, I'd kill you.*

"We have to play this carefully." Gina ran her trimmed nails over the edges of her pale pink lips. "We want the world to know that shades aren't hopeless, but we don't want anyone to think you had something to do with his return."

"I didn't have anything to do with it!"

She frowned at me. "I know you didn't. Calm down."

"Okay, okay." I smoothed the sleeves of my dark green cardigan, swallowing my anger and panic. "So when the reporters grill him, I should translate, so I can censor anything he says about me."

"Exactly. I don't know how long it'll work, but hiding him now will only make people suspicious."

My brief calm evaporated. "'People'? Like the DMP? Will they try to take Logan again?" And maybe me, too, for questioning? I'd heard rumors about humans who got "dumped" and weren't seen for days.

"No one's taking Logan. I have his protective order right here." She patted her bag, tucked tight under her arm.

I gaped at her. "You knew he'd do this."

Gina arched a thin blond eyebrow. "Logan Keeley never met a spotlight he didn't love."

The pub began to play recorded music over the speakers. It was a festive song, matching the joy of the Keeleys as they hugged one another, then their friends, then total strangers.

In the center of the celebration, Logan stood with his head bowed, on the spot where he had exited and re-entered the embrace of his family, friends, and fans. He looked humbled rather than triumphant, as if he thought he might slip away again.

Then he lifted his gaze over the crowd to meet mine. In his eyes I saw an almost desperate gratitude. He'd come back for me, and maybe I'd made it possible. In his mind—and maybe in reality—I'd saved his soul.

So what did I owe him now?

"What was it like to be a shade?"

"It was hell." Logan stood beside me on the Green Derby stage and spoke to the crowd of reporters. "Like a tornado in my head. No one should have to go through that."

He paused while I translated for the pre-Shifters—everyone but Dylan, who stood off to the side with his family. He was the only Keeley I could see from here, thanks to the television crews' lights, which were bright enough to wash out Logan's violet glow.

Megan had left at Gina's request—my aunt thought it would be safer if Logan had fewer potential mouthpieces. Since I worked as a ghost-translator at Gina's law firm, no one questioned why I spoke for him.

Ryan Robertson from the eleven o'clock news said to me, "Ask him how he turned back into a ghost."

"He can hear you," I said. "So ask him yourself."

The reporter next to him smirked. Robertson scratched his head with the capped end of his ballpoint pen, then adjusted his stance. "Logan, how did you make the unprecedented transformation from a shade to a ghost?"

Everyone pressed in to hear the answer, and I resisted the urge to step back.

"I couldn't have done it without Aura," Logan said.

I angled my head, wondering where his answer was going. *If he makes this about me, I'm doomed.* He couldn't lie, but the fact that he was here, putting himself out for public consumption, endangered all my secrets.

I kept my face blank, hoping Dylan was doing the same so the reporters wouldn't know Logan had spoken.

Logan kept going. "She always believed. For eleven weeks, she called to me. She waited. She pulled me out of hell." He paused. "Aura, what are you waiting for? Tell them."

I turned to the reporters. "He says he came back for me."

They frowned, no doubt noticing my use of the third person rather than a direct translation, not to mention the difference in length between Logan's answer and my own. They knew I was leaving something out.

I added, "It was our connection that made it possible. A one-time thing. The miracle of love." I tried not to wince. Logan would never say that.

But scattered "awww's" confirmed my hope: The media were suckers for a love story. I shot him an affectionate gaze, even as my frustration with his selfishness scorched the very love I was touting. If they thought our bond had brought Logan back—which might be the case—maybe they would overlook the weirdness of my own personal history. Like my birthday.

Logan's voice came closer. "That's not what I said. Why won't you tell them what I said?"

"We'll talk later," I told him without moving my lips.

A blond reporter with a shag cut muscled her way in front of Robertson. "Logan, what are your plans? Will you try to pass on?"

"Not yet," he said. "First I need to get the word out about shady ghosts—I mean, at-risk ghosts. I'm proof that they're not hopeless, that they shouldn't be locked up in little boxes. It's fucking cruel."

I repeated his exact words, including his self-correction and pro-fanity, hoping to earn back a little cred with the reporters—not to mention my professional integrity.

Sweat trickled over my ribs, from the heat of the lights and the fear that any moment, my cover as the First would be blown.

"I also want to form a new band," Logan added, "with post-Shifters. I'm dying to make music again. Um, no pun intended."

I recited what he'd said, then realized that his new singing career would bring even more scrutiny. He'd be the subject of interviews and exposés, and sooner or later he'd let something slip. Someone would dig up my records and learn I was born at the Shift. Maybe they would arrive at the same conclusion I had: that my birth might have caused it.

My head filled with a roar of panic. I didn't even hear the next question and answer.

"Aura," Logan said. "Did you hear me? Are you okay?"

I shook my head, wanting to beg him to pass on now before he ruined everything.

"Excuse me." A tall woman with a sleek brunette twist sidled between me and the reporters. She pulled a badge out of her black pin-striped suit and displayed it to them. "I'm Nicola Hughes from the Department of Metaphysical Purity's Office of Public Affairs. Any questions for the Salvatore or Keeley families will henceforth be submitted through me."

One of the reporters raised his hand. "Why can't we—"

"I'm sorry," Nicola said, "no questions at this time." Smiling, she handed a stack of business cards to the reporter on her left. "Be a dear and pass these out? Thank you." Then she turned to me, Gina, and the Keeleys. "Believe it or not, I'm here to help."

We sat at the long wooden table in the Green Derby's private party room. Logan took his place between me and his brother Dylan on one side of the table, with the rest of their family—all pre-Shifters—lined up on the other side. I resisted the urge to move away from Logan, since the depth of my anger could raise suspicion.

Nicola stood at the door, ushering in the waiter, who paused to let his eyes adjust to the darkened room before he started serving drinks.

"This round is on me," she said. "I'm sure you all need refreshment after that episode."

Logan rested his chin on his hand, watching the waiter serve his father a pint of Guinness. He'd once told me that perpetual sobriety was one of the worst parts of being dead, ignoring the fact that it was a combination of alcohol and drugs that had killed him.

After the waiter left, Nicola shut the door. "Now." She strutted to the head of the table. "The last thing you want is more DMP bullshit, am I right? So I'll be as frank with you as I am obscure with the press."

"Hmph," Gina said to my left.

"The department suffered a public relations nightmare when Logan shaded at this bar on January third. And we deserved all the blame. The Obsidian agents who assaulted Aura and Dylan have been disciplined, but the tarnish to the department's image was significant. After all, everyone—not just post-Shifters—can see Aura and Dylan in the online videos."

Yep. Over one hundred thousand views, with five thousand comments, mostly thumbs-up for our flailing attempt to stop the Obsidian agents from locking Logan in a tiny black box.

Nicola continued. "So what better way to boost our image than to help the very ghost we're famous for persecuting?"

"Help him how?" Mrs. Keeley twisted the silver chain of her Celtic cross necklace. "The only thing he needs is to pass on."

"Until he's *ready* to pass on," Nicola said, "he needs protection from the paparazzi. The media have no regard for the privacy of ordinary citizens."

I wrinkled my nose at her hypocrisy. Still, I would do anything to protect my deepest secrets from mass consumption. As much as I wanted to resist Nicola's help, she might be just the shield I needed.

"So let's formulate a strategy," Nicola said, "to decide the nature of Logan's public persona."

"Hang on." Logan put out his hands. "Don't I get a say in it?"

I repeated his words to Nicola, who nodded vigorously.

"This will all be under his direction. If there's one thing we've learned, it's that no one tells Logan Keeley what to do."

He smiled. "Awesome. So I can form a new band?"

"He wants to form a new band," I said, "with post-Shifters."

Mickey snorted. "He's serious about that?"

Siobhan glared at her twin. "I think it sounds cool."

"It'll get attention, and that's all he cares about."

"Mickey, that's enough," Mr. Keeley growled.

I looked at Logan. His expression reminded me of a day at the Keeleys' house just after Mickey had started high school, and Logan, Megan, and I were only twelve. We were annoying Mickey, and he'd slammed his bedroom door in our faces, calling us "stupid kids." In the instant before Logan shot back a better insult, his eyes had turned as hurt as a kicked puppy's.

Nicola clapped her hands once. "A new band is a fabulous idea. It's the perfect platform to show the world, especially post-Shifters, that the DMP is ghost-friendly."

I remembered what an Obsidian agent had said last year when he warned me to make sure Logan passed on. *Recruitment is our number one priority*. In nine months, the first post-Shifters would turn eighteen. Old enough to be dumpers.

So the DMP needed to look good to young people. They would use Logan's band to advertise their own coolness.

"What'll they actually do for me?" Logan said, and I relayed his question to Nicola.

She finally looked in his direction. "We'll manage your PR, handle all your media contacts, and drum up publicity for your gigs." Her smile slid across her face, smooth as a serpent. "You make the music, and we'll make you famous."

I expected Logan to spark with his usual ambition and lust for the limelight.

Instead he seemed to fold further into himself, shrinking under the gazes of those who could never see him.

"I want to talk to Aura and Dylan," he said. "Alone."

The three of us stood on the sidewalk outside the pub, near the place where Dylan had raged and mourned Logan's shading a few months before. I wondered how long the bricks had held the bloodstains from his fists pounding the wall.

"I've got a weird feeling about this," Logan said.

I nodded. "It's too easy. But we need the DMP to protect us from the media." *And from your big mouth*, I wanted to add, but couldn't without triggering Dylan's curiosity. He must've already wondered why I'd mistranslated Logan's answer to the reporters.

The younger brother leaned against the building. "It makes sense they'd want to look better after what happened when you shaded. There was a ton of bad publicity."

"But nothing changed," I pointed out. "They still treat at-risk ghosts the same way. And by February the media got bored, so the public stopped screaming for reforms."

Logan thumbed his lip, looking pensive. "Maybe if I stay in the spotlight, people won't stop thinking about it."

Dylan chuckled. "You'd be like a poster child for at-risk ghosts."

"Is that a good thing?" I said.

"Yeah, people'll see Logan and think, 'He's not so bad. Maybe we should give them all a second chance.'"

"You believe that?" Logan asked Dylan. "I'm not so bad?"

"Of course, dipshit. You're my brother."

"I'm Mickey's brother, too. Look what that gets me."

"Mickey's a douche," Dylan said. "Just forget him."

"I can't forget him."

"Right, 'cause he's the cool brother." Dylan looked past me. "Uh-oh. Aura, don't turn around."

Of course I turned around, then quickly averted my eyes. "Oh, for God's sake."

The ghost of the naked man raised his arms. "It's not like I can put on clothes." He dodged a pedestrian, stepping closer to me.

Since ghosts are frozen in the happiest time of their lives, a lot of men appear in sports or military uniforms—or nothing at all. At least this one was wearing socks.

"What's wrong?" Logan asked his brother. "Is there another ghost here?"

"Yeah, and he's hung like a hippo."

"What? Aura, don't look."

I ignored them both. "What do you want?" I asked the man.

"Simple. I need to know the score of the Orioles-Yankees game. They were in extra innings when I had a heart attack."

"It's preseason," Dylan said. "Who cares?"

"Not tonight's game. Last year, July eighteenth. Rivera was on the mound at the bottom of the tenth."

I kept a straight face. "All this time, you haven't found anyone who could look up the score for you?"

The ghost put his hands on his hips. "It wasn't my only unfinished business. How pathetic do you think I am?"

"Sorry." I waved my hand in the direction of the city. "Try one of the big sports bars. Did you go to them during your life?"

The ghost nodded, then gazed up at the Green Derby's worn wooden sign. "I always liked this place." He disappeared.

"He's gone," I told Logan. "Where were we?"

He stared sadly at the part of the sidewalk I'd been talking to. "I wish I could see them."

I wished he could, too. If ghosts could hang out together, they'd be less lonely, and they wouldn't be so desperate for living company. Then again, they might stick around that much longer.

"Let's do this," Logan said with quiet determination. "I want my afterlife to be more than a rehash. I want it to mean something, and not just for me. But it's gotta be all on my terms, like that lady promised. No DMP recruitment commercials, just our own music and the covers we pick."

"Who's 'we'?" Dylan asked.

"My new band. Let's put an ad online. Here, I'll tell you what to say." While Dylan scrambled for his phone, Logan barreled ahead.

"'Ghost front man seeking talented, all-post-Shifter band.'" He drew his hand across the air, as if the words would be written on a movie theater marquee.

"Wait, wait." Dylan thumbed the text into his notepad function.

Logan started to pace and gesture, the old excitement returning. "Let's say, 'Preferably punk, but accept alt-rock or alt-metal. Covers, originals. Performance experience preferred.' No—'required.'"

My stomach queased as I watched Logan plan his next leap into the public eye. He'd be dragging me with him again.

Dylan spoke as he got it down. "Should I give them my cell number?"

"No, some of them might be weird. Oh! You know what'd be better?" Logan jabbed his finger at Dylan's phone. "Have them e-mail links to their clips or videos. That way we can tell if they suck, and I won't have to reject them in person." He bounced on his toes. "This'll be so cool. I bet we'll get a ton of auditions."

"E-mail them to who? Me or Aura?"

"Aura, would you—" Logan stopped short when he saw the look on my face. "Dylan, go inside. Tell them we'll be in soon."

Dylan sighed, then snapped his phone shut. "Send the kid away. What else is new?"

I watch him go, then whirled on Logan. "Thanks for remembering your new career might have a teeny effect on me."

"You don't have to be a part of this."

"Yes, I do! Everything you say to the press has to come through me. That DMP lady can keep things under control, but only I can keep you from ruining my life." I slapped my hand against the brick building. "Great start, by the way, showing up here tonight. Why didn't you warn me, or better yet, do what you were told and stay home?"

"Because I didn't—" Logan shoved his hands against his scalp. "Because I knew you'd tell me not to come." He clasped his hands behind his head. "I'm sorry for dragging you into all this shit again. Let's just forget it."

"No. This is too important, to you and all the ghosts who need help." I knew that not just any ghost could change the world. The same charm and energy that would've made Logan a rock star in life could make him a hero after death. "Besides, maybe you need to do this to pass on."

"I need to do something bigger than myself."

"Whoa, he finally admits there is such a thing. Alert the media."

"No, don't alert the media." He grinned at me. "Wouldn't want to ruin my diva reputation." When I didn't return his smile, he dropped his hands to his sides. "I really screwed up tonight, didn't I?"

"Yeah."

He stepped closer, his violet form reflecting in the pub's front window. "Can you forgive me?"

I gritted my teeth. "You know not to ask me that while I'm still mad."

"Sorry." He brushed his ethereal hand over my arm. "Do you still love me?"

"I'll always love you, Logan." I moved around him, heading for the front door. "But right now, I don't really like you."

Chapter Six

I flopped into the low seat of Zachary's Mini Cooper, collapsing under the weight of my layered clothing.

"Warm enough?" he cracked as he examined my parka and heavy gloves.

"They call it a killing frost for a reason." I noticed his hands were bare, though the car's heat was off. "It's supposed to be spring, but this is colder than it was most of the winter."

"At least the sky will be clear."

Great, we'd been reduced to talking about the weather. I pulled up my hood, far enough so I couldn't see him from the corner of my eye. As the drive passed in silence, I kept my hands folded in my lap to keep from switching on the radio. Even the Spanish-speaking GPS would've been a relief, but Zachary didn't need directions to our monthly place of work.

We didn't speak again until we got to our sky-mapping site, a small grassy strip next to a field in northern Baltimore County. As we parked alongside the mile-long lane to the farmer's house, I noticed that wheat was starting to shoot up from the field. I wondered if it could survive the freezing night—or if *I* could, for that matter.

We laid out our blanket, then I opened our star map portfolio, my gloved fingers fumbling with the tie.

Zachary slid a piece of paper in front of me. I held it up to the flashlight, which had a red-painted lens to protect our night vision.

It was a website printout, listing the exact minutes of the last several solstices and equinoxes. Zachary had highlighted the two most recent in orange.

> December 21: 10:14 p.m.
> March 21: 12:05 a.m.

"Was he with you then?" Zachary asked.

I nodded, stunned into muteness. Zachary's theory seemed true. Last Thursday night, Logan had come through my window as a shade, then turned to a ghost, then become human. All at the time of the equinox.

If it happened once, it could happen again, on the summer solstice. Theoretically.

"I'll draw." Zachary unfolded the portfolio in front of him. "You find the stars."

I located the first half-dozen constellations while he sketched out the celestial equator and the ecliptic, the course that the zodiac, the sun, and the planets traveled—sort of a superhighway in the sky.

"Leo's a new one this time." I leaned across him to point to the eastern edge of the star map. "So the brightest star, Alpha Leo, is—"

"Regulus," he said. "The Lion's Heart. It's actually a triple star."

I checked the constellation book for Beta Leo, the second-brightest star in the constellation. "Next is—"

"Denebola, in the tail. Got it."

I thumped the book down in front of me. "Well, you seem to know it all, as usual, so I'll just wait in the car, where it's half a degree above freezing."

"Go on, then, if it's that bad."

So much for clearing the air. He wouldn't even take my bait to pick a fight.

Would we be like this until the end of the year? All week in school, I'd bolted every time we came near each other. But sitting with him now in the dark, watching his fingertips trace precise arcs across the paper, and seeing the familiar angles of his face in the flashlight's deep red glow, made me want to do the exact opposite of running away.

He set the pencil in the center of the portfolio. "I'm sorry I was so harsh with you the other night."

I clenched my jaw to stop my teeth chattering, from the cold and from surprise. "I deserved it."

"You were honest with me."

"Lying always makes things worse."

"That doesn't stop people from doing it."

"So you forgive me?" I asked.

"There's nought to forgive. You're not my girlfriend. You can do what you want with whoever you want."

I want you. But to tell him that now, after admitting I'd almost had sex with my temporarily reanimated sort-of-ex-boyfriend, seemed really inappropriate.

It was the truth, though. And if I had the guts to confess what happened with Logan, I could find the courage to ask Zachary to the prom. Even though he'd probably say no.

"Becca said yes, by the way."

My insides turned as cold as the air around me. "To the prom?"

"She says she likes Italian food, so if you could recommend a restaurant . . ." He glanced at me. "Besides the one we went to."

My mouth opened, but the only word I could think of was *NO.*

He picked up the pencil. "Never mind, I'll look it up."

"If you want traditional," I rushed out, "go to Da Mimmo's. But Becca probably likes cutting-edge fusion-y food, so maybe take her to Milan on Eastern Avenue."

"Thanks very much." His voice was void of anticipation, like he was planning a business meeting. "I want it to be nice. It's her last prom and probably my only one, if my dad and I go back to the UK in June."

One word cut through the sirens screeching in my head. "What do you mean, 'if'?"

"His assignment could get extended." Zachary looked at me from the corner of his eye. "You and your boyfriend are making a lot of work for him."

"Sorry."

"Don't be. Dad's never happier than when he's working himself to death." Zachary massaged his wrist. "I think he's close to something big. It must keep him up at night, because he's knackered all day."

He went back to sketching lines, which I noticed were unusually shaky.

I slapped the constellation book shut. "Logan's not my boyfriend."

He stopped drawing but didn't look up. "What is he, then?"

"I don't know. But since that night, he hasn't stayed in my room. It's not like it was between us back in the fall, before he turned shade."

"Except for that small bit on the equinox."

"Yes, except for that! I was happy to see him, okay? I thought I'd lost him forever—again—and then there he was. What would you have done in my place?"

Zachary stared at the edge of the blanket and the dull brown grass that looked pink from the red flashlight. "I don't know what I'd do."

"Right, because you don't know what it's like to lose someone."

"I've lost someone."

His sudden confession took me by surprise. "You never told me that."

"It's not the same. She didn't die, she went to Malta."

Because of his accent or his emphasis, I was confused, until I remembered that Malta was a place. "Is that in Africa?"

"It's in the Mediterranean, but it might as well be on Mars."

"Why?"

He pressed his lips together before speaking. "Suzanne's parents were both MI-X. They wanted to be stationed together, of course, so they didn't have much choice in where to go. When their project in the UK ended, they left for their next assignment, in Malta. And took her with them." He turned the pencil end over end. "We e-mailed and video-chatted for a while, and then . . . she stopped."

I wanted to throttle this Suzanne person for putting that shadow of hurt in his voice. "How long were you together?"

"Eight months, three weeks, and a day. A day and a half."

I didn't mention that it was a shorter relationship than mine and Logan's. If Zachary was measuring the time in half days, she must have meant a lot to him.

"My point is," he said, "if Suzanne had appeared in my room a few months after she left, even after I met you, I probably would've done what you did. And she's not even dead."

All along, he'd been so patient about me and Logan. It wasn't because he was a saint—it was because he understood. "You really do get it."

"I get it. That doesn't make it easier to hear about you in bed with him." He started drawing again, his lines heavy. "It was bad enough when he was a ghost and he couldn't touch you, and I thought, 'If I wait long enough, she'll come round,' and so I waited and waited, but I waited one day too many, didn't I?" The pencil tip snapped against the paper. "Bugger!" Zachary hurled the pencil into the wheat field.

We sat silent as his curse echoed against the distant hills, then faded. My blood raced from his outburst. Maybe we were finally getting somewhere.

"Sorry," he said at last.

"That was our only pencil."

Zachary made another guttural sound, then picked up the flashlight and tromped off into the field.

The loss of his nearby heat made me want to follow him, but instead I pulled my knees to my chest to keep warm—or at least alive.

For five minutes I watched him wander, scanning the rough surface with the flashlight, whose faint red glow reached only a few feet in front of him.

Finally he stopped, picked something up, then came back, his steps as deliberate as they'd been on the way out.

"Did you find it?"

"I found this." He knelt in front of me. "Put out your hand."

I kept my fingers clasped around my shins. "What is it?"

"Never mind." He put the item in his pocket. "If you don't trust me—"

"Hey." I grabbed the front of his jacket. "I trust you more than anyone in the world."

Zachary's gaze dropped to my hand, then rose, burning, into my eyes. "So what are we doing?"

"Nothing. That's the problem." I pulled him to kiss me.

Though my aim was slightly off, and our lips were cold and chapped, I knew in an instant that this was right. Zachary fit me, like the answer to an equation I'd forgotten how to solve.

His groan of relief told me he felt it, too. He slid his arms around my back, and I pressed against him—as much as my parka would allow—wanting to sink into his warmth. I wanted this perfect rightness never to end.

Which of course it did. He broke the kiss, holding my face in his hands. "What do we do?"

My teeth chattered. "Go make out where it's warm?"

"I don't mean right now." Zachary glanced over at the car. "Though that's no' a bad idea." He shook his head. "We'd be too comfortable."

"Not possible."

"We have to think."

"Do we?"

"I asked Becca to the prom."

"So un-ask her."

"I can't un-ask her."

"You un-asked me."

"You deserved it." He cut off my protest. "You did. Hush." Zachary kissed me again, with even more passion and less precision.

I tore off my gloves and slipped my hands inside his leather jacket, the zipper's teeth scraping my skin like icy fangs. The prom seemed a million years away.

His lips left mine again, but only to shift to the edge of my jaw. "Should've given you another chance," he said, his breath coming hard, "talked to you again before I called her."

"You gave me way too many chances. You should've just done this."

He murmured in agreement, moving his mouth to my neck, right below my ear. His fingers threaded through my hair, tingling my scalp. I shivered in a full-on body quake.

Zachary pulled away. "Are we completely mental? It's freezing out."

We left everything behind and ran for the car.

It was warmer there, but more awkward, with the emergency brake between us.

"Why'd we get in the front?" I asked him.

"The back's worse." He peered into the rear seat. "We've never put a living creature there, only briefcases and such."

I had to admit, it seemed about as roomy as my gym locker.

Zachary touched my cheek. "We have a wee problem."

"How wee?"

"We can't be like this in public until after the prom."

"I know." I sat back in the passenger seat with a heavy sigh. "It would be sleazy, not to mention suicidal." Stealing the soon-to-be prom queen's date would get me killed—socially, if not literally. "So what's the deal with you and Becca?"

"We're just friends."

"Does she know that?"

"I'll make it clear. What about you and Logan?"

"Just friends."

"Does he know that?"

"I'll make it clear," I said, matching his cadence, if not his accent.

He didn't laugh. "No more bedroom visits?"

"Only when I'm fully dressed."

Zachary tightened his lips, considering.

"What's in your pocket?" I asked him. When he raised an eyebrow, I added, "The thing you picked up in the field."

"Oh, this?" He reached into his pocket and pulled out a small metal disc. "A message."

"It's a bottle cap."

"It's from one of those fancy iced teas with quotes on the back of the lid. People pay extra for the wisdom."

"People like the guy who plowed that field. He needed some no-littering wisdom. What does it say?"

He flipped the lid over onto the back of his other hand, like in a coin toss. "Oh. Wrong brand, I guess."

There were no words under the lid, just a black-and-white spiral. "Can I keep it anyway?"

He folded it between my palms. "It's yours."

I kissed him again, relieved that nothing was stopping me. Soon the warmth of his mouth made the rest of the world feel that much more frigid, and I shivered harder than ever.

He pulled my coat tighter around me. "I can't wait to snog when it's forty degrees."

"That's not much of a diff—"

"Celsius."

I did a rough calculation. "That's hot enough for bathing suits."

He let his gaze wander downward. "What's your bikini look like?"

"I haven't bought this summer's yet. Ooh, before you go back to Scotland, I'll take you to Ocean City." No, I'd been there with Logan a hundred times. "Or Rehoboth."

"Anywhere would be brilliant. Now back to the bikini."

My shiver turned my laugh into a goofy giggle. "You have a request?"

"I was thinking, red's a fantastic color on you. Besides, I can't stay by your side every minute. Wouldn't want ghosts to chat you up while I'm fetching us french fries."

His words were casual, but the tension in his fingers told me he was thinking of Logan, as I was.

"Maybe we could try Dewey Beach," I said. "I want to go with you somewhere I've never been before."

By the way he pulled me closer, nestling my head against his shoulder, Zachary told me he understood what I was really saying.

"I promise," he said, "I will take you somewhere new."

Before I'd even tossed my book bag on my bed, Logan appeared there, sitting with legs stretched out, like he'd never left.

"How'd it go?"

"Fine." I let my hair drape down so he wouldn't see the flush of my cheeks. "It was freezing. I'm dying to get into my sweats and flannels." I pulled a pair of pajama pants from my drawer. "Can you go somewhere else while I change?"

"Your aunt doesn't know I'm here."

"I know you're here."

Logan drummed his fingers on the bedspread, looking petulant. "Back in ten."

After dressing for bed—no sexy silk nightshirt this time—I went to the bathroom, took out my contacts, and scrubbed my face so that all my skin would glow the same.

Logan was waiting when I got back to my room. "Hey, Nicola scored me a *City Paper* interview today. Her post-Shifter intern set it up."

I put on my glasses. "Be careful who you talk to."

"I know. The article's running next week—might even make the cover. I told the reporter I was looking for band members. Since we haven't set up my new e-mail yet, I gave them your contact info."

Sighing, I went to my desk and opened my laptop. "Let's set you up now."

Logan came toward me. "It'll have to be one of those free e-mail providers since I don't—ow!" He put his hand over his face, as if shading his eyes from me.

"What's wrong?"

He slowly lowered his hand, his violet outline snapping black. "I feel weird. You feel weird."

"No, I don't." That was a lie. Being here with Logan after making out with Zachary? I'd never felt weirder.

"Are you wearing that obsidian necklace Gina gave you?"

I touched my neck, though I knew it wasn't there. "I gave it to Megan."

"Maybe it's your laptop."

"It never gave you problems before."

"I'd never been a shade before." He backed up, near my closet. "Maybe I'm more sensitive now."

"You were fine here all weekend." Gripping the sides of my chair, I watched him brighten to violet again. Then I turned back to the computer, relieved. "What do you want as your username?"

"How about 'Logansghost'?"

A quick search. "It's taken."

"Wow. You think it's a fan?"

I kicked my heel against the chair leg, releasing my irritation. "Think of something else."

"How about 'Logansghost' followed by the numbers of next year?"

Another try. "That works. Why next year, not this one?"

"Class of. It's when I would've graduated."

My eyes drooped at the corners with all-too-familiar sorrow. Logan was annoying, but he was still dead.

"I'll need a fan page, too." He wavered in the corner of my vision. "Can you call Cheryl Titus at *City Paper* and have them print the new e-mail address? That way no one'll bother you. Except me."

My fingertip scraped the white *L* on the black key. "What do you want as your password?"

"How about 'iloveaura'?"

I shut my eyes. "It should have at least one special character and number to keep from getting hacked."

"How about 'aura=#1hot'?"

"How about something you can tell Dylan without embarrassing all of us?"

He paced in front of the closet door. "Let's do . . . 'live' . . . numbers four six . . . slash . . . numbers two zero."

I typed LIVE46/20. "Was this part of your locker combination?"

"The number four is for the word 'for.' Six-twenty is June twentieth, the summer solstice." He paused. "Only eighty-six days left, Aura."

I wished I didn't already know that.

Logan stepped closer, then drew in a hiss. "Ow. Jesus, what is that?"

"What's what?"

"You look red." He squinted at me. "Just part of you. Stand up."

I did as he asked, fighting the urge to flee the room. Logan inched closer, then swiped a hand in front of my body, like a wand-wielding airport security guard.

"It's your head," he said. "Did you get red highlights?"

"Caramel, like usual. And that was three weeks ago. Nothing's changed since last night. It must be you."

He put a hand to his head. "Yeah. Look, I gotta go."

"Fine." I tried not to sound too relieved. "Good night."

When he was gone, I turned on my overhead light and examined myself in the mirror behind my closet door.

Same hair, full of static from the dry night and my parka hood. I pulled aside the long dark waves to see if my neck looked nibbled on. Not at all.

Same brown eyes, cradled by what seemed like permanent bags. But these days, the swelling came from calculus-related sleep deprivation, not from crying.

Same me. Nothing was different on the outside.

On the inside, of course, everything had changed.

Chapter Seven

You and Zach are, like, secret lovers?" Megan whispered across the lunchroom table. "That is so hot."

"Not lovers." I glanced beyond her shoulder to where he sat with Becca and her friends. "Not yet." He'd given me a hello and a secretive smile as he'd passed our table, and I'd resisted the urge to stare as he walked away. Mostly.

"You two're the last people I'd expect to do this. You guys like rules, and not just for the sake of breaking them." Megan clinked her bottle of iced tea against mine. "But it's nice to see you happy."

"I look happy?"

"You're glowing."

"Glowing with guilt, maybe." I snuck another peek at Zachary, who I noticed had sat across from Becca. When he ate lunch with us, he always sat beside me, close enough to touch my arm when I said something funny, or to use my utensils to illustrate a new soccer play.

I popped the lid off my own iced tea and peeked under the cap, hoping it would have the same spiral as the one Zachary had given me last night.

Nope—it had a checkered diamond pattern. But there was a spiral on Megan's cap, lying on the table between us.

"Hey!" Jenna and Christopher arrived, speaking their greeting in unison as usual.

"Oh my God," Megan said, "that belt buckle is a thing of beauty."

Jenna tapped the silver skull buckle with her long black-lacquered nails. "Do you not love it to death?"

While Megan was admiring Jenna's accessories, I switched our bottle caps so I could have the one with the spiral, feeling like an obsessive dork.

"Aura, what the hell?" Jenna said as she slid into the chair next to Megan. "I thought for sure Zach was going to ask you to the prom the other day in the courtyard."

"No, he—" I shut my mouth without telling them he'd asked (and un-asked) me Friday night. No way I'd admit being that stupid. "He just wanted to show me his driver's license."

"Now that he's taking Becca, bizarre as that is, we made you a list of consolation prizes. Chris?"

Beside me, Christopher nudged my arm with a sheet of paper. "Pick your top three and I'll drop some not-so-subtle hints."

I examined the list of guys, all of them juniors on Christopher's varsity lacrosse team. None of the names made me gag, but none of them made me glow, either. "Thanks, but I'm skipping the prom."

I was greeted with a chorus of "What!?"

Megan ripped open her bag of Old Bay–seasoned potato chips. "Aura, don't even think about it."

"You cannot *not* go," Jenna said.

"It's a free country." I squeezed the bottle cap in my hand. "Besides, I've decided the prom is so establishment. You guys should boycott, too. It would be totally punk."

"My dress is totally punk," Megan said. "Prom punk. We're going." She patted the list. "Pick a dude."

"Why would they want to go with me?"

Jenna snorted. "Maybe because you're hot?"

I knew what she really meant. Ever since people had found out that Logan and I had gotten semi-kinky after his death, guys had the wrong idea about me. They figured if I'd take off my clothes for a ghost, I'd do it for anyone who breathed. Especially on prom night, the national holiday for hookups.

I folded the list, creasing the paper hard, as if to smother the possibility of a non-Zachary guy expecting me to kiss him good night—or more. "I'll get back to you."

"By tomorrow, okay?" Jenna pointed at the paper. "Those options won't last."

I shoved the list deep into my bag. *Good.*

As Zachary walked into our seventh-period history class, he set a book on the corner of my desk. "For our project, what we talked about last night." Then he went to his seat by the window, not waiting for my reaction.

I picked up the book, a tourist guide to Ireland's historical sights. One of the four photos on the front was a bird's-eye view of Newgrange. It showed the passage tomb's enormous flat-topped mound, ringed with a brilliant white-quartz wall and covered in lush green grass.

I lingered on the photo, thinking of my mother. Had she carried a book like this on her travels? Had she pored over it on the flight to Dublin, daydreaming of the places she'd see?

A folded index card stuck out of the section labeled Accommodation. On the card's outside fold was Zachary's neat print:

Read the bit in the book first.

He had highlighted the caption under a photo of a small, ivy-draped stone castle. The entry read:

> Twenty kilometres from Newgrange,
> the snug but luxurious Ballyrock contains
> ten charming suites, two on each floor,
> outfitted with twenty-first-century comforts
> while maintaining an air of medieval mystery.
> Enjoy tea on a private balcony
> or cozy up with your beloved in front of an
> open hearth.
> Recommended for over-eighteens, as
> Ballyrock is not BlackBoxed and is confirmed
> to be haunted by a dozen or more ghosts.

I unfolded the index card. Here Zachary had written in a tight, slanted script. Had he made it barely legible on purpose, so no one could read it over my shoulder? Seemed like something he'd do.

Aura,
I dreamed of you last night.

A shiver zinged through me. I imagined his voice rolling the *r*'s, and dropping the *t*'s as if they didn't exist.

You slept in this castle, surrounded by ghosts who all wanted your time, who all wanted your eyes on them. But none came into your room, because I was sleeping beside you. And when you woke, your eyes were only on me.
Someday I'll take you to this place. I promise I'll keep away the ghosts.
Z

I folded the note, then pressed it against my stomach to soothe the jitters. Afraid to look at Zachary, I stared at the photo on the page, wishing I could jump into it with him right now. The way the fog folded around the turrets made me think of how his arms had wrapped around me last night, and how they might wrap again, inside that very stone building.

When I could finally lift my head without spontaneously combusting, I peeked at Zachary's feet. That way I could see if he shifted his weight to look at me, without making it obvious I was staring.

Finally his foot moved, then his hip, then his head onto his fist, in an attempt to look slightly bored, yet politely listening to Mrs. Richards's lecture. All while casually turning in my direction.

I looked at his face as his gaze flicked back to meet mine. He held it, held it, held it, while my entire body turned to flame.

Zachary was waiting at my locker after class. I was grateful he hadn't tried to talk to me at my desk, where my babbling idiocy would've attracted attention. Here the hallway noise would cover up the lust in my voice.

"So what do you think?" he asked, like he was inquiring about the assignment.

I opened my locker, trying not to fumble with the knob. "Possibly doable. The site, I mean." *Not you—you are supremely,* im*possibly doable.* "Can you make it happen?"

"I think so." He draped his arm over the open door, then straightened up, as if realizing he'd fallen into a flirtatious posture.

"Maybe, um . . ." I stared into my locker, drawing a complete blank as to which books I needed for homework. "Maybe we could meet tonight to discuss it?"

"I'd love to." His voice's deep husk weakened my knees, but then he gave a harsh grunt. "No—bugger it, I can't. Becca's family invited me to come for their seder."

My mouth fell open. "Seder?"

"It's the Passover dinner."

"I know what a seder is," I said, too quickly.

"Sorry." He twisted the loose coil at the end of his spiral notebook's spine. "Tomorrow you're going to Philadelphia for Easter, aye?"

"My grandmom's." I retrieved the Faulkner novel I'd barely started reading.

He frowned at his watch. "My dad's picking me up in three minutes. He wants me to take him to the doctor's."

"Everything okay?"

"I think so, but he says I need practice driving. Can't imagine why."

I tried to laugh, but my mind was stuck on him spending the evening with Becca and her family.

"I'll ring you over the weekend," he said. "Or you ring me. Either way." His smile faltered. "Bye." And he was gone.

"Bye." I spoke softly into my locker, wishing it could swallow a scream.

This wasn't going to work.

"Kill me now." I glared at the ceiling of the Keeleys' basement rec room, which doubled as Mickey and Siobhan's rehearsal space.

"So Zach is going to a seder at the Goldmans'. It's not a huge deal." Megan tossed a peanut into the air and caught it in her mouth, then aimed one at Siobhan. "Rachel had you and your aunt over for a seder a couple times. You weren't going out with her."

"This is different." I banged the back of my head into the squishy blue beanbag chair, hearing tiny particles spill onto the floor behind me. No wonder this thing was so flat. "If Zach's meeting Becca's family now, she'll have her claws into him by prom. I am absolutely, definitely not going."

"Want me to find you a guy from our school?" Siobhan asked, then opened her mouth for another incoming peanut.

"Yeah, a pity date for the prom. Because I'm not quite lame enough yet."

"Hey," Megan said, "you know what's a lamer prom night than dancing with a cute guy from Hunt Valley? Sitting in your living room watching a *Law and Order* marathon with your aunt." She lobbed a peanut at my head. I winced and let it bounce off my cheek, my appetite too sour for games or food. "If you don't want a blind date, then get out Jenna's list and we'll do pros and cons of each guy. Siobhan can be the judge if you won't decide."

"Sounds like fun." Siobhan opened her violin case. "But Mickey and I need to rehearse."

The yells of victorious boys came from upstairs.

"Ugh." Siobhan shoved her long, purple-streaked dark bangs back under a plastic headband. "This ceiling's supposed to be soundproof."

Megan fished another peanut out of her trail mix bag. "Nothing can hold back the testosterone rush brought on by Age of Mangling or whatever game they're playing."

I stared at the smooth white square ceiling tiles as a solution dawned on me. My first instinct was to analyze the idea from all angles, to see if it could really be that perfect.

But it was analysis and hesitation that got me into this prom mess with Zachary. I pushed myself off the beanbag chair. "I'm getting a water. You want anything?"

"Yes." Siobhan waved her bow and rosin block. "I want my twin brother to get his ass down here."

Upstairs, Dylan and three of his friends were splayed out on the long black leather couch in the den. Mickey stood behind them, arms crossed over his chest, gaze fixed on the huge wall-mounted plasma TV. I didn't recognize the game, but it involved a lot of pink.

"What is that?" I asked Mickey over the steady *waka-waka-waka* noise.

"Ms. Pac-Man." He kept his focus on the screen. "Dad got Mom a bunch of old arcade games for her birthday."

Dylan spoke up from his reclining seat on the near end of the couch. "Ms. Pac-Man looks all girlie, but it's harder than regular Pac-Man. The mazes have more traps, and the ghosts are smarter and faster."

"Ghosts?" I examined the figures on the screen. "Is that what those blobs are supposed to be?"

"They can kill you," Dylan said, "unless you eat a blinky thing and then you can kill them."

"Guys, shut up!" Rashid jerked the joystick. "Trying to concentrate."

Kyle nudged him with a pale, bony elbow. "Dude, what are you gonna do when you're a fighter pilot—ask the bad guys to hold still so you can shoot them down?"

"This is different, so—aww, you suck." On the screen, the little yellow mouth spun around and flattened like a popped balloon.

"Your parents think eating ghosts is entertaining?" I said.

"They're not supposed to be real ghosts, like in Shade Hunter," Jamal said. "This game's from before the Shift. Duh."

Dylan grabbed the controller from Rashid. "My turn."

Released from the spell of the game, Mickey looked at me. "Did she send you up here?"

"Which 'she'? Megan or Siobhan?"

"Whatever." He slouched his lanky frame toward the basement door.

I scowled, wondering why Mickey wasn't happier, like the rest of the Keeleys, now that Logan had returned from shade. Maybe because Logan was still dead.

I stood next to the couch, watching Ms. Pac-Man make it through the first level. Finally I got up the nerve to do what I came upstairs for. "Dylan, can I talk to you for a sec?"

He grunted, lips pulled between his teeth as he focused on the screen.

"Maybe when you're done," I said. "Or now."

"Something with Logan?"

"No."

"Okay, go ahead."

I glanced at the other boys, all ignoring me. Kyle was paging through a gaming magazine, his long, skinny legs stretched out to prop his heels on the coffee table. Jamal was half-asleep, and Rashid was pawing through a bag of chips that reeked of nacho cheese.

"I'll ask you later," I said.

"Aura, what?" Dylan's voice took on an edge.

I toed the border of the Oriental rug, resisting the urge to fidget with the hem of my faded green Keeley Brothers cami. "Will you go to the prom with me?"

Dylan's hand slipped off the joystick. Jamal woke up. Rashid spilled neon orange chip fragments down the front of his T-shirt. Kyle froze in the middle of turning a page.

Dylan's friends all gaped up at me, looking much younger than sixteen.

Dylan recovered his joystick, muttering "fuckfuckfuckfuckfuckfuckfuck" until he'd maneuvered Ms. Pac-Man through a tunnel that led to the other side of the screen.

"Did you hear me?" I said.

"Yeah." Dylan's knee jerked, making his heel quiver against the floor.

"Well?"

"Okay."

I hesitated. "Is that a yes?"

"Uh-huh."

"Okay." I backed up a step. "Cool."

Dylan's friends were staring at him now, with the kind of awe usually reserved for World of Warcraft Feats of Strength.

I gave up waiting for him to look at me or use a multiword sentence. "Mickey can help you find a tux, and we'll do it all as a group, so you don't need to plan anything."

"Okay."

"Okay, then. Um. Thanks." I started toward the basement door.

"Wait," Dylan said.

I turned quickly, my shoes squeaking on the hardwood. Was he going to back out? Had he heard anything I said? Maybe it would be better if we pretended the last five minutes hadn't happened.

"When is it?" he asked.

"Second Saturday in May." *Please don't say "okay" again.*

Dylan was silent for a few moments, still playing. "Yeah, all right."

* * *

"Are you insane?" Megan threw a handful of peanuts at me. "He's a sophomore."

I batted the flying nuts away from my head. "I'm sure in a tux he'll look seventeen."

"Or he'll look seven," Siobhan said.

"Besides, he's fun to hang out with." I turned to Mickey, looking for backup. "Isn't he?"

He gave a one-shoulder shrug as he adjusted the pegs on his acoustic guitar. "I wouldn't know. He's my little brother."

"So's Logan." I caught myself. "I mean, so was Logan."

"Dylan's different," Siobhan said. "Geeky."

I pointed at their framed original movie poster of *The Empire Strikes Back*. "In case you haven't noticed, we're geeky, too."

"Dylan's a whole 'nother degree of geek. He collects action figures. It's not too late to say you were kidding."

"No way. I'll hurt his feelings." Not that he had shown any feelings when I'd asked him.

"He'll probably be relieved," Megan said. "Dylan wouldn't know what to do with a girl if she came with an instruction manual."

Mickey scoffed. "Megan, you don't have a clue what you're talking about, so just—"

We all flinched, waiting for him to finish the sentence with "shut up." Megan gripped the arm of her chair, looking ready to flee.

"Mickey, you don't think it'll be weird?" Siobhan asked, breaking some of the tension.

"Of course it'll be weird. But at least we know Dylan. It might be weirder to hang out with some Ridgewood asshat we've never even met."

"Then let's set her up with someone from our school." Siobhan turned back to me. "I swear he'll be cute and not stupid. Then that way you can come with us to our prom the week after." Her voice softened. "Like we always planned?"

I stared at Logan's abandoned black Fender Stratocaster propped on its stand like a memorial shrine. We'd planned it all when he was alive, before everything changed.

Now I wanted someone who made things feel the same.

Chapter Eight

So, Aura, do you like any of the boys at school?" my grandmother asked as she dumped a two-pound container of ricotta cheese into a birdbath-size mixing bowl.

She'd asked that question since I was in kindergarten, even when I was dating Logan. But this was the first time she'd asked since he died. Another sign that my life should be turning a corner.

I gave her a tentative smile as I grated a lemon for the ricotta pie. It was four thirty a.m., Easter Saturday, but I didn't mind spending the early hours in the kitchen of her bakery, as long as it meant hanging out with Grandmom and sampling fresh cookie batter.

"Actually," I said, "there is one guy."

"Is he—"

"He's not Italian."

"Hmph." She thumbed a stray dark blond curl back under her

Shift

hairnet. "Well, I guess you gotta try the rest before you settle down with the best."

I laughed. "That's the plan, Grandmom."

"You think you're humoring me, but you'll see." She opened a double-size carton of eggs. "In the meantime, tell me about this boy." Now it sounded like *she* was humoring *me*.

"His name is Zachary, and he's from Scotland."

"Ooh, like Sean Connery?"

"Exactly, except for the old and wrinkly part."

Grandmom faked throwing an egg at me. "Just let me know when you want to meet a nice South Philly boy."

She started cracking eggs, one in each hand, humming along to the oldies station on the radio. Out in the front room of the bakery, I could hear her two assistants sliding trays of cakes and pastries into the display cabinets.

Before they could come back in to interrupt, I asked Grandmom, "Did my mother go out with South Philly guys?"

"Oh, yeah. And not just our neighborhood." She wiped her hands on her apron, which read, THE ~~CUSTOMER~~ BOSS IS ALWAYS RIGHT. "Your mother used to run around with the Sicilians over on Tasker Street."

I smiled at the phrase "run around with," like my mother and her friends were cavorting through the park like a pack of dogs.

Then I thought about my brown eyes and olive skin. The rest of my family was northern-Italian fair, with blue or green eyes. "You think my father's from that neighborhood? Maybe he's Sicilian?" I liked the idea of being 100 percent Italian. "I thought he was Irish, since she was in Ireland when she got pregnant. Did she go there to meet up with someone from home?"

Grandmom sighed and dropped the empty eggshells in the wide trash can beside her. "Aura, honey, you've asked me a hundred times about your father, and a hundred times I've said I don't know who he is. Your mother did a lot of things without telling me. I didn't even know she was going to Ireland until she called me from the airport."

I never knew that bit of gossip, though I was well aware of my mom's impulsiveness. "What did she say when she called you?"

"She said, 'I have to go to Newgrange, Mom, and it has to be now. Life's short.' She said it over and over while I argued with her. 'Life's short. Life's short.'" Her chin trembled. "Of course, in her case, she was right."

Grandmom's assistant Kaye swept in, carrying a pair of empty cake stands. "I know you're talking about me, Ms. Salvatore," she said with a grin, "because I'm always right."

"Hey." Grandmom tapped her wooden spoon against her chest. "Talk to the apron."

I listened to them banter, marveling at how anyone could be so sharp this early in the morning. But when Grandmom turned away from Kaye, I swore I saw her eyes glistening. Questions about my mom burned inside of me, but I couldn't bear to see my grandmother's tears.

Or worse, be the cause of them.

What Grandmom said was true: My mother had been right about life being short. Less than four years after visiting Newgrange and becoming pregnant with me, she had died from lung cancer.

On that rainy Easter Sunday afternoon, I went with my aunt and grandmother to visit Mom's grave. The wet headstones reflected the dark sky, making them look like the black marble Logan once wanted for his own stone (not that his parents listened). A few ghosts wandered between the rows, rain falling through their pale violet figures.

I leaned over to place a wreath of pink and yellow daisies next to my mother's headstone. Based on the photos I'd seen of her, she would've preferred less girlie colors, like red or purple or royal blue. Or maybe that was just me.

My aunt and grandmother stood at the foot of the grave, heads bowed in prayer. Rain streamed off the clear plastic hat protecting Grandmom's brassy perm, and the hood of Gina's lime green jacket shadowed her face.

Instead of praying, I cleaned Mom's headstone, brushing off the wet leaves and fuzzy maple buds that had blown from the trees at the edge of the cemetery.

My cell phone rang. I gave Gina and Grandmom a guilty look as I fished it out of my pocket. "Sorry." My thumb reached for the screen's ignore button.

ZACHARY M.

I hit answer instead, stepping away from the grave. "Hey. What's up?" I said quietly.

"What's up is I miss you. When are you coming home?"

I wiggled my toes in my rain shoes at the sound of his voice. "Gina and I are leaving in a couple hours. We're at the cemetery visiting my mom."

Instead of getting all embarrassed, he said, "That's lovely. Do you like being there?"

"It makes me feel closer to her, even though there's nothing here that really belongs to her. Not like at home, where I can look at her pictures."

"I'd like to see them sometime. If you want to show me, that is."

I felt a rush of dizziness—the good kind, not the imminent-vomiting kind. The thought of sharing my deepest loss with Zachary gave me the same feeling of *right*ness that I got when I thought of kissing him. "I'd like that, too."

"My dad goes to work at five and won't be back until late."

My breath stuttered. "You want me to come over tonight?"

"Yes. And before you ask, we've had the place swept for bugs. No one will hear us."

Because of the solemn setting and the soggy grass, I resisted the urge to jump up and down. "Seven o'clock?"

"Seven. And tell your grandmother thanks very much in advance for the sweets."

We got home in time for me to gather my study materials and change into something a little less Easter-y. I needed to look spectacular, since the last girl Zachary had hung out with was Becca, at her family's seder. Had he seen her again over the weekend? Gone golfing with her dad? Did he even know how to golf? The sport was invented in Scotland, so maybe he was born knowing.

Now I was really going insane.

I searched the rubble under my bed for the left half of my favorite pair of sandals, glad the sun had blasted away the rain and made it seventy-five degrees outside. My skin seemed to come alive anticipating the touch of the warm air—not to mention Zachary's hands.

"Eighty-two days, Aura."

I hit my head on the bed frame. "Ow! Logan, I hate when you do that." I sat up, pulling down my skirt, which had hitched way up when I'd bent over. Logan's glow was invisible in the flood of early evening light through my window.

"It's not like I can creak the floor to warn you." His voice came over my shoulder. "What are you looking for?"

I waved the shoe, then opened the bottom drawer of my nightstand to retrieve a thick purple folder, the one containing photos and a journal from my mother's trip to Newgrange.

"Working on your thesis with Bagpipes?"

"Trying to." I sat on the bed and opened the folder. "I'm missing so many pieces of this puzzle. And the pieces I do have are too jumbled to all fit in my brain at one time." I rubbed my face. "Does that even make sense?"

"Hey, this might sound crazy, but what if the three of us got together and told each other what we know?"

He can't be serious. "The three of who?"

"You, me, and—"

"Don't call him Bagpipes."

"And Zachary." His voice tightened around the name.

"So I can die of awkward-itis? No thanks."

"But it'd be worth it, if we could figure stuff out. I'd do anything to help you, Aura."

"Is that what this is about? Helping me?" I knew he had to tell the truth.

He was silent for a second. "As far as I know."

So at least he thought it was true. That didn't mean it was reality, only that it wasn't a lie. "Maybe Megan should be there, too, to keep things sane."

"Great. She can translate for me so you don't have to."

Since I'll be busy playing referee. "I hate keeping secrets from her, anyway."

"Hey, you lost that red cloud." Logan's voice was closer, coming from the bed beside me. "Remember last week when I had to leave?"

"Yeah, that was weird. At least it's gone now." I closed the folder and slipped it into my book bag. "So, what'd you do for Easter?"

"I went to Mass at St. Patrick's Cathedral in Dublin. I think it was the first time I paid attention since I was an altar boy."

I could imagine how an Easter mass would sound to a ghost, with all the talk of resurrection and eternal life.

"I want to pass on, Aura, I swear I do."

"You don't need to swear. Ghosts can't lie." *Except maybe to themselves.* I zipped up my bag. "I'll ask Zachary about meeting you. I'm going to his place tonight to show him my mom's pictures and journal."

Logan hesitated. "Wearing that?"

I tugged on the end of the short sleeve. He knew I wore this black V-neck T-shirt when I wanted to look hot without looking like I wanted to look hot. I tried to blot out the memories of Logan's hand sliding up under this pleated neon green skirt.

"So this is it, huh?" he said softly. "You're really going out with him?"

"Sort of."

"Then why are you taking Dylan to the prom?"

"Long story. Don't be mad."

"I'm not mad. If anything, I'm relieved." His voice moved back and forth, as if he was pacing. "At least I know you won't hook up with Dylan. Even if he wasn't my brother, you're a million miles out of his league."

I slipped my sandals on my feet, pretending to adjust the strap so he couldn't see my eyes. "I wanted to go to the prom with a friend, not a date."

"Bagpipes isn't your friend anymore? Or he's more than a friend?" When I didn't answer, Logan came closer. "Tell me the truth, Aura. I swear I won't shade out. I just want to know how I fit into your life." He paused. "If I fit at all."

I looked up, where I thought his eyes might be. "You fit. But we can't be together the way we were before, when you were a ghost the first time." I swallowed, wetting my throat to steady my voice. "I can't be your girlfriend."

"But what if I—"

"Even if you come back to life." My chest ached at the thought of Logan's body, full and solid under mine. "Even if it's for good."

He didn't speak for so long, I wondered if he was gone.

Finally he spoke quietly. "Do you want me to leave you alone? Forever?"

He made it sound so simple. But as long as he was here and pursuing his music career/ghost crusade, I had to stick with him, if only to translate his words to protect myself.

Besides, I wanted him here. I wanted to see his smile and hear his voice—whispering, speaking, or singing—for as long as I could. I was still greedy for what I'd lost, then found again.

"Don't leave," I told him. "Not unless it—" I cut off the words, *Unless it hurts too much to be around me.* They would make me sound full of myself, when in fact I felt quite empty.

"I can deal," he said. "After all, we were friends for ten years before we were boyfriend-girlfriend, right? Plus, I have a lot of other . . . stuff to do now, so it's not like you have to babysit me this time around. I'll be okay."

"Good." I smiled at him. "I'm proud of you, for all your . . . stuff."

"Thanks." After a long pause, he said, "I guess I'll go, then."

"Bye."

"Bye."

I waited, holding my breath, wondering if he'd really left. Then a cloud passed over the sun, shrouding the room, revealing no telltale violet glow.

Alone, I finished my makeup and hair, my preparations less frantic than before.

It was true, I was ready to share Logan with the world. Not just because he could do good, but also because as much as I loved him, he could no longer fill every corner of my life.

Some of the biggest spaces were already taken.

Chapter Nine

I heard Zachary's kitchen timer beep as he opened his apartment door.

"Hi." He stood there dazed, absorbing my appearance, then blinked and shook his head. "Sorry." He got out of my way so I could enter. "Tea's just now ready."

Flustered by his admiring gaze, I pushed a flat white bakery box against his chest, probably too hard. "It's *pizza gain*."

"Thanks, but I already had supper." He opened the box. "There's cinnamon on this pizza."

"*Pizza* actually means 'pie' in Italian. So any kind of pie is *pizza*, including dessert." I set my book bag on a dining room chair and rested my hand on the table for support. "I got up at four a.m. yesterday to help make ricotta pies."

"Thank you even more." Zachary reached past me to set the box on the table, but I didn't move out of the way. We stood close together, my heart slamming so strong I could barely speak. From somewhere in the living room area to my left, the latest Radiohead release was playing at a low volume. The singer's haunting murmur made my throat ache.

"I also got you this." I pulled the bottle cap with the spiral design out of my pocket and slipped it into his hand.

He looked hurt. "You're giving it back to me?"

"It's a matching one, off a new bottle. See, it's not scratched like the one you gave me. Not that scratches are—"

Zachary's kiss cut off my babbling. He slid one hand over my waist and the other into my hair, so that I felt utterly consumed by him.

The timer gave a reminder beep, and he pulled away, but only a few inches. "Sorry."

"For kissing me or for stopping?"

"I'll never be sorry for kissing you." He disappeared into his apartment's narrow kitchen, where I heard the rattle of ceramic, then the pouring of liquid.

I stayed in the dining room, shifting my feet. "Logan wants to meet you."

All sound ceased. Zachary appeared in the kitchen doorway. "Why?"

"If we each tell what we know—you and me about the Shift and our funky powers, and Logan about being a ghost and a shade—maybe we can put the pieces together."

"How would we meet when he can't stand to be around me?"

"You'd be in different rooms where I could see both of you, like my living and dining rooms. Megan would be there, too."

"I can't tell anyone about this power of mine. Especially not someone who has a grudge against me."

"Logan figured out you were different a long time ago, and he's never told anyone." Luckily, no one knew to ask him directly. "We should all have the whole picture."

Zachary turned away. I followed him to stand in the kitchen doorway while he pulled saucers, then cups, then plates from a white wooden cabinet. His motions were deliberate, controlled.

When it was all arranged on the countertop, he let out a deep breath, his shoulders sagging. "I'll meet with Logan, if you think it'll help us understand the Shift."

"Thank you."

"Or better yet," he muttered, "help him pass on."

Dessert and tea in hand, we sat on the smooth brown loveseat to look at the photos taken of and by my mom. First came my aunt's scrapbook, then my mother's collection from her longer-than-planned stay in Ireland, starting with Newgrange.

Zachary picked up my favorite photo, preserved in a plastic zip-lock bag, of my mother standing on the hillside next to the passage tomb. He read her sticky note on the back: "Taken by some Irish guy who claimed I looked 'mystical' gazing out at the River Boyne. (Really I was just trying to figure out which road would take me to a breakfast place.)"

"She reminds me of you," he said with a chuckle. "Of course, right now, a ball of dust reminds me of you."

I let my hair fall forward to hide my smile as I pulled out my mom's journal. "This is from her time in Ireland. Most of the pages are missing."

"Are you sure you want me to read it? Seems like a bit of an invasion."

I set the journal in his lap. "Invade me."

I tried not to stare as Zachary read. As far as I knew, only Aunt Gina and I had ever seen these pages.

Even with my mom's sloppy handwriting, it took him less than a minute, since there were so few complete entries.

"This is odd," he said. "The day after Christmas, she writes, 'Went to a St. Stephen's Day party at the local pub. I'm not the one in the family who sees ghosts, or even believes in them, so maybe there was something in the whiskey besides all that whiskey. But I swore I saw' . . ." He flipped the paper. "And the rest of the sentence, of course, is on the next page, which is missing. Small wonder you're frustrated."

In more ways than one, I thought, but kept it to myself, as his brow was low and furrowed in deepest thought.

"So your mum knew this person she thought she saw. She thought they were dead."

"If she meant 'ghosts' literally. Apparently, Mom used to joke about Aunt Gina's paranormal abilities. She was super sarcastic."

"Your mother, sarcastic?" Zachary widened his eyes at me. "I can't imagine."

"Shut up." I bumped my shoulder against his. "Like you can talk."

He smirked as he turned back to the purple folder of photos. "Why did she travel to Ireland in the first place? Not that there's anything wrong with it. Although Scotland's landscapes are much more stunning."

"She went specifically to be at Newgrange for the solstice. According to my grandmother."

"Had she won the drawing for a pair of tickets to go inside on one of the five days?"

I cocked my head. "You know, I always figured she did, but Grandmom said she just up and left. Don't they announce the lottery winners months ahead of time?"

"In October, aye."

"So why wouldn't she tell her own mom, 'Hey, I won this amazing chance to be inside Newgrange at the winter solstice, along with only ninety-nine other people in the world'?"

Zachary touched the photo my mother had taken of Newgrange's dark entrance, surrounded by gleaming white quartz. The picture was date- and time-stamped on that year's solstice. "Maybe she didn't have a ticket when she arrived. Lots of people come to stand outside and be a part of the event."

"But your dad said she was inside with him."

"They never actually met. Maybe he was mistaken."

"But there must have been a record of who was there. Do people scalp their tickets like at a concert?"

"No, I'm sure that's not allowed." Zachary glanced at the coatrack behind the front door, where Ian's hats hung on pegs. "You know, my mum didn't go to Newgrange with my dad. I don't know who did."

I gasped. "Maybe he had an extra ticket and gave it to my mother."

"He could have." Zachary read the final page out loud. "'Monday, April twentieth. Going home tomorrow. My work here is done. Not "done" as in finished. But "done" as in, I can't stay one more minute, not like this.'" Zachary counted on his fingers. "When she says, 'not like this,' you think she means pregnant? It would've been eight months before you were born."

"Probably. I looked it up, and it turns out that most pregnancies last forty weeks, which is almost ten months."

"Forty weeks before our birthday would be . . . early March." He turned the pages. "No entries from then."

"I was born a little premature, so it could've been later, but not much."

"Could it have taken her until the twentieth of April to know she was pregnant?"

"If she wasn't expecting it."

He tapped the journal. "Or your mum knew before that date, but thought your father would help raise you. Maybe she came back to the States when she couldn't find him."

"Or if he refused." My heart twisted. "If he didn't want me."

"Don't say that. If he knew your mum was pregnant—which he might not—he didn't walk out on *you*, he walked out on the idea of you—no, on the idea of a nameless, faceless baby. If he knew you, he'd want you in his life." His voice cracked as it fell. "Anyone would."

The look in his eyes told me he wasn't just talking about my father or some abstract hypothetical "anyone."

He dropped his gaze to his hands as he rubbed his knuckles together nervously. "I'm no' saying that because I want to kiss you. It's just true, so—"

"Shh." I pressed my finger to his mouth. "Don't move." I leaned in and replaced my finger with my lips, brushing them gently over his.

My name was all he said before kissing me, deep and sweet.

I wanted Zachary's mind, to help me figure out who and what I was, and let me do the same for him. But I also wanted his body, to make me feel at home again in my own skin. Though we were finally together in a warm room, I still shivered at the press of his palms against my back.

Under the pound of my pulse, I heard keys rattling. *Not again.*

We broke apart as the front door latch turned. I hurried to straighten my clothes, then realized they were already straight. It was Zachary's kisses that made me feel deliciously disheveled.

The door opened slowly, giving us enough time to pick up our pens and pretend to be taking notes.

Mr. Moore nodded to me as he dropped the keys on the front table. "Aura. How are you?"

"Fine, thanks. How are you?" My voice softened as I realized it was more than a casual question. Ian's face was drawn and pale, and he moved with none of the vigor I remembered. Though his thick salt-and-pepper hair was still more pepper than salt, he seemed to have aged ten years since I'd last seen him in December.

Zachary gave me a worried frown. He'd said his father was working himself to death, but Ian looked positively ghostly.

"How was work?" he asked.

"I wasn't working. I had a meeting with a medical officer." Ian took off his suit jacket, wincing, and hung it over the back of a chair. "Son, we need to talk. Aura, could I trouble you to, er . . ."

"Oh. Sure. Zach, I'll see you in class tomorrow." I reached to gather up the pictures.

"What's this?" Ian moved forward and picked up the two photos—one of my mother and one of Newgrange's front door. His face grew even more shadowed. "I remember that morning like it was today."

"Do you remember her?"

A sad smile touched Ian's lips. "Of course." He winked at Zachary. "The Moore men have a penchant for beautiful American brunettes."

Zachary squirmed. "Didn't you tell us you'd never met Aura's mum?"

"We didn't introduce ourselves." Ian eased into the recliner, supporting himself with both chair arms as he sat. "We spoke only briefly."

"Did you give her your extra ticket?" Zachary said.

Ian raised his eyebrows, probably wondering how we'd figured it out. "I did." He looked at me with bloodshot green eyes. "That's why I feel responsible for you and your troubles, no' simply because it's my job."

"What made you pick my mother?"

"Out of all the people gathered outside Newgrange, she seemed to long for it the most. The way she watched that dark doorway. Like she'd left a part of herself inside."

I wanted to ask what he meant, but he started coughing. It sounded painful, so I quietly collected my belongings, with Zachary's help.

"I'll walk you out," he said.

"That's okay."

"No, it's not," Ian croaked. "Go, son, see her to her car. I won't be running off any time soon."

"Let me reheat you some tea first, Dad." On his way to the kitchen,

Zachary took a handkerchief from his father's suit pocket, then brought it over to him. "Here."

Ian nodded his thanks and coughed into his handkerchief. My core chilled at the fleeting sight of blood. Zachary froze, then turned for the kitchen, his movements quick but stiff.

"Sorry," Ian said when he'd recovered. "How are you getting along these days? With the media?"

"Not too bad. The DMP keeps them off my back—with your help, I take it."

"We do our best."

The microwave beeped, and in a moment Zachary returned to the living room. He gave his father the cup of tea, which smelled of lemon and honey. Ian's hands shook slightly, rattling the cup on the saucer.

Zachary turned to me with fear in his eyes. "Ready?"

I swallowed. "Good night, Mr. Moore. I hope—I hope everything's okay."

Ian managed a hint of his charming smile. "Thanks very much."

At the elevator outside Zachary's apartment, I said, "Call me when you can, let me know what happened."

"I will." His jaw shifted. "I've never seen him like this. He's been shattered lately, but I thought it was from work. This cough only got worse a few weeks ago."

"Then maybe they caught it early."

He jerked his head in a brief nod. The elevator dinged, and when the doors opened, Zachary followed me inside.

"Go be with your dad now," I told him. "I can let myself out of the building."

His thumb jabbed at the *L* button, missing on the first try. "I'd hear it from him if I let you walk to your car alone."

"It's a pretty safe neighborhood."

"It would be rude." He leaned back against the elevator wall. "I'm almost afraid to go back, hear what he has to say."

I moved closer and wrapped my arms around his waist. His own arms enveloped me slowly, and he rested his chin atop my head. I could hear his quick, steady heartbeat through the soft cotton of his shirt.

We said nothing as we descended. When the elevator reached the lobby, he kissed my hair and let me go. We walked out the front door and across the tree-lined island to where I was parked on the other side of the street.

I loaded my book bag into the backseat, then turned to see Zachary with his shoulders hunched, hands shoved deep into the pockets of his jeans. My mind flailed for the exact right thing to say.

"Enjoy the rest of the *pizza gain*."

He scrunched up his face. Definitely not the exact right thing to say.

"Sorry," I said, "that was incredibly Italian of me. Make everything better with food."

A smile softened his eyes. "Thank you. It will help."

"Next time I'll bake you something by myself. It won't be as good as my grandmom's. It might not even be edible."

"It doesn't matter, as long as there is a next time." He opened my door. "I'll ring you."

I sensed he wanted me to leave while he was still calm, so I brushed my hand over his as I got in the car. He gently shut my door.

I watched Zachary walk away, head down, until he disappeared into the building's lobby.

Immediately a violet glow filled my car. "Logan, now is really not the time."

"But I have good news to—*aaugh*!" His form crackled with black static.

"Oh my God, are you shading?"

"No! I don't know! I was fine until now. Aura, why are you so red?"

"I'm not red!" My stomach lurched. "If I'm making it happen, then go. They'll lock you up if you get shady again."

"I know. I'm sorry." He disappeared, leaving only a yellow after-image in my vision.

"Bizarre." I gripped the steering wheel, waiting to see if he would return. I was afraid to imagine where he'd gone or what state he was in.

My phone rang, making me jump. I answered Megan's call.

"Logan's here," she said, "and he's freaking. Something about you being too red to look at?"

"I have no clue. I'm not even wearing red."

"Are you sure? Jenna has this sweater that looks blue from a distance, but actually has little red threads all the way through it. So you can ward off ghosts without anyone knowing you're a post-Shifter who can't get into a bar."

I switched on the interior light to examine my shirt. "Looks totally black to me. Besides, I was wearing this top earlier at my house. Logan was there and he didn't see me all red."

"What were you doing in between?"

"I was—" My breath froze.

Ohhhhh, no.

Zachary was rubbing off on me.

Literally.

I was sitting up in bed, speed-reading the last two hundred pages of *As I Lay Dying* for American Lit, when Zachary called. I'd managed to put Megan off, promising I'd explain everything when the four of us met on Wednesday night. I had a horrible theory in mind, and an all-too-easy way to test it.

"Hey," I said into the phone. "How are you?"

"Cancer," he whispered. "Bloody fucking hell."

"Oh my God. I'm sorry." I sank back onto my pillow. "Is it—I mean, did they say—"

"It's this rare, vicious thing. Mesothelioma. Have you heard of it?"

The word made me think of those late-night, have-you-been-injured attorneys' commercials. "Does it come from asbestos?"

"Maybe. I looked it up online, but I can't remember much except—" His voice shook. "Except that no one lives long."

My hand gripped the phone so tight, I thought it would break. "Can't they do anything?"

"Dad starts chemotherapy on Thursday. But he says—ach, I dunno if he's just being grim, but he says there's not much hope. Aren't parents supposed to make things sound better than they really are?"

"What about your mom?"

"That's the only good part in all this. She's coming straightaway."

"I thought it wasn't safe for her to be here." Zachary's mother had stayed behind in the UK when Ian was assigned here. The danger and instability of being a secret agent's wife had become too much for her.

"It's not ideal, Dad says, but he couldn't leave her in the dark about this. He gave her the choice."

"I'm glad she's coming." I knew Zachary missed her like crazy. "That way someone'll be with him while you're at school."

"And she'll be here if—no. No. He can't die. He's only fifty-eight, for Christ's sake."

I twisted the edge of the dark blue bedsheet around my other hand.

"Oh God, I'm sorry," Zachary said. "You lost your mum to this when she was a lot younger than fifty-eight."

"It's different. I never really knew her." His words "to this" struck me as odd. "What kind of cancer did you say it was?"

He pronounced it carefully. "Mesothelioma."

I wrote it down in the margin of the page I was reading before remembering it was a library book.

"It's ghastly," he said. "One website said the five-year survival rate is almost nil. It's a kind of lung cancer, but it spreads like—"

"Whoa, wait. Zach, my mom had lung cancer, too."

"What kind?" he said in a hushed voice.

"I don't know. I'll ask Aunt Gina."

"How old was she?"

"Twenty-seven."

"That's very young for lung cancer." He fell silent for a long moment. "Aura, do you think—could they have gotten this at New-grange?"

I twitched at the sudden ricochet of his thoughts. "How?"

"Maybe something poisoned them."

"You mean like radiation? Wouldn't it have affected them at the same time? And wouldn't other people have gotten it, too?"

"Maybe they did."

"Eowyn was there, and she's fine."

"So far, aye." He let out a harsh breath. "The Shift might be more dangerous than we know. It might be more than just ghosts."

His last word made me think of Logan and how he'd seen me covered in red after Zachary and I had kissed.

Uh-oh. I wanted to tell Zachary, but he didn't need that on top of the news about his father.

I stared at the framed *Starry Night* poster Zachary had given me and pictured him lying beneath his own copy. I thought of how completely perfect I felt when he held me close, how his touch seemed to make every last molecule tremble and glow and burn to be part of him. How his kiss had changed what I was.

He let out a shaky, shallow breath. "Seems like everything about us has to be part of some bigger mystery."

I closed my eyes. *You have no idea.*

Chapter Ten

Zachary put on a brave front in school the next day, as if his life hadn't just imploded. From the way Becca toned down her natural look-at-me-ness at lunch, I gathered that he had told her about his dad. It made me jealous, and then I felt guilty for wanting to be his only comfort.

I went to his desk after history class. "If you give me a ride to work, I'll tell you a secret."

His faint smile held a touch of mischief. "I can't resist."

You'll wish you had, I thought. As we walked to the parking lot, I noticed with relief that he didn't look for Becca or wait for her dismissal.

"How's your dad?" I asked once we were heading down Roland Avenue.

"Resting. He'll be pure crabbit when I get home, after not working all day."

"I'm sure he could use some time off."

Zachary snorted. "You don't yet understand the heart of a Moore."

I could think of nothing I wanted to understand more (except maybe derivatives). "So clue me."

"Work's important. It's not about 'getting ahead,' as you say here in the States. It's about taking care of your family."

"I get it, I think. It's like my family with food."

We stopped at a light and he looked at me. "So when you bring me biscuits and cinnamon pizza, you're making me part of your family?"

I found the courage to slip my hand inside his. "Something like that."

"It's an honor." He faced forward as the light changed. "A delicious one."

We didn't speak again on the short drive to my aunt's law office, but this time the silence was comfortable. I let myself dwell in the moment, pretending that we could have many more of them.

But I knew it was probably all about to end.

Rather than pulling up in front of the office, Zachary parked the Mini Cooper at the far end of the tree-lined street. "How long do you have?"

I checked my watch. "Five minutes."

"Four and a half minutes of this, then." He leaned across the car and kissed me.

I wanted him to—I'd need my pulse checked if I didn't. But the fact that I needed him to kiss me for more than one reason made me pull away while I could still think. "I have to tell you something."

He groaned and sat back in his seat. "I hate when people say that. It makes me tense."

"Logan couldn't be with me last night."

Zachary glanced out the windshield. "So sorry to hear tha'."

I ignored his sarcasm. "He looked at me and saw red." I waited for his reaction.

"I don't understand."

"I think it's the same red he sees on you."

Zachary blinked. "Still don't understand."

I was hoping I wouldn't have to spell it out for him, but I hadn't given him many clues to work with. "This has only happened after you kissed me, Wednesday night and last night. Yesterday afternoon, before I went to your place, Logan didn't see red on me."

Zachary's head tilted slightly as comprehension dawned in his eyes. Then he scoffed, "That's bollocks. He's lying."

"He can't lie. And it's real—I saw him get shady."

"What?! Did he hurt you?"

"No, he left before it could make me sick."

"So you're saying—" Zachary paused, as if putting the words in the right order. "If I kiss you, it makes your ex-boyfriend go away?"

I put my hand on his arm. "If you kiss me, I become like you. I think."

Zachary shook his head hard, a wave of dark hair flopping against his temple. "No. You can't change someone else's . . . essence or whatever, just by—" He stared at me. "Can you?"

"It sounds insane, doesn't it? Maybe the red was from the way I was feeling toward Logan after being with you."

"How were you feeling?" he asked with a heavy dose of caution.

"Less."

"Less what?"

"Just . . . less."

"Oh." Zachary scratched his thumbnail over a nick on the black rubber steering wheel. "Good."

"There's a way to test my theory." I jutted my thumb over my shoulder. "I have a translation appointment in fifteen minutes with one of our dead clients. If I go in there now, after you've kissed me, and the ghost freaks out—"

"Then it's not just Logan." He faced forward, shoving his hands through his hair. "If the ghosts can't be around you, you'll lose your job."

"I can find another one."

"Working at a coffee shop? That'll look brilliant on your university applications."

I fumbled with the door handle, wishing that for once, he would be selfish enough to fight for me. "I guess we'll see."

"Wait." He touched my shoulder. "To make it an accurate test, you need to be thoroughly kissed."

So he did, the most perfect kiss yet, as if we knew it might be our last. Despite the emergency brake, Zachary leaned in, pressing me into my seat and stealing my breath. I ran my hands over his face and hair, trying to record the feel of him in my fingertips so that later, if I had to, I could replay it in my memory.

Finally Zachary eased back—slowly, stretching the moment as long as he could. But not long enough.

We didn't speak as I picked up my bag and got out of the car. There was nothing to say.

Even after Zachary's engine faded down the block, and even though the trees and buildings cast deep shadows, I didn't see a single ghost.

I hoped it was only because of the tears in my eyes.

I waited in the conference room for Aunt Gina and her client. Unable to sit still, I pulled the thick dark blinds against the late afternoon sunlight. Then I checked the BlackBox switch by the door to make sure ghosts could get in. The attorneys left it on most of the time to keep this room private.

The door opened, and my aunt walked in with her paralegal, Terrence, who handed me a slim folder with the name of the deceased printed on the tab. To stay neutral, I never heard details of the case before an interview.

Gina set a small reading light on the table next to her papers. She turned it on, along with a digital voice recorder.

I sat at the table, trying to slow my pulse through sheer willpower. If this ghost had a bad reaction to me, then Zachary really was changing my essence. If the ghost was okay, then the change only reflected my feelings for Logan. I wasn't sure which possibility troubled me more.

Terrence went to the light switch by the door. "You ready, Aura?" I nodded, and he turned off the light.

I cleared my mind of anti-ghost thoughts—not usually necessary, but I needed every edge I could get. "George Schwartz, come forward."

The ghost appeared on the opposite side of the room, near the window. Though he might have been old when he died, as a ghost he appeared forty, dressed in a simple polo shirt and casual slacks. I wondered what had happened to him that day, to freeze him at the happiest moment in his life. The birth of a child? Promotion to vice president of something-or-other? A hole in one?

I would never find out. Ex-George took one look at me and released a brain-shattering shriek, like tires squealing before a car crash. I covered my ears and closed my eyes.

The noise cut off abruptly, replaced by my aunt's voice.

"Aura, what's wrong? What happened? Is Mr. Schwartz here?"

I opened my eyes. The ghost was gone.

Ears ringing, I wondered if I could invent the client's story to cover my transformation. No, that would be impossible, not to mention illegal.

But I'd promised Zachary I'd never reveal his secret, and there was no way to explain my change without telling Gina who it came from.

She patted the table, her antique gold ring clacking against the wood. "Aura, is Mr. Schwartz here or not?"

I was glad I was sitting in the shadows so she couldn't see my face as I spoke carefully. "I think Mr. Schwartz needs to reschedule."

The moment I shut my bedroom door behind me, I called Zachary.

He answered after half a ring. "Well?"

"The ghost freaked."

Zachary exhaled hard. "Bugger."

"I made up an excuse, so Gina doesn't know anything." I noticed my clean laundry was still stacked on the trunk at the foot of my bed, where I'd left it the night before. Might as well put my nervous energy to good use, I thought, opening my closet.

"What exactly happened?" Zachary asked. "Tell me everything."

I related the short but disturbing incident as I hung up my faded skinny jeans. "This guy's reaction was off the charts. When I've seen you repel ghosts, they just disappear. They don't scream."

"So the power's getting stronger?"

"I think so. The first time Logan sensed you on me, it was painful, but he could stay with me for a few minutes. The second time, he almost shaded."

"Does he know why?"

"He and Megan might guess, based on what happened last night. We'll talk about it when we meet." I thought about the night of my birthday, when Logan had briefly shaded out. I'd kissed Zachary hours earlier, but Logan hadn't mentioned a red cloud. Maybe it had worn off by the time I saw him, or maybe my red sheets and obsidian necklace had created too much static for him to notice. "We should experiment to see how long your effect on me lasts."

"Experiment? Please tell me you're joking."

"Not completely. We need to figure out what's happening." I shook out the dry-cleaning bag with the black-and-white crinkle dress I'd worn on our date, pained at the reminder but glad the tomato sauce stain had come out. "You know, it's kinda nice not having ghosts around. It's nice being more like you."

"I dunno anymore what that means."

The dread in his voice set off my Ramble Reflex. "I'm not saying I want to trade places with you. You've got your own problems with all the—I mean, how's your dad?" I grabbed a plush blue clothes hanger from the closet. "Did I already ask you that?"

"Aura, I saw a ghost."

I stopped, squeezing the clothes hanger. "That's impossible."

"Seems like a lot of impossible things are happening. We may need to redefine that word."

"Where was this? What did it look like?"

"Out my window last night, after you left and after I got the news from my dad. Just a flash of violet on the street."

I held back a sigh. "Back when people first realized that kids could see ghosts, a lot of pre-Shifters thought they could see them, too. But when they were tested, it turned out they couldn't. They were just delusional." *Yikes, bad word choice.*

"I'm not delusional," he snapped. "Why would I want to see ghosts?"

I softened my voice. "Because your father might die, and you'll miss him."

"He wouldn't even become a ghost if he died from this. It has to be sudden, aye?"

"You say that, but deep down, you're scrambling for ways to hold on to him. Maybe seeing ghosts is one of those ways." I switched the phone to my other ear, giving him a chance to respond. He didn't, so I continued. "I'm not trying to psychobabble you. But other people have gone through the same thing. There's no proof that anyone but post-Shifters can see ghosts. You're not like us."

"And you're not like me. But your aunt's client didn't see it that way today, did he?" Zachary's breath rushed out, like he'd sat down hard. "It's too much to take, all at once."

"I know. I'm sorry." I hung up the dress and laid the black silk wrap over it, remembering how he'd drawn it across my shoulders.

"Things are happening very quickly, things we don't understand. It could be dangerous."

I halted with my hand on the wrap. "Dangerous to who?"

"You and me. Your mother and my father both got lung cancer. That can't be a coincidence."

"Yes, it could. Especially since my mom had a different kind. I asked Gina. It was adenocarcinoma." I mangled the pronunciation.

"But she had it, at a young age, which is bizarre. We don't know what we're playing with here."

"Playing with?" He was making me more nervous with every word. I yanked open my sock and underwear drawer.

"You can't deny we've changed each other."

"I'm not denying it, I'm just trying not to lose my shit over it." I jammed a stack of socks into the drawer. "You sound like you're scared to be with me now."

Instead of reassuring me that wasn't the case, he fell silent. I pressed the phone tighter against my ear.

"Zach? You're not saying—are you?" *No.* Not when we'd finally found each other.

"Aura, it's not just about you and me. The Shift affects everyone. And after what happened to our parents—for all we know, there are deadly forces coming out of Newgrange."

My lips trembled as I wondered if the DMP had tapped our lines.

"We shouldn't be talking about this on the phone. Why don't you come over?"

"It'll make this too hard."

This. Breaking up. Not being together. Ever.

Anger trampled my fear. After all these months of denial? After finally discovering how right it felt to be with him? No way I'd let him go without a fight.

"Maybe it *should* be hard. Maybe we shouldn't throw it all away just like that." I snapped my fingers. "Why can't we be together like normal people?"

"We're not normal people. You're the First, I'm the Last. We belong to different worlds, and we're breaching the boundary between those worlds."

"So? Let's breach."

"We don't know what could happen. Look what just kissing has done to change us. What's next? We could tear the whole bloody universe apart."

I rolled my eyes. "God, you sound like the DMP! Maybe you should go join those paranoid drama queens. You'd look so hot in that starchy white uniform."

"How can you be so casual? For all we know, your mother died because of the Shift. My father could die. And who else?"

"But we don't—"

"This is big, Aura. Too big for us to understand."

"It's too big for us *not* to understand." I kicked off my right shoe, letting it fly into the open closet. "It's too important to run away from."

"I'm not running away. But we can't be together until we know it's safe. We can't take that chance."

"Yes, we can."

"I won't."

His words dropped like a pair of boulders. I sank down on the end of the trunk. "You don't want me."

"Don't say tha'." His whisper twisted in pain. "Of course I want you."

"Not enough to fight for me."

"This is *how* I fight for you. I don't want you to be hurt."

"And I don't want you to be noble." I clutched the footboard of my bed. "I want you to be here."

"I can't."

"You won't."

"Same difference."

"No. It's not." I hung up before he could hear me cry.

My body grew heavy, as if gravity had suddenly tripled. I slipped off my other shoe and curled onto my side on the trunk, resting my head on one of the two piles of clean shirts.

Atop the other pile was the black V-neck I'd worn last night. I placed my hand on it, wishing I'd kept it out of the laundry. Maybe then it would still smell like Zachary.

Even as my cheeks flooded and my chest ached at the unfairness of it all, part of me wondered:

Had Zachary seen a ghost? Had the Shift made our parents sick? Could a kiss really change the world?

Chapter Eleven

As I checked my reflection in the dining room mirror for the fourth time, I hoped that tonight would bring answers instead of more questions.

I also tried to forget where I'd been this time last week: in a dark, frigid field, with Zachary keeping me warm.

"Good color choice." Megan tucked in the tag of my royal blue sweater. "Not red, not violet. Definitely don't want to wear team colors tonight."

"Teams? You mean ex-boyfriend versus ex-almost-boyfriend in the World Series of Awkward?"

"Ooh, and I wore black, like an umpire."

"You always wear black these days. It's depressing."

"We were talking about you." She put her arm around my shoulder.

"Don't worry, you look hot. In three minutes, Zach'll be kicking himself for breaking up with you."

The knock at the door made me jump.

"Make that three seconds," Megan added.

I smoothed my hair on my way through the living room, grateful my aunt was working late so she wouldn't interrupt our four-way meeting.

I opened the door for Zachary. Tonight the porch light on his face seemed sallow rather than golden. His eyes drooped at the corners, as if he hadn't been sleeping.

"Hey," I said softly. Despite my hurt, it was hard to stay mad at him, knowing what he was going through with his dad.

"Hi." He glanced past me. "Am I late?"

"You're never late." I stepped back from the door into the living room, as far as the furniture would allow. "There's tea and cookies in the dining room. Sit in the chair at the other end so Logan can't see you."

"Why?" Megan asked me as Zachary passed her. "It's not like they can beat each other up."

"You'll see."

She picked up a cookie and sniffed it. "Mmm, almond. So, Zach, are you really taking Becca Goldman to the prom?"

I glared at her. She knew damn well he was.

"I really am." He sat in the far chair without looking at me.

Megan held her hand under her chin to catch the crumbs as she munched. "I thought she'd get back together with Tyler Watson, since he's way ahead in prom king polls."

"He's with Stacey Sellars now, and before that, Caitlyn Adams—"

"But Tyler and Becca are historic. They were prom prince and princess last year."

"And this is this year." Zachary slapped open his notebook. "Call the ghost."

Megan picked up another cookie and joined me at the bottom of the stairs, where we could see into both rooms. I flicked the wall switch to turn off the living room lamps, leaving a few candles burning, then dimmed the dining room chandelier to its faintest setting. The house looked ready for a séance.

"Okay, Logan," I said. "You know where to go."

He appeared, standing next to the far end of the couch. He cast a wary gaze around the living room, then at the stairs behind me. "Is that guy here?"

"Zachary's in the dining room."

"And he's a pre-Shifter, so he can't hear me call him a dickwad, right?"

"Logan, sit down and shut up." I clanged a spoon against a mug to call the meeting to order. "Before we start, we all have to promise total secrecy."

Megan raised her hand. "Swear."

"You know you can trust me," Zachary said.

Logan winced and covered his ears. "Could he not talk? It hurts my soul."

Since Megan's mouth was full of cookie, I said to Zachary, "Your voice seems to bother him, so maybe you could write your questions and answers."

Zachary scowled as he clicked on his ballpoint pen.

"Wait." Logan raised his hand like a schoolkid. "Ghosts can't lie, so I can't swear secrecy."

"Zach already knows you can't lie." I looked into the dining room. "You sure you're okay with this?"

Zachary nodded and scribbled in his notebook, then tore out the page and slapped it on the table for Megan, who retrieved it.

She laughed, sucking powdered sugar off her thumb. "It says, 'If he tells anyone, I will obsidian his punk violet arse into oblivion.'"

"Very funny," Logan said. "Hey, before I share any secrets with this guy, I need to know if we can trust him." He looked at Megan. "Ask him if he's a fan of Rangers or Celtic."

She sifted through the assorted cookies. "I don't think he gives a shit about hockey and basketball."

"But he gives a giant shit about soccer. Rangers and Celtic are the two big teams in the Scottish Premier League. They're both from Glasgow, like him."

"So?"

"It's not like rooting for the Yankees or Red Sox. Rangers fans are anti-Irish." He looked at me. "Anti-Catholic."

I shook my head. "You really need to enter the twenty-first century."

"Zach," Megan said, "Logan wants to know if you root for the Rangers or the Celtics. Apparently, the fate of the universe depends on your answer."

Zachary gave a silent scoff. His left eye twitched as he scrawled his essay-length response. Then he tossed the whole notebook to Megan.

She angled the paper to the dim light of the chandelier. "It says, 'I don't fancy either of those overpaid packs of bawbags. I support Partick Thistle. *Real* football for *real* Glaswegians.'" She winged the notebook back to Zachary. "I don't know what that means."

"Did he pass?" I asked Logan.

He simmered. "Bastard probably always says the right thing."

"Nope." I noticed Zachary writing frantically. "Now what?"

He held up his notebook to face me: *I get to ask him one free question at the time of my choosing.*

"What is this, the Supreme Court? Just ask."

He circled *at the time of my choosing.*

"I'm bored," Megan said. "Let's spill some secrets."

I launched into the first point before anyone could interrupt. "Zachary and I were born a minute apart. Right before and after the Shift."

"Old news." Megan bit her cookie. "You told me when you guys met. Tons of people are born every minute."

"Not in our minutes. Zach and I were the only ones."

"What happened to the other babies?" Logan glared at the dining room. "What did he do to them?"

"Nothing," I snapped. "They were born earlier or later."

"How do you know for sure?" Megan asked.

"The DMP told me." It was true that they'd confirmed it, but I'd heard it first from Ian. I didn't want to mention him if we didn't have to. "They've been keeping tabs on me."

"Wait." Her eyes and mouth went round. "If you were born right when the Shift happened, does that mean you caused it?"

"I don't know what it means. But I think it gave Zachary this—thing he can do." I waited for him to seize this last chance to back out, but he simply stared at the table in front of him, running his thumb over the corner of his notebook. "He makes ghosts disappear."

"Mr. Red," Logan murmured.

"What did you call him?" Megan asked.

Zachary stiffened. "What did he call me?"

"Ow!" Logan covered his ears. "Tell him to shut up."

"Please don't speak," I reminded Zachary. "He called you Mr. Red, because to him, you look like you're wearing a Santa suit."

Logan snorted. "More like Little Red Riding Hood."

"Wild," Megan said. "So, Aura, if Zach has this power for being the Last, what do you get for being the First?"

"She cures shades," Logan replied. "And she brought me back to life."

Megan's hand halted with the cookie halfway to her mouth. "When you say 'back to life'—"

I explained. "For about fifteen minutes on the equinox, Logan was human again. He was alive."

She shook her head vigorously, a pair of tiny auburn braids sweeping her cheeks. "That's not even remotely possible."

"It happened," Logan said.

"And then what?" She looked between the two of us. "Oh my God."

"No, not *that*," I said. "Fifteen minutes isn't enough time, anyway."

She and Zachary burst out laughing.

Logan squeezed his fists beside his head at the sound. "What's so funny?"

Zachary smirked as he scribbled, then showed me his notebook: *15 mins = > enough time. Trust me.*

I wondered how many times he'd done it with Suzanne in their eight months, three weeks, and a day and a half. Probably a lot, if fifteen minutes was more than enough time.

I quickly changed the subject (sort of). "Zachary's and my powers are sort of . . . fluid." I winced at my choice of words, since it was exchanging fluids that made it happen.

"What do you mean?" Logan asked.

I twisted my hands together, unintentionally making a reverse spider-swear. "When we, um—sometimes I can scare off ghosts. And he says he can see them."

"When?" Megan said. "Is this another equinox thing?"

"No, it's—" I kept my eyes away from Zachary. "It's a kissing thing."

"What?" Logan leaped up from the couch. "You mean the other night, I couldn't be with you in the car because you'd been hooking up with him?"

"Get over yourself!" Megan told him. "Did you expect her to join a convent?"

"This isn't regular kissing," Logan said to me. "He's turning you red."

I felt myself blush, as if to prove his point. I touched the banister behind me, to steady myself if Logan got shady.

"Is that what you want?" he asked me. "For him to change what you are?"

"It doesn't matter what I want, because it's over."

Megan turned to Zachary. "That's why you broke up with her? She said it was complicated."

"Aura?" Logan spoke in a low, almost threatening voice. "Did you kiss him on your birthday? Did you make me shade?"

"Whoa, what?" Megan's hands formed a time-out T. "Logan shaded on your birthday?" She looked at Zachary. "Did you know about this?"

He nodded, then met my eyes long enough for my memory to lock on to that night.

I turned back to Megan. "Remember when I fell off my porch roof and Logan woke you up so you could get Gina?"

"Yeah."

"I fell because he shaded."

Megan looked at him. "But Logan was a ghost when I saw him that night. How'd he make it back from shade?"

"I was so scared I had hurt her." Logan shook his head at the floor, passing his foot through the leg of the coffee table. "I didn't care about myself anymore."

"Awww," she said.

Zachary tapped the corner of his notebook on the table to get Megan's attention, then spread his hands.

She told him, "Logan says he came back from shade for Aura."

"Tell Zachary that seeing Aura fall made me forget myself." Logan stepped as close as he could, keeping his gaze on me. "Tell him it made me forget everything except how much I love her."

Megan quietly recited Logan's words. Zachary's mouth opened, then shut. He wiped his face and picked up his pen. With his elbow on the table, he shielded his eyes as he touched the ballpoint's tip to the blank page. It trembled, but didn't move. I swallowed, my mouth suddenly dry.

Finally he set down the pen, resting his fingers on the barrel as if it were the trigger of a gun.

"What did he write?" Logan snarled. "What can he say to that?"

"Nothing." I closed my eyes, the hurt seeping down the sides of my neck into my chest. "Nothing at all."

"That's because he'll never love you like I do."

"Logan says—"

I stopped Megan. "Please. Don't."

She laid a gentle hand on my shoulder. "Sorry, Aura, but you know it's wrong to censor ghosts." Megan turned to Zachary. "You'll never love her like he does."

Zachary's face went stony, even as his green eyes filled with fire. He swiped a hand across his empty page, then began to write, gripping the pen so hard, the creases of his knuckles turned red.

"What's he saying?" Logan asked.

Megan sidled around the table to read over Zachary's shoulder. "Uh-oh."

He clicked off his pen and sat back in his seat, keeping his eyes straight ahead.

"'For my free question.'" Megan took a deep breath. "'Do you love her enough to let her go?'"

I turned to Logan, expecting an instant "Yes." He'd already told me as much—not in so many words, but in his plans to pass on and his agreement to be my friend.

Yet Logan was struck silent. A cold snake slithered up my spine. I'd never asked him the question so directly, never forced him to search his soul for the strength to release me.

"Logan?" I whispered.

"That's not a fair question." He began to pace. "How am I supposed to answer that?"

"You can't lie," Megan said, "so you give the only answer that'll come out."

"I can't." He put his hands to his head, gripping the once-blond spikes. "Don't make me say it."

I took a shaky step away from him, then another. He couldn't say he loved me enough to let me go. Because it wasn't true.

I met Zachary's eyes, which held sorrow, not smugness. Even though he'd one-upped Logan. Even though his own answer to that question would be a clear, quiet, "Yes."

He whispered, "I'm sorry."

"Fuck you!" Logan bellowed, his voice crackling. "Fuck you, you piece-of-shit coward! You can touch her and kiss her any time you want, but you break her heart because you don't want to see ghosts? What the fuck is wrong with you?" He lurched toward the dining room.

I put my hands up. "Logan, no!"

Zachary stood and moved forward. "What's wrong? Is he threatening you?"

"Augggh!" At the sound of Zachary's voice, Logan dropped to his knees, his outline flickering black. He'd stopped just in time to avoid seeing Zachary.

"Zach, I'm fine! Just stay there." I stumbled, dizzy from turning my head and from Logan's shady energy.

"Aura!" Zachary rushed toward me.

Logan vanished with a shriek. I clutched the banister at the bottom of the stairs, stopping my fall.

Zachary caught me around the waist. "Are you all right?"

"I told you I was fine." I brushed him off. "I also told you to stay over there." I sank onto the bottom step and bent my head, letting my hair veil my face.

"I'm sorry," he said. "But I couldn't let him get away with that. I couldn't let you think I don't—" He didn't finish the sentence. "I hope he's all right."

"Zach, you better go." Megan sat beside me and placed a protective hand on my back.

"Right." He gathered his notebook from the table, then passed the stairs on the way out, so close I could've reached out and stopped him.

At the door, Zachary lingered, fingertips tapping the brass knob. The moment stretched on as I waited to hear his next words.

He had only two. "Good night."

"Tell me how that could've gone worse."

I sat with Megan at the dining room table to smother and drown my dashed hopes with cookies and tea.

"The DMP could've shown up. Or the Channel Four news team." She poured me a cup of tea, which looked lukewarm, based on the lack of steam. "So, I was thinking, you said no other babies were born in the same minutes as you and Zachary, right?"

"Right."

"But instead of you guys keeping all the other babies from being born at that time, what if no one was meant to be born in those minutes? But somehow you guys got in." She licked her finger and used it to dab up her plate's remaining powdered sugar. "It's like at a club, when they stop letting people inside for whatever reason, and they put the velvet ropes up? And then the bouncer's friends, or some hot girls, or famous people walk up, and they get in without having to wait."

I stared at her, then examined the contents of my plate. "What kind of drugs is my grandmom putting in these cookies?"

"Ah. Skepticism from the girl whose ghost boyfriend came back to life just long enough to get laid. By the way, why didn't that happen?"

"It almost did. I'm so sick of almosts." I told her the whole story. It felt good to talk about something as normal as sex (normal for people who were not me).

Megan left an hour later, after I promised she could help me find a prom dress over the weekend.

Once the house was silent, I sat on the couch and turned off the lamp. "Logan, you can come back if you want."

He appeared at the other end of the sofa, in the same place he'd sat before, but now his knees were pulled to his chest. For once, he said nothing.

"I'm glad you didn't shade." My voice was toneless.

"Never going there again." He rested his hands on his knees. "That's the truth, as far as I know."

We sat in silence, contemplating the hardest truths, before he spoke again.

"Why is Zachary letting this power-trading thing come between you? Not that I mind. But I want to know what's worth making you miserable."

"He thinks we're breaching some kind of cross-Shift boundary and that it could hurt us or somehow mess up the world. His father just got lung cancer, like my mom had. So Zachary thinks our power-switching is a sign of something dangerous."

"Sucks about his dad. I know what that's like."

"Yeah, I remember." I'd been with the Keeleys the night Logan's father had his first heart attack.

"So you think Zachary's right about all this?"

"I think he's scared. Not *of* me. Maybe *for* me."

"Huh. I wish I had the guts to be scared."

I thought I knew what he meant, but asked him anyway. I wanted to hear him say it.

"When he gave me that trick question," Logan said, "if I loved you enough to let you go, I wanted to say yes. I wanted it to be true. I know it's what's best for you." He shook his head at the wall between himself and the dining room. "I thought tonight I could prove I was the better guy for you. I thought I'd prove I loved you more, and you would—" He set his elbow on the back of the couch and rubbed his mouth. "But a jerk like me can never compete with someone so fucking pure of heart."

"You can't help what you feel."

"I can try harder to feel something different." His fist tightened on his knee, then let go. "At least I've got the music now to distract me, and maybe help get these feelings out of my system."

"The music?"

"I picked a band Sunday night. That's what I was trying to tell you in the car, but you were too red."

"Who's in this band?"

"Three sixteen-year-olds—Josh, Heather, and Corey." His gloom dissipated as he spoke. "They call themselves Tabloid Decoys."

"Great name."

"It's from that song 'Leech,' by Eve 6."

"I remember that band! We used to love them when we were kids."

"Remember that talent show we did for our folks, where we sang 'Inside Out'?"

I laughed at the memory of us screaming into fake microphones. "We must've been six years old."

"I loved that line about the heart in a blender. I thought it was so funny." He touched his chest, his smile diminishing. "I wonder if Mom still has the video."

"I'll ask Dylan. You could play it on a screen before one of your shows."

Logan's eyes lit up, glowing a brighter violet than the rest of him. "That'd be awesome! But *show*, not shows. We're doing one big concert, on the solstice."

"You mean, with—"

"My real hands, holding a real guitar." He stretched his fingers. "If I turn human again."

"You told your bandmates about being solid? You barely know them."

"Calm down. No one knows about that except the four of us. It'll be a surprise."

"And then what'll you do?"

"Play a few tunes, and probably turn back to ghost, like before. Then I'll pass on if I can. I've got seventy-nine days to make myself worthy."

"What if you stay alive?"

He tilted his head. "Then I guess I'll play an encore."

I tried to smile at his joke. "The DMP won't know what to do with you—what to do with *us*—if you pull this off."

"Kind of funny, since they're sponsoring the whole thing."

A sudden thought occurred to me. "Logan, if it gets out that ghosts can come back to life—even if it's just you—it'll blow people's minds."

"Cool, huh?"

"Not cool. Pre-Shifters have barely gotten used to the idea that ghosts exist. Now you've proven that shading can be reversed. If you show that death itself can be undone, there'll be a massive, worldwide freak-out. It would be like aliens landing, maybe worse."

"Huh," he said. "I hadn't thought about that."

"No, you only thought about how fun it would be for you. I can't be part of this."

"Wait. What if we came up with a way to let people believe it was some kind of illusion?"

"Like a magic trick?"

"Sure. Then they could choose to believe it or not." He leaned forward. "It'd be worth it, don't you think?"

I pictured him standing in the spotlight one last time, his hands bringing magic out of the shiny black Fender, his eyes gleaming with the energy of the crowd and the ecstasy of creation. After months in the shadows, being less than nobody, he could let his light shine forth.

He could be a god again.

I'd have done almost anything to give him such a send-off. It wouldn't erase the tragedy of his death—nothing ever could—but it would leave us both with a memory of glory.

I put my hand over Logan's. "Totally worth it."

Chapter Twelve

So what are we looking for here?" Megan rifled through a rack of prom dresses at our favorite formal-wear shop in Mount Washington. "Sexy, sassy, funky, what?"

"I'll know it when I see it." I picked up a blue dress, then promptly put it back when I saw the skirt was slit up to the thigh. "Probably not sexy."

"You don't want to put Zachary in a world of hurt? I would."

"He'll be too busy drooling over Becca. She always looks amazing in formal wear."

"True. But you're the one he loves. He said so."

"He didn't say so." I'd replayed his exact words in my head the last four nights, trying to decipher their meaning. "He said he couldn't let me think that he didn't . . . something."

"Love you."

"Nope. If he did, he would've come out and said it. Logan says it all the time."

"Logan says everything that pops into his head. Zachary actually thinks first."

"He thinks too much."

She snorted. "At least Zach half said he loved you. Have you even a quarter said it to him? No, you're still at the admitting-it-to-yourself stage."

I grumbled and held up a purple gown with straps crisscrossing the chest. "You think Dylan would like this?"

"If it comes with a Wonder Woman cape. Why do you care what Dylan would like?"

"He's my date. More important, he's not Logan or Zachary."

"Points for him. Ooh, that style comes in red."

"No red." Was Megan still trying to wean me off Logan? "I hear a ton of ghosts show up outside Ridgewood on prom night. I'd hate to ruin their nostalgia-fest."

"But you look so hot in red." She turned me to the mirror and held the red dress in front of me. I had to admit, it was the perfect complement to my tan skin and dark eyes.

I brushed it aside. "I don't want to look hot. It'll give Dylan the wrong idea."

"Good point. You need to look gorgeous, but not ho-baggy. Let's try on the purple one."

The dressing room was too small for two people, so Megan sat outside the door, on the platform with the three-way mirror.

I undressed quickly, wanting to get this over with. I stepped into the gown, almost tripping on the straps.

She heaved a dramatic sigh. "Mickey and I stopped having sex."

I had no clue how to respond to that announcement. "On purpose?"

"On purpose for him."

"Why?"

"He said he couldn't take the pressure anymore. We've only done it twice since Logan died. Twice in six months, Aura. Before that it was twice a day, practically. Not every day, but every day I saw him."

"Wow." My mind flashed to Zachary and his ex-girlfriend again. Maybe Suzanne wasn't even his first. How experienced was he? "I never knew you guys were so bunnylike."

"What was the point in telling you? You would've thought I was pressuring you to do it with Logan."

"I wish I had." I shimmied the dress up over my hips. "I wish a lot of things."

"Me too."

I frowned down at the dress's crisscross straps, trying to figure out where my head went. "What'd Mickey mean, he can't take the pressure?"

"The pressure to be happy, I guess. The pressure to climb out of his everlasting pain." She sighed again. "He can't see past it. It's like trying to see around the sky, he says. It only goes away when he closes his eyes or turns to the ground. Meaning, when he just shuts off."

I paused my struggle to put on the dress, contemplating the wreckage Logan had left behind. "I know."

"Do you?" She was silent for a moment. "Logan's my friend, too. Everyone forgets that. I've spent six months comforting you and Mickey and Siobhan, and not once has anyone ever said, 'Wow, Megan, it sucks that your good friend died, that boy you've known since you were little kids. I bet you miss him. I bet you loved him.'"

I stared at my reflection. "I'm so sorry."

"It's like we're back in the neighborhood playing freeze tag, and Logan's It. Everyone he touches has to stop living, until we're all frozen."

I rested my forehead against the mirror. I'd thawed for a while, with Zachary, but now I felt more cold and alone than ever. To top it off, I'd been a horrible friend, so wrapped up in my own pain that I'd ignored Megan's.

"If Mickey and I break up," she said, "I'll be the last one Logan froze. I guess that makes me It."

"No." I hurried out of the dressing room, holding up the skirt so I wouldn't trip. "Don't be It. Don't start a new misery game."

She looked up at me, sniffling. "Then what can I do?"

I crouched down and took her hands. "Just because you can't make Mickey happy doesn't mean there's something wrong with you."

"If I can't make him happy, then who can?"

"Maybe only Logan can. Or Prozac. Or nothing. But it's not your fault." I squeezed her wrists. "And Megan? I'm sorry you lost Logan."

She burst into a fresh cascade of tears. I hugged her, my unzipped dress falling open in back.

"Seeing Logan at your house the other night," she sobbed, "made me think of the times we all hung out. There were always cookies from your grandmom's bakery, and we'd get on a sugar high, crank up the music, and sing and dance until we puked."

"I'm pretty sure you did all the puking," I said, trying to cheer her up.

She let go of me and swiped under her eyes, smearing her brown mascara. "Maybe we should've stayed like that, just hanging out. Maybe we never should've kissed those Keeley boys."

I tried not to think about that parallel fantasy universe. Maybe we'd all still be friends, even after the Keeleys left the neighborhood. Maybe Logan and I would bring our girlfriends and boyfriends in and out of the group, and maybe we'd always have a crush on each other, just a little.

But at least he'd still be alive.

Chapter Thirteen

Zachary and I had unfinished business.

Having missed the private opening of the ancient-astronomy exhibit due to our aborted second date, we owed our history thesis adviser, Eowyn Harris, a trip to the Maryland Science Center. She'd promised to show us something that would help with our research. Our curiosity—and our desire not to flunk World History—finally overcame our attempts to avoid each other.

I stood on my porch Saturday afternoon, two weeks before the prom, waiting for Zachary to pick me up. Gina was kneeling by the flower bed lining the front walkway, pretending to pull weeds. I knew she just wanted to snoop.

My aunt thought I'd been spending too much time playing publicist for Logan and his band. I didn't have much choice, if I wanted to keep my secrets secret. But watching them rehearse in our basement, hearing the crash of cymbals and wail of electric guitar echoing off the concrete walls, brought back the best parts of Logan's life. Nothing got my pulse pumping like the steady thrum of a live bass guitar.

Well, almost nothing, I thought, trying to shove kissing-Zachary memories into my mind's dark closet.

"Feel free to have dinner at the Inner Harbor." Gina deadheaded a pair of impatiens, then pushed up the sleeves of her denim work shirt. "If Zachary can get enough time off from taking care of his dad."

"No, I'll be back early for pizza-and-sappy-movie night."

A familiar green Mini Cooper stopped on the street in front of the house, beeping its horn.

"Have fun!" Gina said, way too jolly.

I tried to look casual as I made my way down the front walk and through the low iron gate. I tried to make every step scream, *I am not even remotely in love with you, so there. Ha.*

"Hi." I sank into the front seat, hating how close together the car made us sit.

Zachary met my eyes briefly. "How are you?"

"Fine. How's your dad?"

"Tired." He put the car in gear and pulled out into the street. "He has chemotherapy every other Thursday, so by Saturday he's completely shattered. He'll sleep today, because the medicines that keep him from throwing up also keep him from staying awake."

"That sucks."

"At least it lets him rest, and gives Mum a chance to get out for a few hours. It's hard on her."

I noticed he no longer seemed to have trouble driving and talking at the same time. "What do you mean?" I asked him. "Besides the obvious."

"He's a terrible patient. Last night she tried to help him with his bath, and he was like, 'Stop it, I'm no' a wee bairn,' and she was like, 'Well, you're certainly behaving like one. Perhaps I should set you in your pram?'"

I covered my mouth as I laughed. Then I rewound his impersonation, especially the accent he'd used for his mother. "Wait—your mom's English?"

"No, she's a Macdougal. Her great-grandparents moved from Scotland to England."

"So she's as English as I am American."

"Exactly."

"Which is very. So doesn't her Sassenach accent annoy you?" I teased, exaggerating his own dialect.

He chuckled and gave me a sidelong glance that heated my cheeks. "You remembered Sassenach. Good." The light ahead turned yellow, and Zachary hit the brake, a little too hard. The good humor faded from his face. "All this chemo would be tolerable if we knew it would save my dad, but it's not bloody likely."

I fidgeted with the buckle on my messenger bag. "So, how are you doing, with all this?"

He nodded, lips tight, but said nothing.

"I'm sorry." I cleared my throat. "I should've called in the last couple weeks to see how you were."

"Aye—I mean, no, I don't blame you. I'm not angry." He rested his elbow on the window frame. "But I think maybe we shouldn't avoid each other. I don't think that's best."

"I agree," I said, biting my lip to keep from smiling.

"Good." His shoulders lowered as the tension dripped out.

I let myself relax into the soft leather seat. Zachary had admitted, in his roundabout way, that he needed me—at least during this crisis. I would be there for him as a friend, like he'd been for me after Logan died. I would stop pining for him.

Any minute now.

"It's a lot bigger than it looks in pictures," Zachary whispered.

Between us and the entrance to the exhibit lay a life-size replica of Newgrange's main kerbstone, a ten-foot-long rock shaped like a giant loaf of Italian bread. The kerbstone's carved spirals, diamonds, and squiggles made me dizzy, so I focused on the straight vertical line dividing it in half. I stroked my mom's garnet pendant through my red sleeveless top, feeling closer to her now than ever.

Zachary and I had arrived at the museum early, but hadn't wanted to wait for Eowyn to see the exhibit. It felt like we were on the brink of a big new clue or two. Or seven or eight.

He stepped aside, unable to resist reading the nearby informational plaque. I stared past the kerbstone, through the dark doorway to the Newgrange passage tomb exhibit.

Zachary returned. "The sign says that sunlight shines in the chamber on winter solstice for seventeen minutes."

"Uh-huh." I couldn't tear my eyes from the doorway, which seemed to darken the longer I stared at it.

Zachary leaned in close. "On the equinox, how long did Logan have a body?"

"About fifteen—" I blinked hard. "Whoa. It might've been seventeen minutes from the time he came through my window as a shade until—" I gave a slight cough. "Until it was over."

"Could be important," Zachary said in a subdued voice as he faced the kerbstone. "Do you know what these carvings mean?"

I sensed he was changing the subject as much as he was being curious. "There are tons of theories. It pisses me off how archaeologists never agree on anything." I pointed to the left side of the kerbstone. "I think this three-spiral design is only found at Newgrange. Other places in the world have one spiral, or two spirals like that one." I indicated the area on the right side of the vertical line.

"I bet the answer's inside." Zachary rounded the kerbstone and ducked through the faux Newgrange entrance. I followed.

The room beyond the doorway was about fifty feet long. Its walls displayed detailed photos of Newgrange's excavation. *Boring*. Maybe I didn't want to be an archaeologist after all. Or maybe I was just dying to get to the good part, straight ahead of us—a replica of Newgrange's central chamber. The place where my mother and Zachary's father stood a year before we were born. The place where their lives changed forever.

As we entered, we gaped at the towering ceiling made of giant flat stones, stacked overlapping like roof shingles. In real life they would hold up hundreds of tons of rocks and dirt. This one looked like it would collapse if we breathed too hard.

Three recesses branched off the round chamber. They were more like the size of walk-in closets than the cubbyholes I'd imagined. The ones to our left and right each contained a smooth, shallow stone basin.

A trio of tourists wandered in, their jaws dropping at the sight of the ceiling, like ours had. We edged toward the far recess so their yammering wouldn't ruin our mood.

Zachary read another sign. "This is the only recess hit by the solstice sunrise." He leaned forward, examining the walls. "Aura, come see!"

I squatted beside him and saw another three-spiral design carved into the side of the recess. "Wild. It actually looks like two spirals with a third one coming out of them. See how the top one leads into the bottom one, like the letter S?"

"Hmm." His forehead creased into deep vertical lines as he thought. I had the worst impulse to smooth them out with my fingers. Then maybe run those same fingers through his hair, until he let go of all his worries.

I was lost in this daydream when he spoke. "Didn't Eowyn say something about the three recesses representing father, mother, and child?"

"Yeah, but nothing in my reading backs that up. It's probably her personal theory."

"But that's sort of what this looks like. The two spirals joining together, making a third."

I tilted my head to see it from another angle. "You think it looks like sex? You are such a guy."

"That's not what I mean." He glanced at me. "All right, it is what I mean. Symbolically."

I became painfully conscious of the tiny space between us. "At least we're coming up with theories for our paper."

He gestured to the rock face. "Should probably leave out the pornography, aye?"

I laughed. "We'll disguise them so Mrs. Richards thinks they're just spirals."

"Better write this down before we forget." He pulled a pen and a small notepad from his back pocket. Something fell from between the pages and clattered at his feet.

"What's that?"

"Nothing," he said quickly, reaching for it.

My toes tingled as I picked up the small metal circle. It was the bottle cap I'd given him. I placed it in his palm, my fingers brushing his as I let go.

"Er, you must be wondering . . ."

"No." I reached into my bag and brought out the matching cap, the one he'd found in the field.

We held the spiral caps up to the design on the wall, one above the other.

"Odd, don't you think?" he whispered.

"Odd that we found them, or odd that we kept them?"

"Found them." He closed his fingers over his own bottle cap. "I know why I kept mine."

I looked into his eyes, shadowed by the light from above. My own mind seemed to circle—not just right now, but every day, playing the same thoughts over and over. But like the line of the spiral, maybe now I was finally getting somewhere.

"What do you think?" said a voice behind me.

We stood and stepped back to see our adviser, Eowyn Harris, headed toward us.

"Of the exhibit," she added.

"It's brilliant." Zachary had the goofy smile he often wore around her. Though twice our age, she was the most beautiful woman I'd ever seen in person. Her long blond curls fell nearly to her waist, and her flowing periwinkle dress made her look like a flower on legs. If she weren't so nice, I would've hated her.

She watched the tourists move out of the chamber. "Glad it's not crowded. I really need to talk to you both."

I hoped she would give us answers instead of more mysteries.

"Your father called me," she told Zachary. "I'm so sorry about his illness."

He looked confused. "Thanks, but why did he ring you? I didn't know you'd even met."

"Not in person, and this was only the second time we've spoken. Last summer he called me before you came to the States. He was tracking down all twenty people who were here on that day."

Zachary and I exchanged a cautious look. Eowyn had never admitted to being at Newgrange with his father and my mother. When we'd asked her about it, she'd changed the subject. I wondered why she suddenly wanted to talk about it now.

She stared at the recess behind us. "They were standing right there when it happened. Right where you're standing now."

My spine prickled, like a spider had dropped down the back of my shirt. Eowyn had always been a little, um, funky, but this was creepy talk even for her.

"When what happened?" Zachary said.

"I call it the Shine. One year before the Shift. I was over here at sunrise." Eowyn backed up, near the left-hand recess, then pointed to the chamber door. "The light came through, thin like a laser, and stretched along the center of the floor, getting longer and longer, penetrating the chamber like—" She gave a nervous laugh. "Well, there's a reason why they think it's connected to fertility."

"Told you," Zachary whispered over my shoulder.

"Anyway." Eowyn cleared her throat. "It was the most amazing thing I've ever seen. I was only sixteen, but I swore that unlocking Newgrange's secrets would be my life's work. And that was even before it happened."

I fidgeted with my necklace, dying to shout, *When* what *happened?*

She continued. "When the sunlight reached all the way to the spot where you're standing, the tour guide said we could walk through it. He said that some people believe it can heal their spiritual ills, or make a wish come true."

I looked at my feet, imagining them soaked in that magical light, and wondered what I would wish for.

"I was at the back of the line," Eowyn said, "so I could see each person as they passed through the light. A young woman and a middle-aged man were standing together. I didn't realize until later that they didn't know each other."

Zachary shifted closer to me, his hand almost brushing my arm.

Eowyn's gaze went far away. "They passed through the sunbeam—first Ian, then Maria—barely one second after each other. Something happened to them, and no one else." Her hands swept upward, encompassing our bodies. "They were filled with light."

I stared at her. "Filled?"

"Like it was a part of them." She seemed to search for the words. "Like a candle inside a jack-o'-lantern. Except this was no candle, this was—this was the sun itself."

Zachary uttered a word I couldn't translate.

"I had to shade my eyes, it was so bright," she said. "My mother thought I was getting another migraine, which I was. I always did when I . . . saw things."

My heart started racing. "Did anyone else see it?"

"Just me, that I know of." She grimaced. "Please don't think I'm crazy."

"Did you tell my father?" Zachary asked. "Or Aura's mother?"

"Not your dad." She looked at me. "I told Maria right afterward, outside. Then she tracked me down a few years later. The government had been questioning her about you and the solstice. She was scared."

"I didn't know that." My mind boggling, I wondered if my mom had ever shared her fears with Gina.

Eowyn said, "We corresponded off and on until she died."

Zachary flinched at the sound of the word, then passed a hand over his forehead as if he had a sudden fever. "That light—could it have made them sick?"

"Maybe. Maybe not." Her brows pinched in sympathy. "There's much that we don't understand."

"Aye." As he turned away from me, I heard him whisper, "Too much."

When Zachary and I entered his apartment, Ian was sitting in the armchair, watching a soccer game on TV.

He practically sprang out of his chair to greet me. "Aura, it's good to see you again. Of course, in my state, it's good to see anybody again."

"Ian, must your humor be so grim?" A brunette woman made a tsking sound on her way out of the kitchen. "Hello, Aura. I'm Fiona, Zachary's mum."

As she took my hand, I could see where Zachary got his smile that felt like a hug. It lit up his mother's smooth, fair face, reaching her vibrant green eyes.

Zachary made a beeline for the television. "How'd you find the Chelsea-Arsenal match?"

"ESPN's gone World Cup mad," Ian said, "so they're priming their viewers with English Premier League play."

"Brilliant." Gaze glued to the screen, Zachary sank onto the couch, all life's important questions forgotten.

I set my bag on the dining room chair and followed Fiona back to the kitchen, where she had tea already waiting for us.

She smiled at me. "Not a football fan, I assume?"

"I like lacrosse better. Soccer seems like a lot of running around for nothing."

"It seems that way at first." She pulled a polished wooden serving tray from a space next to the refrigerator. "But if you watch carefully, you'll see that one side wears the other down, little by little, finding their weak points, and hopefully in the end, they triumph. It's a game of patience."

I frowned as I helped her arrange the china on the tray. Zachary had shown the patience of a whole realm of saints, but in the end we'd only played to a draw.

"My son seems very fond of you."

I almost dropped a teacup. "Really?"

"Really. So what I want to know is"—she leaned against the fridge and spoke in a low voice—"why is he taking someone else to the prom?"

I looked down, running my fingers along the tray handle's wicker grip. "Because I'm an idiot."

Fiona laughed. "I'm certain he can claim a share of the idiocy." She opened the silverware drawer. "I've met Becca, and she's all right. She likes football, or at least pretends to convincingly enough."

Her revelation bothered me. Maybe Becca was being a fake, but it showed she liked Zachary enough to at least feign interest in something he cared about.

Worse, Becca'd been there for him in the last few weeks, getting him through this ordeal with his father. A lot more than I'd done.

Zachary appeared at the kitchen door. "It's halftime," he said to me. "Let's tell them now."

We went into the living room, where the television had been muted but not switched off. I sat next to Zachary on the loveseat, fighting off flashbacks of our last encounter here on Easter night.

How he'd given me his hands, his mouth, his understanding.

Fiona served Ian his tea, then pulled a dining room chair close beside him. They leaned toward each other almost instinctively, and I had an unexpected pang of jealousy, wishing I could've seen my own parents like that.

They kept their composure as we told them about the events Eowyn had described to us at the Science Center. The only sign of distress was a tight linking of hands when we got to the part about "the Shine."

"I can't help but think," Zachary said when we had finished the story, "that this light did something to you, Dad, and to Aura's mother. Maybe it gave you this disease. She had lung cancer, too."

"Although it was a different kind." I pronounced it carefully. "Adenocarcinoma."

Ian passed a hand through his hair, which had thinned on top from the chemotherapy. "I dunno if it caused that, but it might have had another effect, for the good." He looked at Fiona, who nodded and squeezed his wrist.

"Zachary," she said, "you know we were older than the average parents when you were born. I was thirty-eight and your father forty-one. It was because for a long time"—she shifted on her chair—"we couldn't have children."

"We were told in no uncertain terms," Ian said, "we had no chance. I was—" He waved his hand, apparently unable to utter the word "sterile."

"In any case," Fiona said, her expression slightly pained, "the year after your father went to Newgrange, we had you." She let out a nervous laugh. "Oh yes, there were doubts among our friends who knew of our problems." She pushed her silver hoop bracelet up and down her wrist. "Until you were born, and then no one could deny the resemblance."

Zachary shifted his feet in discomfort. I dropped my gaze to the doily on the coffee table, trying not to squirm at the Moores' attempt to talk about sex in front of their son—and the girl who wanted to do a lot more than talk about it with him.

"So." Zachary placed his hands on his thighs and declared, "I was never meant to be born."

"Bollocks," Ian said. "You *were* born, so you were meant to be. Even if it took a miracle."

"But if you hadn't gone to Newgrange, I wouldn't exist."

Fiona said, "We'll never know that for certain."

"And you wouldn't be dying," Zachary told his father, "from this rare monster of a disease."

"We've discussed the statistics, aye?" Ian said sternly. "It's no' that uncommon for men with my background, who grew up in poor neighborhoods." He set down his tea without drinking it. "My family's flat was probably riddled with asbestos."

"That doesn't mean you didn't get it because of Newgrange."

"No, but any rational person would blame the thing that causes ninety-nine percent of mesotheliomas."

"I'm being perfectly rational." Zachary's strained tone contradicted his words. "But what Eowyn told us—"

"Listen," Ian said. "Having cancer's bad enough, without you trying to explain it with fairy tales."

Hurt scrunched the corners of Zachary's eyes. "Don't you want answers?"

"I just want . . ." Ian pressed his forefingers against his brows. "I want a nap."

Fiona put her arm around him. "Aura, please excuse us."

"Sure. Can I do anything?"

Her sad, tender smile stabbed me with its similarity to Zachary's. "Thank you, no."

She walked with Ian down the hallway, ignoring his protests that he didn't need any bloody help.

Zachary set his elbows on his knees and locked his fingers together. Staring at his father's empty chair, he seemed so alone.

In that instant, I knew it was a giant waste of time to deny that I loved him.

"I'm sorry." I reached to touch his shoulder, but he turned to me, eyes flashing.

"Sorry's not enough. You're like them. You think I'm mental."

I pulled my hand back. "I don't think that."

"You believe me, then, aye?" He said it as a challenge. "Of course not." He swiped the car keys off the coffee table. "I'll take you home."

On the short ride to my house, I pulled out the picture postcards I'd bought at the exhibit. The image in the Newgrange front kerbstone photo was all too clear.

I traced the vertical line that was so deeply carved into the rock, there could be no doubt that it was meant to be part of the design.

"This sounds crazy," Zachary said when we stopped at a light, "but maybe that line is supposed to be the Shift. The builders of Newgrange predicted it."

I couldn't scrub my voice of skepticism. "Five thousand years before it happened?"

"Time is irrelevant. Or it could've happened before, and history repeated itself. Maybe that's why they built Newgrange in the first place." He let his head fall back on the headrest, his eyes rimmed with fatigue. "So many questions."

I gripped the postcard, digging its edge into the webbing between my fingers. These "questions" made me want to run to him so we could find the answers together. But the same questions made him want to run *away* from me. I sensed that the more I argued, the more he would dig in with his doom.

"Bad things may have happened because of it, Aura."

"Good things happened because of it, too." *You happened.*

"If you got hurt, and I was to blame—" He shook his head. "No. Not for anything."

I wondered what horrific scenarios were playing out in his head. Maybe he had gone "mental." But I wasn't about to abandon him to his pain.

As we reached my street, I said, "Call me if you want to talk. Or I'll call you."

He eased the car to a stop. "I think it's best we don't," he said slowly. "To be with you, and not with you—it's too much right now." He lowered his chin, staring through the spokes of the steering wheel. "I'm so sorry."

I managed a weak "okay," then looked down to see I'd folded the postcard in half, separating the two sides of the Newgrange kerbstone. I left it behind as I got out of the car.

If Zachary was right, and that deep, straight, sure line down the middle represented the Shift, then it was a line he would never cross.

Chapter Fourteen

S mile!"

I forced up the corners of my mouth as Dylan held out my corsage, still in its plastic box. Aunt Gina was hovering like a moth, her digital camera flashing every other millisecond.

Megan stood smirking on the other side of my porch, the midnight blue of her gothic corset gown absorbing the light. She elbowed Mickey.

"Dylan," he said in a monotone, "you're supposed to put it on her."

"Oh." Dylan opened the box, tearing the plastic with a crack that hurt my ears. His awkwardness clashed with the bold design of his tux, black with gray pinstripes, that made Mickey and Connor look ordinary. It fit with the dark, straight swoop of hair over his right eye. Dylan was on the verge of serious cute.

"Ooh, a dendrobium!" Gina exclaimed, then leaned in for a close-up.

Dylan pulled out the corsage's long pin with the pearl tip. He glanced at Siobhan's flowers, which were fastened to the single wide strap of her black mermaid-style dress.

He turned back to me, face full of confidence, then stopped when he saw how my purple gown's satin straps crossed my chest, providing no convenient corsage landing strip.

I lifted my left hand. "Try the wrist?" He looked at the pin with confusion. "Use the strap," I said.

"Oh! Got it." He stretched the white silky band over my hand. Then he straightened the purple flowers so that they lay flat against my skin. "Good?"

I smiled up at him, willing us both to relax. "Perfect."

He sent back a grin. The camera flashed.

"Finally! A nice shot of you two." Gina elbowed her way between us and displayed the picture on her camera screen. "Sweet, isn't it?"

My reply lodged in my throat.

Captured in pixels, Dylan's smile looked just like Logan's.

At the restaurant, the Keeleys sat on one side of the table, and the non-Keeleys on the other. It hurt to see the three remaining siblings all lined up, missing the brother who'd brought so much life. But when I mentally substituted Zachary for Dylan in the seat across from me, the image didn't fit.

Logan was rehearsing with Tabloid Decoys tonight, teaching them the songs he'd written since he died. It was a slow process, since he couldn't write down the notes or play them on the guitar. They had to transcribe them from his voice alone—not easy for a trio of sixteen-year-old amateurs, and not as much fun for me to watch as a full-blown practice.

I tried to think of a nonemotional dinner topic besides sports and the weather. "Do you two have gigs lined up for the summer?"

Siobhan shot a deadly glance at Mickey to her left. "Our last show is in Catonsville on June fifteenth."

"The last show?" My throat lumped at the thought of losing another Keeley tradition. "Why?"

"Because only one of us is serious about music," Mickey said through tight lips.

Siobhan clattered her fork against her plate. "I'm serious about music, I just don't want it to be my life. I never did."

"That's why we named the band the Keeley Brothers," he said, "because we never knew whether you were staying or going."

I exchanged a look with Dylan. Was he also wondering how many times they'd refer to Logan without using his name?

"It was because you wanted it to sound like the Clancy Brothers." Siobhan adjusted her corsage, which had already wilted. "Music isn't fun anymore. Why do it if we have to treat it like work? I might as well be an accountant."

"The point is to succeed, so you never have to feed yourself by being an accountant."

"God, Mickey, would you give up the starving artist routine? We've been millionaires since the settlement."

His response was almost a growl. "I'll starve before I spend a dime of that blood money."

"Mom and Dad are using it for your fancy music college."

"No they're not," he said. "I'm deferring enrollment. I won't go unless I can pay for it myself."

"What if you can't?" I asked him.

"Then I'll get a job and focus on my music."

Siobhan snorted. "He'll be a busker in a subway station."

Mickey folded his hands together, elbows on the table, and met no one's eyes. "I might move to Seattle."

A hush fell. Megan stopped cutting her salad and stared across the table at Mickey. This was obviously news to her, too.

The normally quiet Connor was the first to speak. "No, dude. Seattle's where people go to kill themselves. I read that someplace."

Mickey gave a single nod. "I read that, too."

Dread stole my appetite. Was Mickey thinking of ending his life, with all he had to live for?

"What about Austin?" Connor said. "Better scene, better weather."

Mickey picked up his water, but instead of drinking it, he stared through the side of the glass. "I like rain."

Scattered amid the sleek black limousines in the Ridgewood parking lot, the white Department of Metaphysical Purity vans looked like the losing side of a chess game.

My school's front courtyard was swarming with ghosts, who had no doubt returned to reminisce about their own prom night, and to watch the seniors and juniors pass by in our formal wear. Their ghostly light was reflected in the water of the courtyard's center fountain, turning it a deep violet.

Strolling down the front walk with Dylan, I scanned the crowd of ghosts, who were waving at us like children at a parade.

"I don't see him," Dylan said to me.

"Who?"

"Duh. Logan. Who else would you be looking for? Who else would I be looking for?"

We climbed the stairs and walked through the peaked stone archway into the school. I didn't glance back at the ghosts.

"Our Hunt Valley hotties are here!" Dragging her boyfriend, Christopher, Jenna Michaels hurried down the hallway in her red-trimmed black gown that rivaled Megan's dress in its gothy goodness. They joined Connor and Siobhan, acting as their Ridgewood dates so they could get into the dance.

We went to line up at the registration table—or as I thought of it, the point of no return. From here I could see into the dark cafeteria, where a pair of DMP agents patrolled the wall of windows, maybe making sure the BlackBox was keeping out the larger-than-usual crowd of ghosts. As if they could even know without one of us telling them. Maybe they were really there to check up on me or Zachary or both.

Behind the table, our class president, Amy Koeller, greeted us with a wide grin, her hand looped through a giant roll of raffle tickets. "Welcome to your Midsummer Night's Dream, aka the best Ridgewood Junior-Senior Prom ever!" As she bent to cross our names off the list, Christopher peered down her lilac fairy dress, provoking a jab in the ribs from Jenna.

"Where's your boyfriend?" I asked Amy. I'd figured he would come home from college for the prom. Assuming he existed.

"Freaking MIT physics final. On a Saturday, can you believe it? Next year, he says, he'll be here for my senior prom." She smoothed a long blond tendril away from her glittery face and glanced at her silver-and-diamond watch. "Hey, Aura, I know I can count on you for a huge favor. You know how the junior class council is in charge of putting on the prom?"

"I guess." I had not known that, but whatever.

"Molly Sachs, your homeroom's council member, is sick with the flu, and she was scheduled to take tickets from ten to eleven. Frankly, you're the only person from your homeroom I trust not to screw it up." She put her hands out to fend off my protest. "All you have to do is check off names and make them buy a raffle ticket."

I considered pleading mental incapacity, but the task would let me escape the dance floor's inevitable heartache.

"No problem. We'll trade places."

She looked up at Dylan. "Sweet."

He fidgeted with his tie as his face turned to panic.

Dylan and I moved to rejoin the others, who were standing together near a fake pear tree, looking down the hallway.

Mickey shook his head. "Man, that's hard-core."

"Takes some serious balls," Connor agreed.

Megan and Siobhan were just staring, mouths open.

I pushed past them so I could see. "What are you all—oh."

Under a trellis bedecked with swoops of green ivy and white holiday lights stood Zachary and Becca. They were surrounded by a semicircle of drooling senior girls, who were in turn surrounded by a semicircle of sullen senior boys.

Becca was wearing a strapless steel-silver gown with a subtle rhinestone trim that made her look like the ultimate ice queen. She was also wearing the world's smuggest face, because Zachary was wearing . . .

A kilt.

Yeah.

The short tuxedo jacket covered none of the kilt, whose background color picked up the dark forest green of his vest and eyes—or at least the color of his eyes as I remembered them. Not that I ever thought about that.

My gaze dropped to his off-white knee-high stockings. The laces of his black shoes crisscrossed his instep, ankles, and shins, tied in front with perfect bows. Around his waist—at his crotch, to be exact—hung a black leather pouch with silver accents that glittered in the trellis's white lights.

On its own, each piece of the outfit would have looked girlie. But together, they formed the most masculine package I'd ever seen.

"The green is for the forests of the Highlands where my clan comes from." Zachary pointed to the kilt's vertical threads. "The yellow line is for the sun that shines once every three weeks." He winked. "Luckily, we keep busy with lots of indoor activities."

The girls laughed. The boys glowered.

Behind me, Mickey whispered to Dylan, "Is that the guy?"

"Must be. I'm supposed to watch out for him."

"I can see why."

Zachary's face turned serious. "The red thread is for the blood my ancestors shed, kicking out the Sassenachs, the pasty weak English."

"So what's the blue?" asked Rachel Howard.

"The blue is for the water. In Irish Gaelic, Moore and Muir mean 'sea.'" He cocked his head. "But in Scottish Gaelic, it just means 'big.'"

The girls covered their mouths and cackled.

"What a tool," Mickey muttered.

Becca merely laced her arm through Zachary's and gave a quiet, knowing smile. I wanted to smack it off her face.

As if hearing the shrieks in my head, Zachary turned in my direction. When he saw me, he broke into a smile—a real one, not the arrogant smirk he'd been wearing for the last minute. I ducked behind the pear tree.

"What's that say on your belt thingie?" Hailey Fletcher asked Zachary.

"Er, it's the family herald."

"I can't read it."

"Hailey, get away from his crotch," Becca snapped, before her voice turned sweet. "Zachary, tell them what it says."

I peeked out from behind the branches.

"It's the family motto," he said. "*Durum patientia frango.*" Zachary looked at me from the corner of his eye as he translated. "By patience, I overcome difficulties."

I stared at him, frozen with regret. He'd asked me first. It could have been me standing with him. Even if we'd kept it painfully platonic to soothe his fears, I could've at least kept him out of Becca's clutches. If I hadn't been an idiot.

Her hand slid up his biceps. "I don't think you'll have difficulties tonight."

My eyes and nose began to burn, and I almost expected smoke to pour out my ears, like a cartoon character's.

"Forget him," Megan whispered to me. "Let's go dance."

I took Dylan's arm, steadying myself as we proceeded past Zachary and Becca's crowd, on into the gym. *Don't look back. Don't look back. Don't look back.*

I looked back. This time, Zachary wasn't watching me at all.

Chapter Fifteen

When did you get taller than your brothers?"

After three minutes of slow-dancing with Dylan—one hand on his shoulder and one in his hand, like people our parents' age—*that* was the best conversation starter I could conjure up.

"I don't know," he said.

Silence fell again.

I considered pleading sore feet so we could stop. In fact, my brand-new shoes were chafing like crazy. Thank God I brought blister bandages.

But as I loosened my hold, I saw, not ten feet away, Zachary and Becca dancing, next to another sparkly fake tree. Their bodies were melded together from chest to thigh, her arms draped around his neck, her fingers playing with the back of his hair. They were laughing together, at ease in each other's arms. Like something more than plain old prom dates.

Over Zachary's shoulder, Becca caught my eye. Her smile turned sly and triumphant.

I wanted to run away more than ever, but wouldn't give Becca the satisfaction. I twined my arms around Dylan's neck. "That's better."

His eyes widened at the sudden press of my chest against his. He looked away quickly, but his Adam's apple bobbed with tension.

People walking by did a double take at the sight of us, no doubt remembering Logan from when he went to Ridgewood before the Keeleys moved. Before bleaching his hair, Logan had looked a lot like Dylan did now.

My regret deepened. Only a total basket case would take her dead boyfriend's little brother to the prom.

As the song ended, Dylan practically pushed me away, then looked at his watch. "It's ten o'clock. Don't you have to do something?"

"Crap!" I said, the way most people would say, *Hallelujah!* "Come with me."

I hurried out to the hallway.

"Right on time!" Amy handed me a ballpoint pen and a thick roll of raffle tickets that looked no smaller than before. "Almost everyone is here, so you'll be catching the stragglers, aka the drunks." She picked up her purse. "Right now I am dying to dance."

"So is Dylan. He's a friend of mine." I put extra emphasis on the *F*-word, then pushed him in her direction. He gave me a panicky look as Amy dragged him off.

I sat at the table, grateful for the solitude. Alone, I didn't have to pretend to have a good time. I didn't have to pretend to ignore Zachary and Becca. Or pretend I didn't miss Logan more than ever.

At eleven o'clock, the class treasurer, D'Wayne Singletary, showed up to take the cash box and the raffle tickets. I thanked him and headed for the girls' room.

In the stall, I examined my right foot, grimacing at the red welts beneath the shoe's strap. "Ow." Luckily, the bathroom was empty, so no one heard me whine.

But then a trio of new voices sounded from the hallway outside. *Please keep walking. Please keep walking.*

A hand thumped the outer door, swinging it open.

Hailey Fletcher's squeal echoed in the tiled room. "Becca, how do you keep from humping that boy on the dance floor?"

"Massive self-control." Becca's footsteps stopped near the sink. "Gross! Look at the shine on my face."

"Powder. Now." Chelsea Barton snapped her fingers. "You have to look perfect for your prom queen picture."

"Don't jinx it," Becca said.

I heard the zip of a purse, then the clatter of makeup components, so I decided to stay put. I slipped off my right shoe, then quietly unwrapped a blister bandage.

"Becca, don't worry," Chelsea said. "The polls say you won by a mile."

"That's because everyone's scared of me. You never know how they'll vote in secret." She groaned. "My nose is like an oil spill. Zach really makes me sweat."

"He makes us all sweat," Chelsea said. "I am so hating you."

"I know. And Hailey, if you don't put a leash on your boyfriend—"

"What's Nate doing now?" Hailey asked as she entered the stall next to me.

"His cracks about Zachary's skirt and pantyhose? I can*not* be held responsible when Zach smashes Nate's head against the bleachers."

"He knows Nate's just bullshitting."

"First of all, Hailey," Becca said icily, "Nate isn't bullshitting, he's threatened. Second of all, Zachary seems calm, but he's tough. He's from inner-city Glasgow."

No, he's not, I thought as I pasted the bandage over my blister. Zachary was from Maryhill—a working-class Glasgow neighborhood, but with university types. Not "dodgy," as he would say.

"And don't forget," Becca continued, "those football hooligans get into huge fights—rows, they call them—and people get beaten to death. For all we know, Zachary's killed someone."

I rolled my eyes as I refastened my shoe. Dylan was probably wondering where I was by now.

"Fine, I'll talk to Nate," Hailey said. "Speaking of kilts, what's Zach wearing under there? I've always heard they go commando."

"I can't tell yet." Becca's words were distorted, as if she was putting on lipstick. "I tried to feel him up while we were slow-dancing, but that kilt is made out of wool."

"Did he grope you, too?"

"That's not his style." She sighed as she snapped her lipstick cap. "This is going to be the single greatest night of my life. I will be crowned a queen, and then I will wear that crown—and only that crown—while Zachary Moore finds out what it means to be royally screwed."

There was a chorus of hoots, following by the slap of a high five.

In your dreams. Becca had probably seen me walk in here and was saying all this to torture me. No way Zachary would sleep with her. Right? No.

"You have to give us the play-by-play," Chelsea said.

"I wouldn't do that to him." Becca's voice was almost vulnerable. "Whatever happens is between us."

Hailey whimpered. "But you'll tell us what he wears under the kilt, won't you?"

"Of course. It's my duty as an American."

The next voice belonged to Rachel, who I hadn't even realized was there, since she hadn't taken part in the catcalls. "Becca, have you two even kissed yet?"

"No, we were saving it for prom. I think."

"Uh-huh. You know who looks even hotter than Zach tonight?"

"Trick question," Becca said, "because the answer is no one. But who are you talking about?"

"Tyler Watson."

"Oh my God, yes!" Hailey exclaimed. "That boy is wasted on Stacey Sellars. And what is she wearing? Panda skin?"

Chelsea snickered. "I didn't know Lady Gaga had a line of prom gowns."

"Stacey can have Tyler," Becca said with a sneer. "For now."

"Oooh . . . ," they crooned.

"Tyler is so next month," Becca murmured. "After Zachary flies home with some pure dead brilliant memories." She mimicked his accent better than I ever could.

"You really think you and Zach'll do it?" Rachel said. "I thought he still liked Aura."

"Fuck Aura." Becca's purse zipped shut with emphasis. "By the time I'm done with him, he won't even remember her name."

As soon as I was released from Bitch Central, I hurried back to the gym, hoping to find Zachary. As I entered, the hip-hop tune's pounding bass seemed to crush my skull, even though it was a song I usually liked.

On the far end of the gym, Megan and Mickey stood side by side against the wall, shoulders not touching. I scanned the dance floor, where Siobhan and Connor were jamming with Jenna and Christopher.

I had no idea what I would say to Zachary ("I like your outfit"? "My heart is disintegrating"? "Please don't have sex with Becca"?), but I had to say something.

A hand waved in front of my face. "I'm right here."

I started at the sight of Dylan, then took the cup of punch he offered me. "Thanks. Have you seen the guy with the kilt?"

"Why?" His voice was full of caution, and I thought of Logan's warning to him, to watch out for Zachary.

"I have to tell him something." I didn't meet Dylan's eyes when I added, "It's for school."

"Riiight."

"So have you seen him?"

"You want something to eat? They have these awesome chips, I think they're crab-and-ranch flavored."

"I'm not hungry."

"I know that sounds gross, crab and ranch? But it works." He adjusted his tie again, maybe noticing he was rambling. "They also have plain chips."

"I said I'm not hungry." I bit my lip at the sound of my crankiness. "Sorry. I'm a little distracted."

He seemed to come to a decision. "You know, I saw Kilt Guy go through there." He pointed to the door leading to the boys' locker room.

"Be right back. Promise." I handed him the punch cup and scurried off.

Walking down the locker room hallway, I heard nothing but the clack of my heels and the soft thump of bass. For some reason I recalled a science lesson that said lowest frequencies travel the farthest. I imagined the sound waves rolling out from the speakers, curling around the corners, and finding me here alone, like a victim in a slasher film.

I hesitated at the outer door, but only for a second. Maybe it wasn't too late not to lose Zachary.

The bleachers of Ridgewood's athletic field gleamed a dull silver in the moonlight. Since there were no ghosts, I figured Zachary had to be nearby. But the stands were empty.

I sighed, feeling stupid for my impromptu wild-goose chase. Could Zachary have left the prom entirely? Not with Becca—she'd never leave before they crowned the king and queen. Maybe they'd had a fight.

I couldn't give up. I pulled out my phone to call him.

That's when I heard Becca's low, sultry laughter.

I inched behind the bleachers, staying in the shadows and softening my footsteps. Soon I saw Zachary standing against the small wooden snack bar with his back to me. Two silver, high-heeled shoes appeared around his calves, along with two hands on his back, descending lower.

I was too late. Becca had drowned him.

I shrank back, afraid to watch and even more afraid to be discovered. The thought of Becca directing her victorious laugh at me shot spikes of fear across my shoulders.

Then I heard Zachary's voice, soft and low, which gave me hope. If he was using his mouth to speak, it wasn't doing anything else.

I peeked at them again. Becca was seated on the snack bar's condiment counter. I couldn't hear Zachary's words, but the tender way he held her face said it all.

Finally he lifted her from the shelf and set her on her feet. She dusted off her butt, then his, though his didn't need it. Then she took his hand as they headed back toward the building. He looked down as if surprised, but didn't pull away.

I stumbled to the front of the stands and sank onto the bottom bleacher. My lungs seized up, but if I cried, my mascara would turn my face into a muddy mess. So I swallowed my sobs until my stomach ached.

A familiar whisper came from behind. "Aura."

I gasped and turned. Sitting on the top bleacher, glowing violet in the night, was Logan.

Chapter Sixteen

Remember how we used to sit up here freshman year," he said, "at football and lacrosse games? Far enough we could pretend we were too cool to care whether Ridgewood won?"

"Somehow we always cheered anyway." I got to my feet and resisted the urge to run to him, knowing I'd break my ankles in these heels.

"This is where I first asked you out." He put his hand on the seat beside him. "You were eating an ice-cream sandwich. It was dripping down your wrist, and I had the worst urge to lick it."

"I don't remember you asking me out here."

"I asked you to come to our first gig. Where we kissed for the first time."

Now *that* I remembered like it was yesterday. Though Logan had been full of fire onstage, his kiss was soft and sweet, almost shy.

"That doesn't count as you asking me out. I would've come to your show anyway."

"Just because you didn't know what I was asking doesn't mean I didn't ask."

I grinned up at him, then realized my neck was getting stiff. "Can you come down here?"

He didn't bother walking. In a flash he was next to me. "Wanna dance?"

"Let's go closer to the school so we can hear the music." I looked at the assortment of ghosts on the athletic field, going through the motions of their respective sports, unable to act as a team. "And be alone."

"You look amazing, by the way." He touched the tail of his open shirt as he walked beside me. "I'm way underdressed."

"I don't care."

He beamed at me. "So how much are you hating prom night?"

"Let's see, Megan and Mickey aren't speaking, Dylan keeps step-ping on my toes, and—" I cut myself off, not wanting to reveal the worst part.

"Let me guess: Bagpipes and the Bitch?"

"Good guess." I told him what I'd overheard in the girls' room and then seen at the concession stand.

"I don't remember Becca being that desperate," he said. "Aren't guys usually throwing themselves at her, not the other way around?"

"She wants Zachary because he made her chase him. Looks like she finally caught her prey."

"Did you actually see them kiss?"

"No, but they were—"

"What, talking?"

"While glued to each other," I said. "They could've been kissing before I walked up."

"Or she tried to kiss him and he had to talk her down from her horn-doggedness."

I snorted. "If Becca could hear you say that, you'd be twice dead."

We stopped off the side of the front courtyard, close enough to hear music floating from the gym's high windows. It was a song from last year, one that Logan and I had danced to at Homecoming.

He held out his hand, palm up. I placed mine in it, willing my fingers to feel his. He drew me close, and I clasped my hands behind his neck. To any pre-Shifters watching, I had my arms wrapped around nothing, but I didn't care what anyone thought. I was at home in Logan's ethereal embrace.

"Look," he said, "I don't know this Zachary guy, and I don't want to know him. But if he was really into you—and it sounds like he was—I don't see how he could like Becca, too. Maybe as friends, but not in a hookup way."

I wanted to believe him. After all, Logan had zero motive for making me think well of Zachary. He could have told me to surrender the fight. But he spoke as if he only wanted me to be happy, and as if he realized he might not always be the source of that happiness.

"Who wouldn't want Becca?" I asked him, still insecure. "She's gorgeous."

"She's scary. Something about her always made my balls wish they were internal organs."

A much-needed laugh burst out of me. It was rare that Logan said the exact right thing.

We swayed in the shadows, and when I closed my eyes, I could pretend the other ghosts weren't watching me, maybe remembering when they'd danced at their own prom. I could pretend I felt Logan's arms around me.

"You have *got* to be kidding."

We broke apart at the sound of Dylan's voice. "Dude, what's up?" Logan said. "Hey, my tux looks awesome on you."

Dylan descended the front stairs and stalked toward us. "What's up, *dude*, is that I didn't say you could dance with my date."

"I don't need your permission."

Dylan brought his face within inches of his dead brother's. "Why can't you just leave her alone?"

"I would if she wanted me to."

"How can she know what that's like, when you won't let her find out?"

"She had a life without me when I was a shade."

"When you were a shade, none of us did shit but sit around waiting. There was no life-without-you." He scowled at the space between me and Logan. "Obviously there never will be."

"What's the big deal?" I asked Dylan. "Logan's been a part of our lives, even after he died."

"I thought for one night he could leave us alone."

My neck prickled as I realized the reason for his anger. "Dylan, do you mean all of us, or—"

"I mean you and me." He jerked at his tie to undo it. "But there's no such thing as you and me."

"Holy shit, you like her." Logan lowered his head like a bull as he moved between us. "My own brother. You couldn't wait until I'd passed on to make a move on my girlfriend?"

"I'm not your girlfriend," I said.

"And I didn't make a move," Dylan added. "*She* asked *me* to the prom."

"As friends," Logan said.

"We didn't feel like friends when we were slow-dancing."

Logan turned his head toward me. "What's he mean by that?"

I covered my face, too cowardly to see the hurt in Dylan's eyes. "I'm sorry. I didn't mean to give you the wrong idea. I was just—"

"Trying to make Kilt Boy jealous. Yep. I should've known I'd never have a chance with you."

"Only because it would've been like hooking up with my own brother. You don't like me that way. You just think you do because I'm safe."

"*I'm* playing it safe?" Dylan shouted. "You're the one dancing with a ghost. You're the one who asked your dead boyfriend's brother to the prom because you were too scared to be with the guy you really wanted. A guy who is probably right now getting blown by the prom queen."

My insides curdled at the image. "She's not queen yet. And there's no way they're—they went back inside."

"Good idea." He grabbed my hand and started to pull me toward the door.

"Wait!" Logan said. "Where are you going?"

"Anywhere you're not!" Dylan yelled.

"Aura!" Logan shot forward, then hissed and leaped back. "Fucking BlackBox." He shifted to the side, as if searching for an opening. "Aura . . . stay with me."

My heart felt like it would rip in two. "Give me a minute," I said to Dylan as I slipped my hand out of his and walked over to Logan. "I can't just leave your brother after the way I've treated him."

Logan wavered. "Okay, but—maybe we can meet up later?"

"We'll be out late. I came with them."

"With my family. You're more a part of them now than I am." He shoved his hands in the pockets of his baggy shorts and looked up at the school's clock tower. "I loved Ridgewood. I wish we never moved out to the County. The teachers here were amazing, and we actually learned stuff that mattered, instead of obsessing over state tests all the time." His gaze fell on me. "What if I pass on and forget all this? What if I can't even remember what it was like to touch you? What kind of heaven is that?"

I clutched my purse, running my fingers over the silk and sequins the way I once stroked his skin. Behind Logan, the other ghosts crowded closer, blending into a giant violet mass, unable to sense one another.

Logan noticed my shifting glance and looked over his shoulder. "I'm not the only ghost here, am I?" When I shook my head, he groaned. "God, I'm so pathetic. Hanging around my old school on prom night. I need to get a life."

"Logan—"

"Scratch that. What I really need is to get a death."

He vanished.

Dylan came to my side. A prom couple passed us on their way to the courtyard for a cigarette break.

"They must be seniors," Dylan said as we watched them light up in the midst of the ghosts.

We turned and went inside, stopping in the school's stone foyer. "What did Logan mean by 'his tux'?" I asked Dylan.

He passed a self-conscious hand down the pin-striped jacket's lapel. "He picked it out before he died. Showed me last month." He thumbed the black silk vest's bottom button. "I knew that anything I picked would be dorky or boring."

"Logan was right about one thing. You look awesome."

Dylan gave a half smile and glanced at his feet. "Forget what I said outside, okay?"

"So you don't like me?"

"What's the point?"

"There doesn't have to be a point. I want to know how you feel."

He took a couple of steps away, then turned to face me without meeting my eyes. "You asked me to the prom. I figured it was as friends. But I thought maybe . . ." When I didn't interrupt, he continued. "Since we were kids, we always had the ghosts. We could see them and no one else in my family could. And after Logan died . . ." He scraped the side of one shoe against the other. "You were the only one I could talk to about it."

I should have sensed Dylan's feelings sooner. Maybe I had, but just couldn't deal. "I know what you mean," I said. "No one else missed Logan like we did, even though he was still here."

He nodded. "The rest of my family could be sad. But I couldn't, not with his ghost around."

"Like it would've insulted him. Like he wasn't enough anymore."

"Exactly! I feel like an asshole for saying this, but . . . I wish he would go. Now that he's not a shade and we know he's okay."

"He'll go soon." I frowned. "Here we are, together at the prom, still talking about Logan."

"What else do we ever talk about?"

"Nothing. But maybe we should start." I fumbled for something to say, then spied what Dylan was holding. "Are you going to put your tie back on?"

"Nah, it took half an hour to tie it the first time. Here, hold out your hand." Dylan looped the tie around my right wrist, the one without the corsage, and tied a double knot. "So you'll remember who you're leaving with tonight."

His fingers brushed the back of my hand as he let go. My breath hitched at the sudden zing of connection. *Whoa.*

Applause and cheering burst from the gymnasium.

"They must be crowning the royalty," I said.

"Lame."

"Totally." I shifted my feet. "Although I am kind of curious."

Onstage, Justin Harlow and Christina Wilkes raised their fists like they'd won the heavyweight title instead of prom prince and princess.

Dylan helped me stand on a chair to get a better view. From the back of the gym I could see Zachary's and Becca's profiles, touched by the edge of the stage light's glow. The smile plastered on her face couldn't cover the terror. He brushed his hand over her back in a soothing gesture, and she eased her body against him.

Principal Hirsch opened the envelope in slow motion, drawing out the fake suspense. "Your prom king and queen are . . . Tyler Watson and Becca Goldman."

Becca put her hands to her neck, closed her eyes, and mouthed, *Thank you.*

Tyler shrugged at his girlfriend, Stacey, who seethed as he moved toward the stage, holding out his hand for Becca.

I had to admit, they looked pretty regal as they mounted the short flight of stairs. Becca's silver dress shimmered and sparkled in the gleaming white lights. The assistant principal placed the crown on her head, then applauded with the rest of the crowd.

The dance floor cleared for the royalty as a sappy country-and-western song cued up. Becca and Tyler began to dance, as close as when they'd been girlfriend-boyfriend.

Dylan helped me down off the chair. "Looks like Scotty's beaming his way over here. Now's your chance."

I gaped at him. "You don't mind?"

"Not if I get the last dance. That's a rule, right?"

"It is now." On an impulse, I stood on tiptoe to kiss his cheek. Then I turned and smashed into Zachary.

"Sorry." He steadied me as I stumbled against him. "Am I interrupting?" he asked Dylan.

"No. I think Amy needs my help with, um . . . stuff." Dylan disappeared into the crowd.

Suddenly I found my purse's zipper fascinating. "Congrats on Becca's victory."

"Thanks. I think." Zachary angled his body toward the center of the floor. "Will you dance with me?"

My face flared hot. "I think this dance is supposed to be for them."

Principal Hirsch spoke into the microphone. "Everyone is now welcome to join the royal couples on the floor."

Zachary reached for my hand. "Please."

I struggled to breathe. "What's the point?"

He dropped his hand, but stepped close so his mouth was at my ear. "The point is that we want to."

The song eased into the second verse, the singer softly declaring her faith in things unspoken, in the power of a single touch.

I moved forward as Zachary's arms slipped around my waist. Then I was holding him close, my hands on his shoulders and my face pressing the silk of his vest. My eyes shut, lashes brushing the place where his heartbeat thumped.

We didn't speak. I knew that later, alone, I would think of a million things I wished I'd said, all the questions that burned inside me about him and Becca—and him and me.

But at that moment, I let my mind go blank. For once I barely heard the music. We were in a dark, soundless bubble, with touch the only sense remaining. I could feel each of his fingers on the bare skin of my back.

My hands slid up, thumbs brushing the nape of his neck. He sighed and pulled me tighter against him. I remembered the first time we'd kissed, how I'd threaded my fingers through the soft waves of his hair and thought of Logan's short, sharp spikes. If Zachary kissed me now, who would I think of? Would I think at all?

The song ended, and we let go as the last note faded. When I opened my eyes, the floor swam and blurred.

"Thanks very much," he whispered.

I blinked as I watched him walk away. Becca glided forward to greet him with a gleaming smile, caressing her stupid silver crown. She linked her arm with his and swept him toward the other side of the dance floor for pictures. Then she turned and gave me a look that could cut glass.

Dylan appeared beside me. "That girl hates your guts."

"So? She can't hurt me any more than she already has."

He laid a protective hand on my back. "I wouldn't bet on it."

Chapter Seventeen

The limo was about ten feet off of school property when Mickey unzipped the cooler and started passing out bottles of beer.

I drank quickly, wanting to block out the evening's lowlights—Becca's bitchery, Logan and Dylan's fight, and my all-too-short dance with the guy I couldn't have.

Mickey passed Dylan a Coke.

"Screw that," Dylan said. "Gimme a beer."

"You're too young."

"You and Siobhan drank when you were sixteen," I pointed out. "So did—" I rubbed my upper lip, hoping they hadn't heard me almost say Logan's name, especially connected with alcohol.

Mickey zipped the cooler, then rested his feet on it as he lounged on the limo's black leather couch across from us. Megan snuggled up to him, kicking off her shoes. They looked like they'd made up, at least enough to touch each other again.

As Megan stretched out her feet, I noticed I'd left my purse on their seat on my way into the car.

I was about to ask her to pass it to me when Mickey groaned and banged the back of his head against the window. "I'd kill for a cigarette. Siobhan, why did we quit smoking?"

"It was ruining our voices, which people can actually hear now that we're not singing backup." She scratched her nose and gave me a panicky look—another near mention of Logan.

"Mickey, don't sulk." Megan thumbed a button on his dress shirt. "It's prom night."

"Prom night, part one!" Siobhan raised her beer bottle and draped her legs over Connor's lap. "Next week is the sequel. The rehash that can never top the original."

"Some sequels are better than the original," Connor said. "Like *Empire Strikes Back*. Or *Two Towers*."

"That's different, my dearest darling dear. Those were middle parts of a trilogy. We're not getting a trilogy."

"We could," Megan said, "if we crashed a third school's prom week after next."

Siobhan laughed. "Oh my God, that's brilliant. Then when we get kicked out, we can just party someplace in our formal wear."

Connor took her empty bottle and exchanged it for a new one from his own cooler. "I can't afford a third tux."

"I'll pay for it." Siobhan kissed him. "You can be my kept man."

"Mmm, sounds kinky." He scooped her into his lap, making her laugh harder.

"Mickey, what do you think?" Megan asked. "Fake third prom in two weeks?"

He smiled at her, but his eyes were tinged with sadness as he brushed a tendril of red hair off her cheek. "It's a date."

"Yay." She cuddled against his shoulder and couldn't see how quickly his smile faded as he stared over her head at the limo's dark carpet.

I wanted to tell Mickey that Dylan and I had seen Logan tonight, but knew it would upset him. Yet it seemed wrong not to talk about the person we were all thinking of.

Mickey reached for the stereo controls above his head and cranked up the radio, cutting off all cross-limo conversation.

I eased back in my seat next to Dylan. His shoulders were pulled in as he held the Coke can in his lap with both hands.

"You okay?" I asked him.

"He should be here," Dylan said. "Not me."

"Don't say that."

"He should be in this tux. He should be with this girl. Not me."

I scrambled for comforting words. But what he said was true. We'd planned this seven months ago—Siobhan and Connor, Mickey and Megan, Logan and me. Dylan was the replacement part, one that looked and felt enough like the original that he almost fit. The "almost" was worse than "not at all."

And yet, when I thought only of the here and now, I realized . . . I liked being with Dylan. Simple as that.

"I'm glad I asked you," I told him, and it was the truth. "I'm glad you said yes."

He looked at me from the corner of his eye. "You're shitting me, right?"

"I shit you not." I held up my free hand to swear, then tugged on his shirtsleeve. "And just because someone else picked out this tux doesn't mean you didn't make it your own."

"Thanks." He glanced down. "Your flowers are dying."

I flourished my right wrist. "But my tie corsage is fresh as ever."

He laughed. "I need that back, or they'll charge me."

"No, I'm keeping it." I extended my arm away from him. "As a souvenir, since my flowers are dead."

"Gimme." He reached around me, snatching at my hand as I waved it high, then low.

"Come and get it," I teased.

Dylan lunged forward and seized my wrist, planted behind me on the seat. The motion pressed our bodies together and brought our faces inches apart. He loosened his hold a fraction, running his thumb along my pulse in a motion that made me shiver.

Though no one around us said anything, I could feel them watching.

"This can't happen," I said, though of course it could.

Dylan sighed and let go of me. "I know."

We spent the next ten minutes in silence, angling ourselves to look out through the tinted glass behind our seat. On the other side of University Parkway, spots of violet winked on and off like fireflies as we passed ghost after ghost. They blended with the reflection of the limo's multicolored interior lights.

"Aura, I know this is just about prom," Dylan said finally. "Fun for one night. I don't expect anything else."

I took another sip, trying to decode his meaning. Was he saying, "I get that we're just here as friends"? Or was he saying, "If we hook up tonight, don't worry. No strings"?

Major danger zone. The fact that I was even considering it meant the beer was affecting me. But maybe for once I should stop thinking so much.

My phone rang. Megan grabbed my purse on the seat next to her. "I'll get it!"

"Don't answer if it's Gina. You sound drunk."

She pulled out my phone. "It's Zachary."

"Great," Dylan muttered.

My hand shot out. "Give it to me."

Instead she answered. "Zach-jack! What's up? Zach? Are you there?" She shook the phone, as if that would help. "Zach? Aura, I think he pocket-dialed you."

The curse of having a name that starts with A. "Just give it to me."

She plugged her other ear with her finger. "Someone's talking in the background. Mickey, turn the music off." The car went silent. "Zaaaaaaach! Why can't he hear me? Does he have the earpiece turned all the way—" Her face froze suddenly, then her mouth formed an O.

I lunged across the limo and snatched the phone from her hand.

"Aura, don't!" she said.

"Shut up. Everyone." I put the phone to my ear and turned up the volume. And knew in a moment why Megan had freaked.

Becca's voice sounded a few feet away from the phone. "Mmm, Zach. That feels amazing."

"I've hardly done anything." His low laugh rumbled. "Yet."

Every cell in my body turned to ice water.

Becca moaned again. "I love it when you use your teeth."

My stomach tied itself in a knot. I regretted having even one beer, much less two.

"Too hot for this," Becca said. I heard the sound of heavy cloth hitting the floor. His tuxedo jacket, or maybe his kilt.

"What's wrong?" Dylan whispered behind me. I shook my head, and he reached around to grab the phone. I knocked his hand away. "Ow!" He rubbed his wrist.

I heard whispers that weren't coming from the phone. The other four were staring at me, eyes filled with pity.

Could I ever have a private heartbreak? Or would I always be the president of the public humiliation club?

Yet I couldn't stop listening. I waited to hear Zachary reject Becca and proclaim his feelings for me, or at least for him to realize what she'd done: turned down his earpiece volume and dialed my number so I could hear them but he couldn't hear me. My fists clenched with the need to knock out her perfect teeth.

Soon there were no more words between Becca and Zachary. Just noises.

"Should I?" Megan said. I looked over to see her showing her own phone screen to Mickey.

His brows lowered. "Do it. Boy deserves it for being an idiot." He gave me a look of brotherly affection that I hadn't seen on his face since before Logan died.

Do what? I mouthed.

A harsh rattle jarred my ear. I yanked the phone away. "What the hell?"

"He just got a text." Megan smirked. "A little coitus interruptus, courtesy of *moi*." She enunciated the syllables with relish. "Or hopefully pre-coitus interruptus."

Something creaked on the other end of the phone, maybe a mattress.

"Where are you going?" Becca said. "Don't answer that."

"I'm not." Zachary was out of breath. "I'm turning it off."

"No!" Becca shouted, and I knew she'd set me up.

"What the bloody hell?" Zachary spoke into the phone. "Aura, are you there?"

Panicking, I hung up, then dropped the phone like a hot coal. It bounced on the limo carpet at my feet, where I stared at it.

Dylan put a hand on my back. "You okay?"

I was too stunned to shake my head. Not only had I heard Zachary and Becca almost have sex—and I couldn't be sure the "almost" applied—but he knew I was listening. He could check the time count on the call and see *how long* I'd been listening. And know what I'd heard.

I shouldn't have hung up. If I'd stayed quiet, he might've thought I'd pocket-answered his pocket dial and never heard a thing. What kind of pathetic pervert did he think I was?

"I want to die."

Dylan's hand tensed. "You don't really mean that."

"Not literally. I'm not going to throw myself out of the car or anything."

"Good. But if you change your mind, wait till it stops, okay? So I can catch you."

I couldn't help laughing. And then, I couldn't help kissing him.

Dylan jolted in surprise, but didn't pull away. He kissed me back, his lips new and foreign—in a good way, like an exotic food I never knew I wanted to taste.

"Aura—," Megan started to whine, but Mickey cut her off.

"Leave them alone. It's none of our business."

"Yuh-huh, because we'll have to pick up the pieces."

My phone rang. I ignored it. Dylan didn't.

He leaned forward, and if I weren't holding on to him I would've spilled off the seat. He scooped up my phone and answered it.

"What the fuck do you want?" After a pause, he said in a firm voice, "This is Dylan Keeley, the guy who would've killed to trade places with you until five minutes ago." He met my eyes. "She doesn't want to talk to you. Now why don't you go back to screwing your prom date and let me do the same?"

Dylan hung up the phone and pressed it into my palm. The limo erupted into applause.

"Dylan, you rock!" Megan said as Siobhan let loose a piercing whistle. Connor and Mickey shared a "Yeah!" and a high five, like after a Ravens touchdown.

"Thanks," I whispered to Dylan.

He shrugged. "I didn't mean that part about screwing you. I just wanted to piss him off."

"I know."

"So if you want to get wasted to forget about him, which I'd totally understand, don't worry. I won't take off your clothes, even if you pass out."

I tried not to laugh. "That's . . . really noble, Dylan."

"So while you're still sorta sober—" He gave me a quick, sweet kiss.

"Thanks." I meant it.

"Oh, and I really do need this." Dylan pulled gently on the end of my tie corsage. It slowly slipped off my wrist, and my pulse quickened, as if he were undressing me. Which I guess he was, a little.

Dylan stuffed the tie in his pocket, then put his arm around my shoulders. We settled back against the seat as Mickey cranked up the music. I finished my second beer and started a third while Dylan sipped his Coke. The city lights whizzed past as the limo raced south toward the Inner Harbor.

"It was cool of that guy to call back," Dylan said a few minutes later. "I never would've had the guts."

I smiled up at him, feeling strangely at home. "You're braver than you think."

Chapter Eighteen

I woke the next morning to the distant sound of my phone ringing. I realized that last night I'd left it on top of my purse on the bathroom counter.

Please don't answer it. Please don't answer it.

"Hi, Zachary!" Gina said brightly.

I shoved the pillow over my head, wishing I were strong enough to smother myself. But I knew that I would let go when I passed out. Still, it would give me a few minutes of relief, and maybe kill the brain cells that were holding last night's memories. Becca and Zach. Me and Dylan. Way too much beer.

A knock came at my door. "Guess who's calling?" Gina said as she swept into the room.

I put my hand out.

Gina walked over, bare feet thumping the rug. "Are you hungry?" She put the phone in my hand. "When you're off, I made—"

I hung up the phone and tossed it under my bed.

"I see."

I heard Gina rub the backs of her hands like she did when she was nervous. The sound of skin against skin made me press the pillow harder over my head.

"So . . . I made blueberry muffins. The berries aren't really in season yet, but—"

The phone rang again.

"I'll just go away now," she whispered. On her way out, the door slammed behind her.

The monster under the bed finally stopped ringing. A minute later, a bleep told me he'd left a voice mail.

"Go to hell," I whispered.

It rang again, with the tone for a calendar reminder. Which never turns itself off.

I oozed onto the floor, hating life. Did I schedule a study meeting for the day after the prom? Was I that much of a masochistic workaholic?

Worse: Did Zach and I have a meeting with Eowyn? My gut twisted at the thought of seeing him again one-on-one. At least at school I could hide in the crowds.

I squeezed myself halfway under the bed to retrieve the phone.

MOTHER'S DAY, the screen said.

I rested my forehead on the floor, hot shame washing over me like lava. Then I shambled to my desk and pawed through my book bag until I found the small drugstore bag.

Inside Gina's greeting card I wrote, "They didn't have any 'sorry I've been such a bitch' cards. They would sell really well. Anyway, I wanted you to know that I know how lucky I am to have you, even though I don't always—okay, never—tell you, except in these cards once a year. So it's good that they invented this holiday. I love you."

I pulled the second card out of the bag. Crap, it was for Grand-mom, and I'd forgotten to mail it. I whapped myself in the face with the card, then set it aside. I'd write "Belated" between "Happy" and "Mother's Day" and mail it tomorrow.

The third card, I left in the bag.

I slunk down to the dining room, where Gina was sitting with her laptop and paperwork. "Shouldn't you take the day off?" I asked her.

"What for?" she said without looking up.

"For this?" I handed her the card and kissed her cheek.

"You remembered!"

"We have two o'clock brunch reservations." I wondered if the restaurant had a hangover special.

Gina read the card and sniffled. "You're so sweet." Then she looked at my empty hands. "You have something to put in the box?"

"Later." I gripped the back of the dining room chair, calculating how much more sleep I could get if I went back to bed. Probably none, because I wouldn't sleep either before or after I listened to Zachary's voice mail.

As if reading my mind, Gina said, "Sorry I answered your cell. I know you hate that. I figured you wouldn't want to miss a call from Zachary."

"I'm not speaking to him." I stalked out of the dining room. I never wanted to hear his voice on that phone again.

Alone in the kitchen, I dug my nails into my palms to keep from yanking every plate from the cupboard and hurling them against the wall. After the way Zachary had been with me—in his car, on his sofa, *on the dance floor*—how could he want someone else so much?

I wanted to hate him. I wanted to wipe him out of my life. I wanted to rewrite our story to make him the villain.

I wanted it to stop hurting.

I forced myself to breathe. I'd survived Logan's death, so this should be easy. After that, everything should be easy.

I poured a cup of coffee, trying to talk myself out of the pain. *Zachary's not your boyfriend, he's never been your boyfriend, and he never will be. Not after this.*

He'd made it clear we couldn't be together without endangering ourselves or the world or whatever. Did I really expect him to save himself for me?

Yes. I did. I expected him to help me find a way.

Upstairs in my room with an uneaten muffin and an undrunk cup of coffee, I sat at my desk and began to write the final Mother's Day card.

Dear mom,
How are you? Wow, it's been quite a
year. I bet you're wondering

I stopped writing.

No. This year, meaningless platitudes weren't going to make me feel any closer to the dead mother I couldn't remember.

I exchanged the blue pen for a black one and started again.

Why didn't Dad want us? Was he married?
Was he a priest? Was he dead by the
time I was born? Did he ever Know I
existed?

My pen scrawled faster.

I'm so pissed at you, mom. Why
didn't you try to give me a father?
Why didn't you leave me your whole
journal? Don't I have the right to Know
who I am?

I can live with a hard truth. I can't
live with this absolute nothing you've
left behind.

Until next year, Happy mother's Day.

Love, Aura

I put the card in the envelope, licked it, then pounded it shut along the seal, rattling the paper clips on my desk.

As if in echo, my phone vibrated with a text message. Zachary.

DID YOU GET MY VM? PLS REPLY.

I trashed the message, then after a brief hesitation, dialed my voice mail.

"Aura . . ." Zachary's tone twisted in agony. "I don't know what I can say that won't make it worse."

"Then don't say anything." I erased the message, then disconnected and stared at the phone. "Shit." I dialed voice mail again, hoping I'd accidentally hit save instead of delete.

"There are no messages in your mailbox," the robot lady informed me.

I set the phone down quickly so I wouldn't throw it through my window. *Should I call him back?* I wondered. *No, that's insane. How desperate am I?* I needed to show him I didn't care, and I'd never be able to do that on the phone.

I tapped out a quick text message, which thankfully wouldn't reflect how hard I was thumbing the keys:

NO WORRIES! :-)

I hit send, then wrote *Mom* and today's date across the front of the card. My phone buzzed again with Zachary's reply:

???

I stared at the screen. If his voice mail was nothing but "Sorry about last night," then why would my "No worries!" confuse him? What had I missed? Curiosity gnawed at me, but calling him back— and admitting I was so upset I'd deleted his voice mail, then pretended I'd heard it—was not an option.

Shift

I switched off my phone, then went to my aunt's room and slipped the card into the shoe box on her nightstand, the one that held every card and letter I'd written to my mom since her death. I vowed that one Mother's Day I would open them all.

But not today.

Chapter Nineteen

Monday at work, Gina and her partners put the final touches on the case for George Schwartz, the ghost I'd scared off over a month ago after kissing Zachary. Since that life-shattering day (for me, at least), Mr. Schwartz and I had met twice, with no ill effects. He didn't even seem to remember I had blasted him with red. Mostly he wanted justice.

I wished I could have been a ghost today. My classmates had heard about the No-Pocket Pocket Dial, probably from Becca herself, who ate lunch with none other than her maybe-no-longer-ex-boyfriend Tyler Watson.

Zachary was the quietest I'd ever seen him. Unlike me, he wasn't used to scandal. He hadn't realized that the moment he asked Becca to the prom, he'd stepped into a snake pit, one he couldn't charm his way out of.

When I got off work at six, I called the Keeleys' house.

"Hey," Dylan said on the first ring.

"Hey." Sitting in the car outside my aunt's office, I watched a mismatched pair of ghosts cross the tree-shaded street, through a small blizzard of maple seed "helicopters." "What are you doing?"

"Um . . . I don't know. Nothing, I guess."

A car drove down the other side of the road, and one of the ghosts leaped out of its way. Obviously a newbie. The other ghost plodded on, letting the car pass through it.

"Who all's there right now?" I asked Dylan.

"Mickey and Siobhan are out. Not together, though. My parents are out, too."

"But you're there."

"Yeah." His voice fell as he said the word, as if his presence put the house in a state of lameness.

"Can I come over?"

Dylan was red faced and panting when he answered the door.

"Did I interrupt your workout?" I asked him.

"No—I mean, yeah." He wiped his forehead. "I'm done. For the rest of my life. See?" He flexed his biceps in an erratic move that made me laugh.

We got sodas and chips and headed for the long black couch in the den. Dylan took the left middle cushion instead of sitting on the end, so I sat next to him. To avoid scaring him off, I set the chip bag between us.

He started flipping channels, so fast I couldn't see what was on each station before he skipped to the next. "We have some back eps of *Get a Life* on the DVR."

"You still watch that reality show? Even after Logan died?"

"No, we just record it. Not sure why."

"I know how the season ends. The ghost passes on."

"I bet they'll all end that way. The ghost probably has to sign a—"

"Wait, stop. What was that?"

He turned the channel back to a cable news station, which showed an overhead view of the DMP headquarters building in Arlington. Police cars were parked outside at odd angles, as if they'd screeched to a halt, like in the movies.

The Breaking News caption read: GUNMAN KILLED AT DMP STANDOFF.

Next to the shot was a photograph of a middle-aged guy with his arm around a young man in a graduation cap and gown. Under the photograph it said, STUART WEXLER, AGE 47.

"You didn't hear about this?" Dylan said.

"No, I went to work right after school." I'd been listening to my own music in the car—my worn-out heartache playlist—instead of the radio.

"This dude walked into the DMP office today with a Glock, started taking hostages. Couple of them got shot." He turned up the volume. "I guess the SWAT team finally took him out."

"What did he want?"

"Get this: His son was an at-risk ghost. They put him in a box last year, and this guy went nuts. He said if they didn't let his kid go, he was going to blow up the whole building."

"Like that guy a couple months ago in Michigan?"

"Yeah, except this one was bullshitting about the explosives." Dylan waved the remote control at the TV. "That could've been us. Those Obsidian agents would've put Logan away if he hadn't shaded."

"I can't see your dad holding up a government building."

"Nah, it'd be Mickey and Siobhan and me. But no way I'd use a handgun. Submachine would be the way to go, probably an H&K MP5. That's what the FBI uses for hostage rescue, so . . . I'm saying this out loud, aren't I?"

"Yep."

"You know I'd never do anything like that."

I nodded. "It's always pre-Shifters' brains that short-circuit when it comes to ghosts. We're a lot saner than they are."

"We better be."

The news anchors mentioned the stats of the slain gunman's son: Ryan Wexler, age twenty-three, civil engineer, killed in a construction site accident two years ago.

"I guess Ryan's in a box on a shelf in that building." My insides shriveled at the thought. It could happen to Logan. It could happen to any of us after we died.

As we watched the rest of the news report, I noticed Dylan's fingers twitching atop his knee, the one closest to me.

The commercial came on, and he muted the television. "You want to go upstairs?"

Dylan's room looked like the "in-between" shot of a home remodeling show. Thumbtacks peppered two of the bare walls, scraps of paper hanging off them, as if posters had been ripped down. One sign remained: STOOGES PARKING ONLY, ALL VIOLATORS WILL BE SLAPPED. I assumed it referred to the comedy troupe, not the classic punk band.

The narrow shelf lining the far wall was swept clean, and so was the top of his dresser. I wondered if their contents were now in one of four storage containers stacked on the floor.

The top container was overstuffed, its lid askew. I peeked in to see action figures lying in a haphazard jumble. The people-pile reminded me of a mass grave I'd seen in a documentary.

"Why are you packing these up?"

"I'm not a kid anymore." He shoved the lid down on the container until it snapped shut.

"Plenty of grown-ups have collectible action figures."

"I haven't liked this stuff for a long time, but I didn't feel like taking it down. Plus, my friends would be all, 'What's up? Don't you like *Naruto* anymore? Who the fuck *are* you?' Not like they don't ask that already."

"So why are you getting rid of them now?"

"Duh," he said softly as he turned away.

I noticed his walls were painted the same dark, rich blue as Logan's old room, the color of the sky at dusk. Dylan's room in their last house had been a bright, Tweety Bird yellow (or what he probably would've called a Wolverine yellow).

"I wanted to show you something." He reached into a half-open drawer and pulled out a spiral notebook with a black cover. "You should probably sit down."

I glanced at the bed. Dylan turned his desk chair around and dropped the notebook on it. Then he sat on the edge of his bed, hunched forward, arms folded.

I opened the notebook, angling it toward the sunlight coming through the window.

Logan's name and phone number were scrawled on the inside front cover, along with a note: *If this is found by a total stranger, please, please, PLEASE call me. I'll give you any reward you want. But if you throw it away or keep it, your soul is TOAST.*

The first page read, in neat letters: *This page left blank on purpose.*

The date and time on the second page made my eyes blur with tears. October 17, eleven thirty p.m., the night before his last birthday. The night before he died.

Fame Journal, Volume 1

I'm starting this tonight so I can look back someday and remember what life was like before It happened. It might not happen tomorrow when those label guys come to our show, but it will soon. My life is going to change.

And then, my life is going to end.

A chill seeped up my fingers into my arms, as if the notebook were made of ice.

It's a fact: when guys like me get famous, they fall apart. They forget who they are. (Maybe because there's nothing to remember. Outside of the music, I don't know if there is such a thing as me.)

It'll be great at first. Everyone will love me. But eventually "everyone" won't be enough. And the more they love Onstage Logan, the more they'll hate Offstage Logan. Especially people who really know me.

(It's already started. Mickey thinks I'm a poseur. Siobhan thinks I'm a diva. Aura thinks I'm a slut-in-waiting. Dylan's the only one who still thinks I'm a hero. I guess that's what little brothers are for.)

So I'll fill the place that used to have a real me with whatever I can drink or snort or shoot or smoke, until one night I'll be too wasted to remember how much of each I've done.

My sob hitched at the image, but I couldn't lose control. Not yet.

I can tell myself and everyone else that I'll be different from all those other rock star losers who burned out and one day instead of waking up in a puddle of their own puke and piss, just didn't wake up at all. But that last page will come. Way too soon.

Anyway, if anyone's reading this after I'm dead (and that should be the only reason why you're reading this, okay? If I'm still alive, put this down or I swear I will punch you in the teeth), I just want to say I'm sorry. I'm sorry I turned out to be such a total fucking asshole.

After a space of four blank lines, he wrote:

I love you all, so much more than you should ever love me.

I turned the page, knowing what I would find.

Emptiness.

Logan ended as soon as he started.

I searched the blank pages faster and faster, finally thumbing the edges like a flip book. "That's all?"

"No." Dylan knelt before me and opened the notebook from the back. He flipped forward three pages, then pointed at a list in the left margin, between the middle and bottom holes.

Aura Keeley

Aura S. Keeley

Aura Salvatore Keeley

Aura Salvatore-Keeley

Aura Keeley-Salvatore (??)

My tear fell onto the list, blurring the months-old ballpoint-pen ink. "When did you find this?"

"The night he died. It was in his desk. After the cops left, I snuck into his room to look for stuff he wouldn't want Mom and Dad to find."

"Was his ghost there to tell you what to hide?"

"No, but this was pretty obvious. I asked him later, though, and he said not to show anyone."

"Why are you showing me now?"

"I don't know." He looked up at me, eyes shining with tears. "I hate this house, Aura. He's never been here. Sometimes it's like he never existed, and this stupid piece of shit"—he gripped the sides of the notebook, his fingers touching mine—"is the only thing that makes him feel real to me. Except for you."

I pulled my hands off the notebook, wanting to tuck them away. But instead they reached for Dylan, sliding over his cheeks and into the flop of silky brown hair.

As he knelt frozen under my touch, I studied his face, searching for some shadow of Logan. Every edge of Dylan was softer—cheekbones, mouth, jawline—as if he'd been carved from wax instead of stone.

His eyes were a deeper blue, like the walls of this room, the kind of blue that slips you into a dreamless sleep. Logan's eyes always made me want to stay up and party; even after death, they sparked with endless light and life. I could fall into Dylan's eyes and never get up.

"It's a bad idea," he said, and kissed me anyway.

I moved forward into his arms, faster than he seemed to expect. We lost our balance and tumbled onto the floor.

"Are you okay?" he gasped.

"Uh-huh." I pulled him to kiss me again. He rolled half atop me, crushing my right thigh. I curled my other leg around his to bring our bodies together.

Our mouths melded, as if we'd die without each other's breath. Unlike Zachary, who had been careful and deliberate, Dylan was raw, reckless, his hands everywhere.

And unlike with Zachary, this felt nothing like love. It felt like lust and sorrow rolled into one. It terrified me, and the only way to fight the fear was to kiss Dylan harder, hold him tighter, let my own hands roam farther.

I shoved aside every thought—of Logan, of Zachary, of our friends and families. It was time to stop feeling guilty.

Stop feeling angry.

Stop feeling.

Time to stop.

"Stop." I think we both said it, and we did.

Stopped making out, at least. And started crying (again), and talking, and holding each other, lying on our sides on Dylan's checkerboard rug.

"He knew, didn't he?" I sobbed against Dylan's shirt. "When he wrote that note. He knew he would die."

Dylan wiped his eyes. "He just didn't think it'd be so soon. He must've figured he'd at least get through four or five notebooks."

I thought of the pages of white space, nothing but one sheet of doubt and self-loathing, and one tiny hope in a margin.

"You guys never did it." Dylan said it like a statement, not a question, so I guess Logan had told him. "Are you still—"

"Pretty much. No, not pretty much. I'm still a virgin."

Dylan's gaze traveled down the front of my half-open shirt.

"I know," I said. "You're thinking we could change that in about ten minutes."

"More like two minutes."

I snickered, then fell silent. Why were we still lying on the floor, clinging to each other? Was it because we couldn't cling to Logan? Or was there something more between us, something that made us want *nothing* between us but skin and sweat?

I tried to lower the tension. "You probably don't have any condoms, anyway."

"I have half a box left."

"Are these hand-me-downs from Mickey?"

"No, they're mine."

"What happened to the other half of the box?"

He laughed. "You know, just because I'm a total dork doesn't mean I've never gotten laid."

"By who?"

"You don't know them. They're from my school."

I snorted. "How convenient. When was this alleged laying?"

"Last fall. After—you know. Girls felt sorry for me."

"You used Logan's death to get sympathy sex?"

"I didn't use it, it just happened. He was happy for me, said he was glad he could do some good in this world. But after he shaded I felt too shitty to talk to anyone, especially girls."

"Except me."

"Except you." His face turned thoughtful as his hand drifted down my back. "I could always talk to you."

I became intensely aware of the trail of heated skin his hand was leaving. I angled my head to look at his model airplane mobile hanging in the corner. "You brought girls here?"

"No way, not with all the action figures." His hand left my back and stroked my hair. "You're the first."

I wasn't sure if I wanted to mean something special to him, or if that would be the worst thing possible. But I was almost sure that if Dylan kissed me again, I would shut off my mind and give him my body.

And I was absolutely positively sure that later, alone, I would hate myself.

We lay intertwined, chest-to-chest, for more heartbeats than I could count. Finally Dylan took a lock of my hair and pulled it forward, running his fingers all the way to the end, until their tips stopped above my heart.

"Aura, what do you want me to do?" he whispered.

I wrapped my hand around his, fighting the urge to move it lower. "Be my friend."

He closed his eyes and let out a long, hard breath. "I was hoping you'd say that."

I laughed, feeling the pain and tension loosen their hold.

"'Cause frankly," he added, "I really suck at sex so far. I'd hate to suck at sex with you."

"Not that I'd know the difference." I focused on slowing my own breath. Panting would send the wrong signal. "Do you want to go watch TV or something?"

"Yeah." Dylan rolled on his back, wincing. "Soon as I can stand up without hurting myself." He nudged me with his elbow. "Maybe in a few months, if you change your mind—"

"We'll see."

He stood slowly, pulling down his shirttail, like I didn't know what he was hiding.

I picked up the black notebook from the floor where it had spilled.

"Do you want to keep that?" he asked.

I longed to tear out the page with all the iterations of my married-to-Logan name, maybe preserve it for the day he'd left this world for good. But it was a future that belonged to the past.

"No." I pushed the notebook into Dylan's hands. "He didn't even want me to read it."

"Are you sorry you did? Are you sorry . . ." He looked at the rug where we'd lain entangled.

I smiled up at him, feeling oddly light and free. "I'm not sorry for anything."

Chapter Twenty

Using the curve of my arm to hide my writing, I scrawled the solution to the final calculus problem across the page. With one last eraser-chewing scan, I checked my work.

Yep. If this wasn't correct, I was never in a billion years going to understand the subject, which meant I would never be an astronomer.

I lifted my arm, letting Logan's violet glow spill over the page. "How's that?"

He leaned forward, so bright in the dark bedroom I had to squint.

"Perfect." He smirked. "Told you it was easy."

"Easy?" My laugh pitched up to a giggle, I was so giddy at my breakthrough. "If you still had eyes to poke out with this pencil, you'd be blind right now."

"So you're set for the test tomorrow?"

I slapped the book shut and rested the side of my head on it. "Think so. I'm glad finals aren't until next month. No way I could fit parametric equations in my head along with everything else we've studied this year."

"You'll ace it."

"Thanks to you." I curled my arm under my head. "How'd you get to be such a math genius?" Usually only juniors and seniors took calculus—luckily for me, Logan had it last year as a sophomore.

"Why are people so surprised when I know anything about anything?" He smoothed his hair and gave me a wicked grin. "It's the cuteness, isn't it?"

I scoffed, even though that probably was the reason. Girls aren't the only ones who have their smarts judged on looks.

"Besides," he said, "music and math have a lot in common. I read somewhere they use the same part of the brain."

"Really?"

He nodded, giving a sullen frown that reminded me, disturbingly, of Dylan. I hadn't told Logan I'd hooked up with his brother—and didn't plan to. The confession would give me only a brief relief from guilt, but it would tear them apart for good.

"I hate when people act like music is nothing but wild creativity," Logan said. "That's bullshit. It's also about counting and measuring and calibrating. If you do it right." He passed his hand over my MP3 player sitting on the bed between us. It was playing Mozart to help my concentration. "And if you do it really right, no one can tell how hard it is for you. You can let them believe it's magic, because that means *you* must be magic. You're worth worshiping."

His frown deepened, making him look much older than his frozen-at-seventeen.

In the week and a half since the prom, Logan had fielded another flood of interviews (which meant *I'd* fielded a flood of interviews, hence my calculus panic). The reporters all asked the same questions, most of which had nothing to do with the music. They were more fascinated with Logan's ghosthood and return from shade. They thought the music was just his "platform."

Logan was growing disillusioned with the attention. Nobody'd ever questioned his "motives" for writing a song, but once he started speaking out on behalf of at-risk ghosts, he got more politics than he'd bargained for. He was an artist, not a crusader.

I had a question for him, sparked by his one-page journal that Dylan had shown me. A question no one had asked. "If you hadn't died, and by some bizarre chance had not become a rock god, what would you have done?"

I expected him to say "music producer" or "sound engineer," something that would've kept him close to the famous.

"Easy." He patted my calculus book without sound. "I would've taught. Music, probably."

"At a high school?"

"Or middle school. Probably not elementary—they'd fire me the first time I accidentally said 'fuck.'"

I laughed out loud. "On your opening day? Yeah."

His eyes literally gleamed, then faded. "Doesn't matter, because it'll never happen. I'll leave college to Mickey. He can go get his PhD in Musical Twattage or whatever it is he thinks is good enough for him."

I cocked my head. "Didn't Dylan tell you? Mickey's not going to college next year."

"What? No. Why isn't he?"

"He says he doesn't want to spend any of your blood money."

Logan's face twisted. "So he's missing college and using me as an excuse?"

"I don't think that's how he sees it."

"Of course not." Logan got off the bed and started to pace. "He probably thinks he's being noble and superior."

"Have you talked to him at all since you've been back? Through Dylan or Megan?"

"Mickey doesn't want to talk to me."

"Maybe, but he *needs* to talk to you. Logan, I think he wants to—" I wished I could swallow the words. "I think he might hurt himself."

Logan stopped pacing. He stopped, period.

"No," he whispered. "He can't do that."

"Megan's tried to help him, or convince him to get help, but—"

"He can't do that! With all he has to live for? Hell, he has *life* to live for. I'd do anything to have that! Even if it sucked every single day. At least it would be life."

He started pacing again, clutching the pale violet spikes of his hair. I noticed that despite his agitation, he showed no signs of shading— not so much as a flicker of black.

"Let's talk to Mickey," I said.

"Not you. I'll find someone who doesn't know us."

"Why?"

"Because he'll say things I don't want you to hear."

"You mean like secrets?"

"No, just—things. You remember the way he'd cut me down when I was alive. Can you imagine how he'll be after seven months of sulking, when he can't even see my reaction?"

I had to admit, I didn't want to be in the middle of that conflict. "I could ask one of the other translators at work."

"Maybe." He wiped his hands on the sides of his shirt, and the motion seemed to calm him. "Siobhan's not so bad. I should talk to her. Will you help me?"

"Sure. That's a good start."

"Start?"

"You should settle things with your parents, too."

"My parents barely admit I'm a ghost. All they care about is me passing on."

"Because they love you. And part of them still can't grasp the whole idea of ghosts without going totally batshit. A lot of pre-Shifters are like that. But I think we should try."

"Fine, fine. Set it up." He sat on the bed and rubbed his arms. "Wow, I'm more nervous about that than any interview."

"You never know, it might be fun."

"Fun? You've hung out with my parents, right?"

"Yes, and all eleven hundred times, they were fun." I bit back my resentment at the fact that he at least *had* parents. That wasn't the point.

I opened my bag next to the bed and slid my calc text and notebook inside.

"I guess I should let you sleep," Logan said, but stayed where he was. Not that he had to physically walk out the door, but he usually stood up to say good-bye. Habit, I guess.

I brought my bag to my desk to collect my laptop. "Where are you going tonight?"

"I don't know." He traced the stitching on my bedspread. "Aura, do you ever get tired of this world?"

I considered his question. As miserable as I'd been after he died, and after he shaded, and then after Zachary broke up with me, I'd never felt like I didn't want to exist.

"Not really."

"Maybe because you sleep. I think that's why ghosts either pass on or go crazy and turn shade. It's not the bitterness. It's the boredom." He set his palm on the mattress, as if it had finished a task. "Don't freak out, but sometimes I think about staying here for years, turning solid every three months. What would I do with those seventeen minutes? Play guitar? Eat pizza?" He glanced at me. "Have rampaging rabbit sex with my best friend?"

I laughed, though I didn't want to encourage that line of thought. At least he no longer called me his girlfriend.

"One of those times," he said, "I think I'd take a nap."

I went to sit beside him. "You want to rest. We all do." I thought of the grueling emotional and academic journey this year had been. After all the angst and hard work, I felt no closer to the answers I sought—about me, about Zachary, about the Shift. "Sometimes I just want to shut off my mind. Music helps."

"Music helps everything. Usually."

I reached behind him and picked up the MP3 player, then set it on my nightstand. With a few button clicks, I started my pre-exam playlist, the seventy most soothing songs I owned.

"You can rest with me," I said.

Logan gave me a sad, grateful smile. "I'd like that."

He lay back against the pillow, almost gingerly, like he thought he would break it, or vice versa.

"That's where I sleep now," I said.

"You've always slept on the left side."

"I used to, but then I wanted to be away from the window."

"Why?"

I stared at the dark brown blinds. "Because it hurt too much to watch it, every night, waiting for you to come back."

"When I was a shade?"

I nodded. "And I couldn't just roll over, because then I'd be looking at the empty space where you used to lie." I pulled back the covers and slid underneath. "But you're here now, so I should sleep on this side again. It's closer to the clock, anyway." I reached to set the alarm.

"Aura, sleep wherever you need."

"I need to sleep here." I lay down, the pillow cool beneath my head. "I need to feel normal again."

He placed his violet hand around mine in a facsimile of touch. "I'll do like I used to, leave once you fall asleep."

"You can stay all night."

"Won't it be creepy for me to watch you sleep?"

"Then don't watch me sleep. Just be here. Tonight, tomorrow

night, whenever you need a quiet place to rest. Leave when you want."
I curled my thumb over his. "If you want."

"I won't overdo it, I promise."

I believed him. His lack of shadiness was a sign that he'd changed. The last time I could remember him losing his temper was the night we met with Zachary and Megan. Since then he'd grown sadder, more serious. In other words, more grown up.

"I have to turn over," I said. "Your light keeps me awake."

"Sorry, I can't help the shine."

As I rolled to lie on my left side, his last word echoed in my head, reminding me of what Eowyn had called the Newgrange sunrise a year before my birth. The Shine.

Which in turn reminded me of how much work Zachary and I still had to do on our project, and how much I dreaded seeing him again. I forced my mind to stay here and focus on the soft music, hoping it would carry me away.

But my eyes wouldn't stay shut. I squirmed, my limbs searching for a comfortable configuration.

"You can't sleep?" Logan whispered.

"It's weird being on this side. It's like my arm doesn't fit."

We switched places, and immediately I felt myself relax into the mattress.

"Better?" he said.

"Mm-hmm," I murmured.

"Good. I love you, Aura."

"Love you, too."

I snuggled my face into the pillow, feeling at home again. This right-side, right-side-of-the-bed position—one of hiding and mourning—had become normal to me. Facing the window meant facing the world, something I'd thought I was ready to do.

Obviously not yet.

Chapter Twenty-one

Zachary and I drove separately to our next meeting with Professor Harris. I'd told him—via text message, since we weren't speaking complete sentences to each other—that I had another stop to make on the way back from the University of Maryland. It was easier to lie in a text.

As I approached her office, I could hear him and Eowyn laughing.

"Sorry I'm late." I sat beside Zachary in front of Eowyn's wide cherrywood desk—after pulling the chair farther away from him. "Hope I didn't miss anything."

"Not at all." Eowyn smiled at me. "Zachary was just telling me about the international soccer rivalry at home, and how if England advances in the World Cup and Scotland doesn't, his mother will be the filling in a resentment sandwich."

"Heh." I unzipped my messenger bag and pulled out my project materials, glancing at Zachary. He was eyeing the Keeley Brothers and Tabloid Decoys stickers on my notebook and folders.

"So tell me." Eowyn folded her hands. "Why are you two falling behind schedule? Is there a research roadblock I can help with?"

"We're fine," I said, "just busy."

Zachary nodded at my notebook. "Aye, busy with the rock star and his paparazzi."

My mouth dropped open. *Ouch.*

"Ooo-kay." Eowyn sat back in her chair. "So it's not a research roadblock, I take it."

"Our biggest problem isn't the ragged schedule." Zachary muted the edge in his voice. "To be honest, we have several theories that we can't prove. We aren't even sure if it's safe to report them."

Her usual smile dissipated. "I'm sure that what I told you at the exhibit didn't help. But that's outside the scope of your thesis, which Mrs. Richards insists is a history paper. Your assignment is to focus on the people who built Newgrange and used it throughout the centuries. Not its hypothetical connection to other things."

"You mean the Shift," I said.

She looked at my right hand, which I noticed was clutching the arm of my chair so tight, the knuckles were turning white. I let go and rubbed my wrist.

Eowyn pulled a set of keys from her top desk drawer. "Let's take a walk."

On our way out, she closed and locked her door, checking the knob twice to make sure it didn't turn.

As we exited the building, Eowyn's cell phone rang. She looked at the screen. "Oh! Excuse me for a second."

She answered the phone, leaving me and Zachary to walk beside each other in silence toward the wide grassy expanse of McKeldin Mall.

After a few yards, he spoke quietly. "Did you really listen to my voice mail?"

I startled at the suddenness of his question and the vulnerability of his voice. "Which one?"

"The one I left the morning after the prom," he said with a touch of annoyance.

Eowyn gasped into the phone. "Are you kidding me? For a one-way ticket? Is that coach or business class?"

I turned back to Zachary. "I told you I listened to it. I said everything was fine."

He walked backward, with an athlete's easy grace. "What did my message say?"

"Um." I swiped at the hair blowing across my cheek. "That you were sorry about the night before. Can't we just move on?"

Eowyn groaned. "I don't have an exact date yet, I'm just shopping for rates and schedules."

Zachary kept his eyes on me, his dark hair tossed at his temples. "What else did I tell you in the voice mail?"

"That . . ." I sucked at improvising, and besides, he knew the right answer and I didn't, which gave him an advantage. "Uh."

"I knew it," he said with a mix of triumph and anger. "You didn't listen to it." He faced forward again, a few paces ahead of me.

"Was it about your dad?" I shouted over the whistling breeze. "How is he?"

"No, it wasn't," Zachary said, "and he's the same, thanks. But his work visa's expiring next month, because he can't work."

My feet slowed, almost stumbling. "When are you leaving?"

"The twenty-second of June."

Two days after the solstice. I would lose both him and Logan in one weekend.

"Frankly," he said, "I don't know whether to be mad or relieved you didn't hear my message. I think I'm both."

Now he was torturing me on purpose. "I accidentally deleted it, okay? I was tired that morning, and my thumb slipped and hit the wrong key."

He shot me an *oh, please* look over his shoulder. "Doesn't matter."

"You've been so helpful," Eowyn said into the phone. "You'll be the first I call when I set a date. Thanks again!"

She hung up as we approached the long, rectangular fountain in the center of the mall. It reminded me of the Reflecting Pool on the Mall in DC. But because the landscape here was sloped, this one incorporated several stairlike waterfalls, creating a background murmur.

Oh. Maybe she'd brought us here so no one could overhear us over the fountain and the wind. Or maybe I was paranoid.

"Aura. Zachary." Eowyn took one of our hands in each of hers. "The time is coming soon when I must leave you."

"Are you sick?" Zachary blurted.

She squeezed our hands and let go. "I'm fine, despite a severe lack of sleep. I just need to leave the country. I'm in trouble. I haven't done anything illegal, I simply need to be out of the DMP's reach so I can continue my research in peace." She looked at Zachary. "Your father says I'll be safe in the UK."

"Why is the DMP after you?" he asked.

"They think I have information that might lead them to the mysteries of the Shift."

My muscles jolted. "Is that true?"

"Not sure. I have the documents, but I can't read them."

"Are they in some ancient language?" Zachary asked.

"They're in English, but I can't unlock them." She pressed her lips together, as if sealing in the words. "Only Aura can."

I jerked my head to look at her bag. It wasn't big enough for papers. "Where are they? Can I have them now?"

"I promised to wait until you were eighteen, or until I could no longer personally protect the information."

Great. I wouldn't be eighteen for seven months. "Promised who?"

She squared her shoulders and faced me head-on. "Your mother."

"I was right." I kicked a stone down the sidewalk ahead of me as Zachary and I walked toward the university's visitor parking lot. "My mom was hiding secrets from me."

"Not *from* you," he said. "*For* you."

I kicked the stone again, with more force. "But not until I'm eighteen! What's so horrible that I can't handle it now?"

"Maybe it's a legal matter. What can you do once you turn eighteen?"

"I can use my cell phone while I'm driving. I can vote. I can buy cigarettes and lottery tickets and porn."

"It's probably not one of those. Don't you become an official adult at eighteen?"

"Duh." I kicked the rock, but it spun off the side of my foot. Zachary saved it from shooting off the sidewalk.

"So think. What would that mean for your mother, you being a real person?"

I stopped. "Oh my God. I think that's the age when adopted kids can hunt down their birth mothers."

"You know who your mother is."

"But I don't know my father." I grabbed his arm. "Maybe that's what's in the documents—my dad's name. Which means I can find him!"

He gave a wistful smile. "I hope so."

"I will." I tilted my head back in triumph. The sky suddenly looked bluer, the clouds puffier.

I noticed I was still holding on to Zachary's arm. I dropped my hand but didn't move away. My excitement gave me a shot of courage.

"Please tell me what your voice mail said. The part I missed."

His gaze dropped to the notebook I was gripping, the one with the stickers for Logan's bands. His smile disappeared, making my heart plummet to my shoes.

"Sorry." He turned and gave the rock an extra-hard kick, shooting it across the street. "Not today."

I gave a defeated sigh and followed him toward the parking lot. As we walked, we divided our thesis into sections, each of us choosing the parts we would polish into a final form.

When we reached my car, he said, "I'll send you the outline and maybe we can meet next week?"

The thought of spending more time with Zachary, seeing up close the hands and mouth that had been all over Becca—and trying to decode his mixed signals—sounded downright masochistic. I had to get over him.

"There's a lot going on right now." I scraped my shoe against the mud splash on the bottom of the car door. "With finals and band rehearsals and all of Logan's interviews, plus the show next month."

"And?"

"In my aunt's firm there are these two guys who work down on the Eastern Shore." To avoid Zachary's narrowing eyes, I stuffed my notebook back in my bag, which I took my time refastening. "We hardly ever see them, but they do a ton of work for us by e-mail and videoconferencing and remote desktopping. Maybe you and I could do that, so we wouldn't have to—"

"See each other?"

Exactly. "No, it's not that. I just think, with our crazy schedules, it would be—"

"Brilliant. Let's do it."

I watched him walk away, trying to convince myself that this was easier. If it was just a matter of time before I could read my mother's secrets, then I didn't need Zachary to help me figure things out.

I turned back to my car, fumbling with the keys on Gina's giant metallic Italian flag key chain. I couldn't look at Zachary and think of my birthday—either the last one, when we had first kissed; or the next one, when I had hoped we'd go to Newgrange for the solstice.

Another dead dream.

Chapter Twenty-two

The school year ended, and I officially became a senior—a senior who could look forward to an entire year without calculus. With Logan's help, I'd aced the class final.

It was the least he could do, since wrangling him and Tabloid Decoys had become my part-time job, one that was interfering with my real job, which actually paid me. The band members—Josh, Heather, and Corey—agreed to give me a portion of their CD sales for the next year. Since their previous year's sales only reached mid-double digits, I figured my royalty checks would maybe buy me lunch. At McDonald's.

But the money wasn't the point. As always, I needed to monitor Logan to keep him from spilling my secrets. Plus, I needed to wring every moment out of his time on Earth.

Because this time, I knew it was ending. This time, I knew he was ready.

However, his band—and its new "lead singer"—were not. Tabloid Decoys had only two rehearsals left before their big solstice concert. Logan and Mickey—finally communicating—had figured out the ultimate fake magic trick, one that would make Logan's return to solidity less believable and thus less likely to cause a universal freak-out.

Now they just had to get it right.

"If you want to be me," Logan told his older brother at the end of the song, "you have to be less cool."

Sitting beside us in the second row, Megan repeated his words toward the stage.

Mickey glared at the ceiling of the high school auditorium, where he was rehearsing the finale. "I can't help it if I'm naturally cooler than he is."

"For the fortieth time," I said, "don't talk about him like he's not here." I gestured to my left, where Logan sat with his feet propped on the seat in front of him.

Mickey's hand tightened on the neck of the black Fender. "What do you mean by 'less cool,' *Logan*?"

"Try smiling for once in your life. And bounce more. Work those Vans."

After I translated, Mickey frowned at the blue-and-black-checkered high-tops on his own feet, but thankfully made no comment. He and Logan had been bickering all afternoon, as they had when Logan was alive. But at least they were speaking again.

We'd found an outfit that matched what Logan had been wearing the night he died, and which he still wore, as it was apparently the happiest moment of his life. The day after tomorrow, on the morning of Logan's solstice show, Mickey would get a temporary Aura tattoo over his heart, then bleach his hair blond with black streaks. Their faces and lanky builds were so similar, people used to think they were twins.

After Logan's death, Mickey had rejected his own punk image. He'd dyed his jet-black hair back to its natural medium brown and stopped spiking it. He'd also abandoned the electric guitar.

Seeing Mickey plugged in again was like bringing a piece of Logan back to life—and Mickey with him.

Mickey turned to his temporary bandmates. "Let's take it two measures before the first bridge. Josh, watch your tempo—you sound like you're on crack heading into that chorus."

Corey, the drummer, counted off, and they crashed into the rolling, swerving bridge, my favorite part of "Shade," Logan's new tune. If he became human again on Friday night, he would play it himself. It would be his swan song.

Logan watched intently as Mickey tried to mimic his frenetic onstage energy, transforming from his own dark, cool, brooding self into Logan's passionate, boisterous, heart-on-his-sleeve persona. As Mickey made the Fender wail, Logan played along, his fingers forming the chords and picking out the solo.

But he hid his hands below the seat in front of us so his bandmates couldn't see. Like the public, the members of Tabloid Decoys thought Logan would run offstage and Mickey would take his place in a "magic trick" made to look like a miracle. Only Megan, Logan, Mickey, and I knew that the miracle would be real.

All this so that Logan could play guitar one last time. I glanced over at his violet hands, weaving a spell on an imaginary instrument, and knew it was worth it.

The song ended, flawlessly this time. We hooted and cheered.

"Very nice!" came a voice from the back of the auditorium. Nicola Hughes strode down the aisle, clapping as she walked. She was more casually dressed than on her usual visits to rehearsal, in a pair of jeans and a tight top that showed off her skinniness. "Are we all ready for Friday?" she asked me and Megan. "Anything I can do?"

Logan beamed at her, though she couldn't see him. "Ask her which radio stations are coming."

We shared his question, and she replied, "The three major rock stations from Baltimore and DC, plus one each from Frederick and Harrisburg. I've also got calls in to the punk, indie, and alternative satellite radio stations."

"Tell her she rocks," Logan said to me, then faced the stage. "Let's round out the set list. Which two songs should Mickey play after 'Shade'?"

Josh said, "Why not play the other songs first and end with 'Shade'? It's our big number."

"Yeah, but I know from experience, shit happens. If things get wild after my alleged transformation, and they shut us down, I want to make sure that song's been played."

"Who'll shut us down?" Heather turned to Nicola. "The DMP? I thought you said all this was approved."

"Of course. There'll be plenty of security." Nicola looked at me. "Does Logan have a concern?"

"My only concern," he said to me, "is not screwing up that solo. Be right back." He disappeared, then reappeared onstage.

"He's fine," I told Nicola. "You can go."

Instead, she took a seat at the end of our row and pulled out her cell phone.

"She's a hoverer, isn't she?" Megan whispered to me.

"I'll be glad to get rid of her, if we ever do. But she's probably the only reason we've had any peace these last few months. She's like a mother bear and we're her cubs."

Logan reappeared beside me. "We settled on 'Little Lion Man' by Mumford and Sons as an acoustic solo, then finish off with AFI's 'Bleed Black.'" He lowered his voice so only the two of us could hear. "That gives us a little cushion in the seventeen minutes."

"Good," Megan said. "It would suck if you dropped that expensive guitar when you turned back to air." She smirked at him as she climbed over the seat to go talk to Mickey.

I watched Logan run through a series of chords, nodding his head and setting his fingers in the proper configurations.

"You're ready, aren't you?" I asked.

He looked up from his air guitar and gave me a serene smile. "Almost."

I wondered how I would feel Friday night, seeing Mickey looking so much like the live Logan. If Logan failed to turn solid at the moment of the solstice, his brother would take his place onstage. He would sing the notes, play the chords, and touch the fans that were meant for Logan. Maybe Logan would still pass on, but he'd be doing it in sadness instead of triumph.

Since the band was on a break, I switched my phone back on. The screen told me I had a missed call from Eowyn.

Before I could dial my voice mail, the phone rang. Zachary. We hadn't spoken since we'd turned in our paper almost two weeks ago, on the last day of school. We'd briefly discussed getting together before he left for the UK next Sunday. For research purposes on the Shift, I assumed. I didn't dare to hope for anything more.

"Hey," I said casually, as if it didn't still hurt to hear his voice.

"Aura, Eowyn's gone."

Zachary and I met outside the computer and space sciences building on campus, then dashed up the stairs to Eowyn's office.

My heart pounded from more than exertion. According to Eowyn's hasty phone calls to me and Zachary, she'd had to leave the country quickly or risk having her research materials confiscated. The DMP was closing in.

At quarter to five, we ran into the astronomy office, where the department secretary, Madeline, was waiting for us.

"Just in time." She opened the top drawer of her desk and pulled out a slim envelope and a set of keys. "Professor Harris said to let you alone in her office as long as you needed. But I have to lock up and leave at five. My kid's day care charges extra if I'm late."

"Thanks very much," Zachary said.

Madeline gave me the envelope. Then she led us over to Eowyn's door and unlocked it with a "Good luck."

We turned on the light and shut the door behind us. I opened the envelope, my sweaty fingers catching on the slit.

Inside was a half sheet of notebook paper. In unusually shaky handwriting, it read,

AURA AND ZACHARY,
THE TRUTH ISN'T ALWAYS BEAUTIFUL, AND IT'S
ALMOST NEVER KIND. THE TRUTH JUST IS.
    BE AS STRONG AS I KNOW YOU ARE,
    EOWYN HARRIS

I turned the paper over, her words filling me with dread.

#1 OF 3: BENEATH THE TREE WE DIDN'T DRINK.

We stared at the paper for several moments.

Finally Zachary said, "Huh?"

"It must be some kind of scavenger hunt."

"Seems like something she'd do. It would keep the DMP from finding whatever we're hunting for. Of course, it might keep *us* from finding it, too."

I repeated the clue under my breath. We'd drunk trees?

I scanned the office, hoping some detail would trigger a memory. Her books and papers were gone, but her decor had been left behind—the midnight blue ceiling tapestry with golden stars, the blue and lavender woven rug, the low, Japanese-style tea table. The room even smelled faintly of her honeysuckle perfume.

Wait—the table.

I remembered our first meeting, less than two days after Logan had died. Eowyn had served us tea in mugs decorated with ogham letters from the old Irish alphabet, letters that each held a special meaning.

I flapped my hand. "The mugs! The symbols on them—they had something to do with trees, right?"

"They corresponded to different trees and meanings, I think. The clue says it's the one we didn't drink from." He went to the table and stood next to the cushion we'd sat on together. "There were three of us that day. So there's a fourth mug?"

"She kept them in here." I hurried behind her desk and opened a small cabinet. Four white mugs sat upside down on a woven cloth, next to a twilight blue teapot. I yanked out the mugs, two in each hand, their ceramic clink hurting my ears. I peered inside and underneath each cup. Nothing.

Zachary knelt beside me. "The symbols appear when the mugs are filled with hot water, remember? So we can't know which one she means until we fill them."

An invisible clue only we could find. Eowyn Harris had just topped Zachary as the coolest and most frustrating person I'd ever met.

The astronomy department's coffeemaker was empty, so we said goodbye to Madeline and took an all-too-long elevator ride to the vending machines in the basement.

The soles of my creepers and Zachary's sneakers squeaked on the empty hallway's freshly waxed floor. It seemed like we should skulk so no one would see or hear us, but maybe the adrenaline rush was just cranking up the drama in my head.

We stepped up to the tall, humming coffee machine, relieved that it gave us the option of using our own cups.

I unzipped my bag and retrieved a mug, trying to forget that Zachary and I, once again, made a great team. Even Mrs. Richards had proclaimed it in front of our history class, giving our junior thesis the only A+. I'd been amazed, considering that during our entire joint presentation, all I could think about was jumping my partner's bones.

"What do you want?" Zachary said in a low voice.

I twitched. "Huh?"

"To drink?" He fed a dollar bill into the vending machine slot. "No point in wasting money. Besides, our brains need caffeine to figure out these clues."

I couldn't argue with that, though Eowyn's letter—and Zachary's presence—had made me plenty jittery. "Mocha."

The machine spat out a rancid-smelling approximation of my favorite drink. Before the mug was even full, the ogham letter *quert* appeared—a straight vertical line with four lines connected to it. It looked like a toothbrush facing left.

The apple tree. Signifying love.

"I had that one." My chest tightened as I remembered how much seeing that symbol had hurt, so soon after Logan's death.

"No, I had it," Zachary said.

"That's because you traded with me, the Love mug for your Strength." The first in a long line of kindnesses.

"Aye," he said softly. "I remember now."

I didn't look at him as we inserted the second mug and fed the machine more money. Sure enough, a bitter-smelling tea poured into the mug with the letter *duir*—the oak, signifying Strength. It was like *quert*, but with only two horizontal lines. A toothbrush that's seen better days.

"Eowyn had the mug for Healing," I said. "I don't know the letter's name, but I remember it looked like a telephone pole."

The ogham letter on the third mug looked nothing like a telephone pole. It looked just like *quert*, except facing the other way.

"There." I pointed to it. "The only one we didn't use."

"I'll look it up." He opened the web browser on his phone. "Good memory, that."

I remember everything about that day, I thought as I sipped the mocha, which tasted like chocolate-flavored battery acid.

"It's *nuin*," he said, pronouncing the Gaelic like the native speaker he was. "The ash tree. Supposed to signify Connection, if that helps."

"So the second clue must be under an ash tree. Or inside one? I don't even know what they look like."

He turned his phone so I could see the screen. "There's a picture."

"Great—big and green, like a tree. There must be a hundred of them on this campus."

He thumbed through the text and let out a soft curse. "Says they were all but wiped out by a beetle the past few years."

"That's sad for the trees, but it might make our job easier."

"Let's see if anyone's home in the botany department." He called information, subduing his accent so the directory robot could understand him.

When the call went through, though, Zachary turned on his Scottish charm. "Aye, hello, lassie. Might you tell me where we could find an ash tree on the College Park campus?" He chuckled. "No, I promise it's no' for an exam. It's for an article in *Tree Huggers* magazine, a wee independent UK publication. We're doing a feature on universities maintaining viable populations of threatened species." Leaning against the vending machine, he smirked at my silent laughter. Then he put the phone to his chest and spoke to me. "She says there's none on campus, but one at the National Arboretum. Where's that?"

"In DC. Maybe half an hour away."

He spoke into the phone again. "Aye, I know where tha' is. Brilliant. Cheers for the information." He hung up. "Thank God a woman answered. American men are immune to the accent."

I waved off his arrogant but accurate statement and dumped the rest of my drink in the water fountain. "Let's go."

The ash's leaves waved their pale underbellies above my head, as if cheering on my frustration. The thick canopy allowed only glimpses of the bright early evening sky, white with the haze of Washington, DC. We'd been lucky to slip into the National Arboretum twenty minutes before closing. Any minute now they'd be kicking us out.

For the third time, I ran my hands over the ash's smooth gray trunk, then searched the area around its roots. No secret box or compartment.

"What did you expect," I asked myself, "Keebler elves to the rescue?"

"Who?" Several yards out, Zachary was pacing an outward spiral around the tree, shuffling his feet and examining the grass, which was begging for a good mow.

"Keebler elves. They make the cookies that taste like cardboard."

He grunted without looking up. "I miss the packaged biscuits from home. No one makes junk food like the Brits."

"Better than my grandmom's cookies?"

"Does your grandmother make dark chocolate HobNobs? No. So yes, better." He stopped. "Here we are."

"What'd you find?" I scampered over, practically on all fours.

In front of his toes lay a small brass plaque bolted to a six-inch-long concrete frame. The plaque read WHITE ASH, *FRAXINUS AMERI-CANA*.

Zachary tapped the edge with his foot. Two of the plaque's bolts had come off, and the other two were loose. I pried up one end and stuck my hand in.

Zachary grabbed my wrist. "What are you doing? There could be anything down there."

"Like what? An angry leprechaun?"

"Like a snake or a vole."

"What the hell's a vole?"

"A rodent. They bite." He tugged on my wrist. "Let me get it."

"Your giant man-hands won't fit." I tried to ignore the way his touch was sending ripples of zings across my shoulders.

He wrenched the plaque off all its bolts. "Now they will."

We leaned over to peer into the hole. It was so narrow and dark, I couldn't see the bottom.

Zachary's hand flashed out. "Got it." He pulled from the hole a thin steel box the size of a TV remote control, with a piece of laminated paper attached. I ripped off the card to read the clue:

#2 of 3: Alpha and beta to the proud queen of the sky.

Zachary shook the box. Something rattled inside. "It's locked with a combination. Six numbers."

I flipped the clue card. On the back it read, *If this note isn't meant for you, put it back now or be forever cursed.* The last two words were underlined in red. It reminded me of the warning at the beginning of Logan's notebook.

"So this clue will help us figure out the combination," I said.

Zachary turned the card over without taking it from my hand. "Alpha and beta. The two brightest stars in a constellation?"

"Ooh, yeah." I pondered how a star could be numbered. "The combination could be the magnitude of the stars' brightness. That's three numbers each."

"Fantastic." He lifted his phone to open the browser. "But which constellation? Who was the proud queen of the sky? Andromeda?"

"She was a princess. Her dad tied her to a rock to sacrifice her to a sea monster, because—" I thumped the side of my head, hoping to shake a memory loose from our eighth-grade mythology segment. "Some god—Poseidon?—was pissed off because the king's wife had said she was prettier than the nymphs."

"The king's wife would be the queen," Zachary said flatly.

"No shit." I tapped the edge of the card against my chin. "It's the one with—oh! Oh!" I jumped to my feet and pointed at the sky. "The constellation that looks like a W."

"Oh. Cassiopeia."

"Cassiopeia!" I pumped both fists in the air, then put a hand to my head, suddenly dizzy. I realized I hadn't eaten since breakfast.

While time crawled, Zachary touched his phone screen to look up the stars' magnitudes. To occupy my nervous hands, I tossed the box into the air, flipping it end over end and catching it.

"Whatever's inside better not be breakable," he muttered.

"She would've marked it 'fragile,'" I said, almost dropping it.

"Here's Alpha Cassiopeia's magnitude: two-point-two-four."

My hands shaking, I punched in 224.

"Beta Cassiopeia is—oh, that's interesting. Two-point-two-eight."

I tabbed 228 onto the box's buttons, then tried to turn the latch. It wouldn't budge.

Zachary stood to look over my shoulder. "Try it again all at once. Maybe it didn't like the pause."

I steadied my hand and plugged in 224228. The latch sprung. "Yes!" I lifted the lid. The box held a small key with a tag that said "308."

And another laminated card.

#3 of 3: The place that holds your treasure box of truth shares five digits with Ruis.

"Another ogham?" Zachary brought out his phone again. "I've still got that page open. *Ruis* means 'elder,' which stands for Transition. So there's a treasure chest under an elder tree? How tedious."

"Trees don't have digits. That key could be for an apartment. But where the hell is it?"

"It's too small. And since when is an apartment a 'treasure box of truth'?"

I groaned and stamped my foot. "It could be a metaphor."

"All right. Calm down."

"I can't calm down!" I kicked at the grass. "What if I never find out this truth because I was too dumb to figure out the clues?"

"Eowyn wants us to know. She's given us the hints in our work."

"But why not just tell us where it is?" My breath started to come fast. Too fast.

Zachary reached out. "Here." He eased me to sit. "Head between your knees."

I stared at the shadowed ground beneath my legs, silently begging my guts not to empty.

He sat beside me. "Are you afraid we won't find the answers about your father and the Shift? Or are you afraid we will?"

I dug my fingers into the dirt. "Yes."

Zachary set the open box between us. "We could give up. Protect ourselves."

"Protect ourselves with ignorance? It would make us weaker."

"Possibly." He nudged the box with his foot. "Whatever you decide is whatever you decide. But I thought I should remind you that you have options."

With my chin on my knees, I looked around the grounds of the arboretum. Over by the azalea garden, a young couple held hands as their little girl chased a butterfly—free from ghosts, thanks to Zachary's presence. Besides them, we were alone.

"What have we gotten ourselves into?" I whispered.

I glanced at the key in the box. It would open up my past and probably my future. Once I learned the secrets, I could never unlearn them, never go on living like I didn't know.

Maybe I couldn't figure out this last clue because deep down, I didn't *want* to know.

Zachary spoke softly. "I wish I had all the answers so I could give them to you." He adjusted the sleeve of his polo shirt. "In exchange for dessert, of course."

Despite my fear, I couldn't hold back a semi-smile. "Doesn't sound like much fun for me."

"True, adventures are better with both of us." He leaned back on his hands and nodded to his car. "And it's good practice for me, driving from town to town, not crashing."

My chuckle faded as his words tickled my mind. "Wait, what did you say?"

"About not crashing?"

"Before that."

"Er, it's good practice? Driving? Town to town?"

The puzzle piece slid into place. "Towns!"

"All right, towns," he said, exaggerating the vowel so that it didn't sound like "toons." "Don't take the piss out of my accent."

"Towns! Five digits! Maybe it's a zip code."

He snatched the key from the box, shaking the tag with the number. "Could this be for a postal box?"

"Maybe." Excitement rushed to my fingertips, and I turned the clue card over. "'Shares five digits with *ruis*.' Elder."

"Is there a town called Elder?"

"Eldersburg! It's—I don't know, somewhere near Baltimore. I've heard them say it on the traffic report."

"Let's search for the post office." Zachary thumbed the screen of his phone. "No results."

"How can it not have a post office? Every town does. What's the zip code?"

"21784. Hold on." A grin spread across his face. "Sykesville. Same zip code, and that's where the post office is."

"'Shares five digits with *ruis*.' We did it!" I reached out to hug him, then stopped myself and offered a high five. We clasped each other's hands for a long moment, then Zachary helped me to my feet. As we walked toward our cars, he didn't let go of my hand right away.

But he did let go.

Chapter Twenty-three

Where were you when I called earlier?" Zachary asked me once we'd dropped off my aunt's car at my house. "It sounded loud."

"Dress rehearsal." Since we had an hour's drive ahead of us to Sykesville, I told Zachary everything—about Nicola's publicity help, Logan's concert, and even what he planned to do at the end: turn human, then pass on once his seventeen minutes were up.

"Sounds risky," Zachary said. "What if everyone finds out he's really solid?"

"They won't. Mickey will be backstage dressed as Logan. They look enough alike that people will assume they've switched places, especially since Logan will run backstage before coming out again with a real body. I'll be back there, too, since Logan needs my help turning solid."

"What kind of help?" Zachary's voice was almost a growl.

"Whatever it takes."

His lips tightened, and he switched on the radio to listen to a World Cup match. Discussion over.

We reached downtown Sykesville none too soon. Judging by the empty side street where we parked, it was the kind of place where not much happened after six on a weeknight.

Luckily, the lobby where the PO boxes were located was open all night, and right now was totally empty.

Once we'd found Box 308, I inserted the key and opened the door.

A large manila envelope leaned against the interior of the box. I pulled it out, almost reverently. The front bore Eowyn's name and this address, but no postage. She had put this here herself.

Inside were two more envelopes—a thick nine-by-twelve one and a small white one bearing a READ ME FIRST! sticky note.

I slipped my thumb under the piece of Scotch tape, my heart hammering so hard I could feel my pulse against the paper. The envelope contained a single folded sheet.

DEAR AURA,
WHEN YOU READ THE CONTENTS OF THE OTHER ENVELOPE, YOU'LL BE THE ONLY LIVING PERSON TO KNOW YOUR MOTHER'S SECRET. I HOPE SOMEDAY YOU'LL SHARE IT WITH ME.
    I'M VERY PROUD OF YOU AND ZACHARY. TOGETHER YOU WILL DO GREAT THINGS. IF THEY LET YOU.
    WALK IN PEACE,
    EOWYN CYNTHIA HARRIS

Beneath her name was a phone number with a 00 prefix.

"Now she tells us how to reach her," Zachary muttered.

I traded him the letter for the larger envelope. Across the wide adhesive seal was my mother's handwriting: TO BE READ *ONLY* BY AURA, IF EVER. At either edge the seal was reinforced with red candle wax, like a letter from a hundred years ago.

"We're the first people to read this," I whispered.

"And we should do it somewhere private."

"There's no one here, and I can't wait." I broke the seals.

A peek inside the envelope showed a mass of loose pages, so I hurried to the table near the self-service postage machine. There I dumped out the contents all at once.

The missing pages of my mother's journal. I wanted to cheer. Or cry. Maybe both.

"Eowyn had them all these years," Zachary whispered.

The pages were arranged chronologically, starting with an entry marked "December 21 (cont.)." My toes wiggled inside my shoes as I realized *this* was the remainder of the entry I had at home, which I'd memorized months ago:

> *December 21*
> *There are no words to describe what happened this morning in Newgrange. But so, so, SO many questions.*

I scooted closer to Zachary so he could read over my shoulder. I didn't want to go through this alone.

Shift

This morning before sunrise, twenty of us huddled inside that chamber. I felt lucky to be here on the day of the actual solstice, unlike the eighty lottery winners whose tickets got them access on one of the two days before and after. (I wouldn't have been inside at all, if not for a gorgeous Scotsman who gave me his extra ticket.)

Let's be honest. I'm lucky to be alive, period, but now more than ever, for having seen this place.

As the time approached, we all hushed, as if our words could keep the sun underground. I imagined how prehistoric folks must have felt as the sun spent less time above the horizon each day, maybe wondering if it would one day stay away and never come back.

At the visitor center they said that

I flipped the page, and Zachary put out his hand. "I'm not done."
"Did you get stuck on my mom calling your dad gorgeous?"
"I don't read as fast as you. But aye, that was odd."
I waited while he finished. Then I turned over the page.

"solstice" means "sun standing still," because for three days the sun seems to trace the same pattern in the sky. At one precise moment, it switches from "leaving" to "returning."

But the light doesn't really return on the winter solstice. That day is still pretty damn dark. Solstice is just a promise.

But it's a promise kept. Light always returns. Unlike people. When they're gone from this world, they're just gone.

Not anymore, I thought. Logan was only one of thousands, maybe millions, who had returned as a ghost since the Shift. The way Mom described the meaning of the solstice made me think its connection to ghosts couldn't be a coincidence.

I read on.

While I was standing there, thinking thoughts as deep and dark as the chamber itself, it happened.

A red-golden beam appeared, like a laser shooting down the corridor onto the chamber floor. When it touched the far-thest spot on the floor, in the back recess, they even let us step through it. I felt giddy for the first time in months.

Right then, I believed, to the bottom of my soul, that anything could happen. If the sun could return from death, anyone could. I had done it (from the brink of death, anyway).

Why couldn't he?

"Whoa." I looked up at Zachary, wishing my hands would stop shaking.

"She almost died?" he said. "Did you know that? And who's 'he'?"

I shook my head. "I'm so confused. Let's keep going."

Afterward, we all gathered outside, none of us wanting to leave this place and what we'd shared. An American teenager with long blond curls told me the strang-est thing—when I'd passed through the solstice sunbeam, she saw me lit up from the inside, like my skin was a lampshade.

On any other day, that image would've creeped me out. But at the time, *my mind was soaked in belief, the kind I'd had as a kid, when I thought that God granted our prayers the way Santa Claus grants wishes.*

So to commemorate our shared awe (and because the morning light looked exquisite on Eowyn's golden hair), I took her picture and promised to mail it to her.

Now that it's dark again—the sun set at four, how depressing—my soul feels heavy. God and Santa Claus are fairy tales, and wishes don't make anything come true.

My hands trembled harder. In her pictures, Mom always seemed so carefree. I'd always envied the way she breezed through life, even as it was ending. I never knew how much pain her heart had harbored.

I took a deep breath and turned to the next page. At the top, it read "December 26 (cont.)." The entry had been torn out midsentence. The first word was "Anthony."

I thought back to the journal pages I had at home. Anthony must have been the possibly dead person my mom couldn't believe she saw at the St. Stephen's Day party.

Even though I knew it couldn't be him, I tried to get closer, maybe ask if I could take his picture. Then me and Not-Anthony would have a good laugh and he would think I was trying a lame pickup line ("Don't I know you? Haven't we met? You look like a guy I wish I'd slept with"), and he'd smile and buy me a drink, and after that, who knows?

But when I got to that side of the pub, he had disappeared. No one else had seen him.

So I'm re-evaluating my disbelief in ghosts. As long as I'm in Ireland.

I drummed my fingernails on the table while Zachary finished reading the page. "Do you know who Anthony is?" he asked.

"Please stop asking questions. I don't know anything but what's in front of us."

"Sorry."

"I'm going to keep reading ahead. You can catch up."

"No. We can't do this here, where anyone could walk in." Zachary scooped up the pages and headed for the exit.

I had no choice but to follow.

* * *

Zachary's car was parallel parked on the wrong side of the street, facing traffic—not that there was any traffic. We got in and locked the doors.

He put the key in the ignition. "Where should we go?"

"Nowhere. If I read in a moving car, I get carsick."

"Then you read out loud here, while I keep a lookout."

"Whatever." Luckily, there was still plenty of sunlight. I started reading to Zachary.

> "December 31/January 1
>
> I'm writing these two entries together because it feels like one day. I haven't slept since night before last. Now I wonder if I'll ever sleep again.
>
> New Year's Eve night was warm enough that we could stand outside the pub to drink and smoke and look out at the party boats on the River Boyne.
>
> That's when I saw Anthony. Walking atop the water. His long coat brushed the river's tiny waves, making no ripples.
>
> He looked just as he had the night before the car accident, when he was alive. But now he was serene and determined, like a man with a mission.
>
> When Anthony reached the shore, he disappeared."

The next entry's handwriting was even sloppier than the others', the words leaking off the lines as if written by the left hand of a right-handed person.

"January 2ish

Holy, holy, holy shit, it's true. It's really him.

I'm under the covers. (Coward.) A's out there in my room, which doesn't feel like mine anymore. This whole real world—whatever that means—doesn't feel like mine anymore.

Why me? Why not Gina? Her love for Anthony ruined her life. All I did was get on a plane to learn about my friend's favorite place in the world, to feel close to him after his death.

And now I am. Closer than I ever thought possible."

I looked out the window, my eyes strained from deciphering the bad handwriting. "She must be talking about the guy Aunt Gina had an affair with. Gina used to see ghosts, so she saw him after he died. She told me my mom had a crush on him."

"Sounds like more than a crush," Zachary said. "So he was with your aunt and mother at the same time?"

"I don't know if he was," I said defensively. "It's hard to tell for sure what happened when." I continued reading aloud.

"January 3

Not flying home tomorrow. I'm staying here to be with him. I can always make up school later, if I stay healthy. I can do anything later.

But only this is now. Life is short."

What did she mean, *If I stay healthy*? I swept my hair off my face, wishing for a ponytail holder in the hot, stuffy car.

As if reading my mind, Zachary turned the key halfway in the ignition and rolled the windows all the way down. The radio came on automatically, but he switched it off.

> "January 20
>
> It seems so unfair, so WRONG, that Anthony helped me escape death, only to be yanked there himself.
>
> I would give anything if we could be together now, like we never were in life. But it's impossible. His flesh is now spirit, and my flesh is, well, flesh.
>
> But it hasn't stopped me from falling in love."

My chest ached. Everything my mother wrote rang so true to the way I felt after losing Logan. The endless longing and review of missed opportunities. The sense that I would've done anything to feel his skin against mine once more, and that with another chance, everything would be different.

I skimmed the next several pages, tossing them onto the floor in front of me. They held nothing but snippets of conversation between Mom and ex-Anthony, plus lists of places they'd gone.

One day these pages would help me put together a full picture of my mother's time in Ireland, but right now I needed to know who my father was. A cinder of fear smoldered as I began to grasp one possible, horrible truth.

"Slow down," Zachary said.

"I have to know." I flipped the stack over. "I'm starting from the end."

I read the final entry to myself, in silence.

April 19

I'm pregnant. This is impossible.

Last year they told me the cancer treatments would make me infertile.

But it's happened. I don't know how.

I wish I didn't know who.

What in the world is growing inside me?

My spine froze. "She called me a 'what.'" My voice almost squeaked.

Zachary took the page and read it. "Christ . . ."

"Why didn't she call me a 'who'? Why was I a 'what' to her?"

"Aura." Zachary's voice was urgent. "She said the cancer treatments should've kept her from getting pregnant."

I nodded, making my head pitch even worse.

He shook the page. "The cancer she had *before* she went to Newgrange."

I tried to listen to what he was saying and understand how it fit with my tumbling thoughts. The pregnancy, the cancer, the timing of it all . . .

"Oh my God!" I sat up straight. "The disease must have gone into remission and come back after I was born." I scoured my memory, trying to recall the course of Mom's disease. All Gina'd ever told me was that Mom had had cancer that killed her when I was three.

"Aura." Zachary started to reach for me, then pulled his hand back. "If it's true, then it means that what happened at Newgrange didn't make her sick. It didn't make my dad sick, either."

"It made us possible." I raised my gaze to meet his. "We shouldn't exist."

"But we do exist. We're here." His whisper shook. "Do you know what this means?"

I couldn't say it out loud, but my mind shouted the truth I'd wished for all these weeks. If the Shine didn't hurt his father and my mother, then maybe the Shift couldn't hurt us, either. Crossing that boundary—with a kiss, or maybe more—couldn't hurt anyone.

We could be together.

I broke our gaze, the intensity in his eyes more than I could bear.

I turned over the previous day's entry.

April 18
    Off to the chemist for a pregnancy test. That way I can prove it's a stomach virus.
    Or stress. Why wouldn't I be stressed?

I passed the page on to Zachary and flipped the next.

April 11

I'm a week late. Probably because I'm not eating enough. The money's running out, and I have this room to pay for.

I can't leave. He might come back.

My lips formed the word *Who?* even as the name painted itself across my mind.

March 23

He's really gone.

March 22

He's gone.

Her words were a desert. My chest felt like it would collapse. The next page seemed to weigh a hundred pounds as I slowly turned it over to see . . .

March 21

If anyone finds this . . . who would believe it? I can't.

We were sitting. Talking. His hand around mine as if he held it.

Her scrawl grew shakier.

> (No. If I write this, even if no one reads it, it will be real. So I can't write it. I can't, can't, CAN'T.)

The pen tore the paper, the end of the last word shooting off to the right.

The entry began again, blue ink replacing the black.

> Something happened. Not something amazing. Not something incredible, stupendous, or any other word ever invented.
>
> I was touching him. He was touching me.
>
> Anthony was alive.

A vortex opened inside my head. My hand dropped to my lap, crumpling the paper.

"Aura, are you—"

"Not okay." My head and stomach lurched in opposite directions. "I feel sick."

"Put the seat down."

I grabbed the handle and sank backward when the seat released. "Here, read it out loud. I can't finish." I shoved the paper at him.

He started from the beginning of the March 21 entry, his voice faltering at "I was touching him," as the meaning sank in.

"My God . . . ," he whispered.

"Keep going."

He read on out loud: "'We didn't wait. We had no idea how long it would last. A minute? An hour? Forever?'"

Hearing my mother's words in Zachary's deep, lilting voice made it all too real.

My father was a ghost.

"'About fifteen minutes was what it turned out to be. Long enough to'—Aura, are you sure you want me to read this?"

I gripped the sides of the leather seat. "I need you to do this for me."

Zachary cleared his throat and continued.

"'Long enough to make love, barely, breathlessly. He tasted like'— 'like a living man. He was real. I know it wasn't a dream or a hallucination, because someone pounded on the other side of the wall, saying, "You two hush!" so I knew I wasn't alone having a delusion.'"

Please no more details. I wanted to cover my ears at any hint of my parents having sex, but I had to hear it all.

"Then, just as we were saying, 'I love you,' for the tenth or eleventh time, his body became air again. I could put my hand through him and not touch his beautiful skin.

Anthony's gaze turned distant, and he smiled

in a way I'd never seen before. I spoke his name and reached to touch the air that framed his face, wanting to capture that smile in my memory.

But his form turned golden-white, then disappeared."

I closed my eyes and heard Zachary flip the page, the paper rustling in his hand.

"'All day I lay in bed, wondering. Why he died. Why he came to me. Why he left. Now I no longer wonder. Now I just feel numb.'

"That's all," Zachary said softly.

"My father was a ghost." I sucked in my breath, as if I could pull back the words. "What does that make me?"

"It makes you, you. There's nought you can do about who or what your parents are."

I opened my eyes to the car's gray ceiling. "But if my father was dead when he—when they—Zach, am I even alive?"

"How can you doubt it?" He leaned over and squeezed my hand between his. "You feel this, aye?"

"Am I half-ghost? Is that why I could help Logan turn back from shade? Is that why—" My heart thumped to a halt. "Oh God."

"What?" he whispered.

"I shouldn't be here." I pulled my hand from his and rubbed my arms against the sudden half-dead feeling. "When I came into the world, I caused the Shift. It's wrong, and it needs to unhappen."

"How?"

My throat turned cold, but I forced out the words. "When I die."

"No." It wasn't a plea or denial, just a statement of fact. As if his stubborn self could stand between me and death. "Aura, you belong in this world."

I stared up into his green eyes, fixed in fear and determination. It was the only place I could look without feeling like I was falling. But how could I hold on to him when he'd be gone in four days, maybe forever?

A knock came at my car door. I let out a yip of surprise.

Nicola Hughes bent down to my open window, an almost garish smile on her red-painted lips. "Hi, Aura! Funny, I happened to be in the neighborhood at the coffee shop and caught a glimpse of you."

Zachary's window started rolling up. He was watching a man in a suit who stood on the curb using a cell phone. Another DMP agent working with Nicola?

She put her hand over the edge of my window. "I thought maybe we could go over some last-minute details for Friday's show, hmm?"

I pulled my seat up and shoved the papers onto the floor, out of her sight. "Maybe tomorrow at lunch? We can meet with Logan and his brother."

"I think now would be better."

"Put on your safety belt," Zachary whispered.

I didn't question. The moment felt balanced on a knife's edge. The coffee shop on the corner was closed, its windows dark.

"Sorry," I told Nicola, checking that my door was locked. "We're on our way to a movie, and we already bought the tickets online, so—"

"I'll pay for your tickets. Maybe you can catch a later show. Or tomorrow."

Or never, I thought as the agent on the sidewalk moved toward Zachary, motioning for him to get out.

Zachary turned the ignition and slammed the car into gear. The tires squealed as the Mini Cooper shot forward, through the empty parking spaces in front of us.

A white van pulled out of an alley, blocking our path. Zachary stomped on the brake pedal and jerked the steering wheel to the right. We skidded, so fast I couldn't scream.

The Mini Cooper screeched sideways to a stop, leaving Zachary's door only inches from the van.

He let out a harsh Gaelic curse, then stared at me with wide, dark eyes. "Are you all right?" he asked, breathless.

"I think." My cold, shaky fingers slipped on the seat belt latch twice before I clicked it off. "Glad you warned me. Are you okay?"

Zachary nodded jerkily. His fingers looked glued to the steering wheel. "So much for our big getaway."

"At least we didn't crash. That was amazing dri—"

He pointed past me. "Look out!"

A hand was reaching through my open window. It unlocked my door and swung it open, revealing a hulking DMP agent. Not the one who had been with Nicola. This one wore a bright white uniform. A dumper.

"Are you injured?" he asked.

"No, we didn't—"

"Step out of the car, miss. Your friend, too."

I tried to kick my mother's journal pages under the seat with my heels, but the agent leaned in and offered his arm to help me out.

"Now, please," the dumper said with an unsettling calm.

"Can I get my bag?"

"We'll take care of that. Just step out of the car."

I did as he asked, hoping they would retrieve my bag and assume that the scattered journal pages were trash.

Unless that was what they were looking for. If they'd somehow followed us all the way from Eowyn's office, they knew what we had. She'd said the DMP was closing in.

Behind me, Zachary climbed over the center console and out of the car, keeping a wary eye on the second dumper approaching. He was smaller than his partner, but had that I'm-in-charge look.

Nicola dashed up to us, shoes clicking on the street. "Are you hurt? For God's sake, what were you thinking?"

"What were *we* thinking?" I pointed to the van, which bore a DMP logo on its side door. "They pulled in front of us, on purpose. We all could've been killed."

Nicola frowned at the first uniformed agent, who was gathering up—*oh no*—my bag and journal pages.

"Let me handle this." She strode toward Zachary's car. "I'm Nicola Hughes, from the Office of Public Affairs. My partner and I have the situation under control, so if you'll—"

"Hey, drop that!" The second agent pointed past Nicola at Zachary, who had his phone to his ear. Speed-dialing his dad, I hoped, since my own phone was in the bag the agent had grabbed.

The agent moved forward and grabbed the phone from Zachary's hand. "I'll hold on to that for you." He slipped the phone into his own pocket. "If you'll come with us."

"What are you doing?" Zachary looked up and down the street, then raised his voice, though there were no bystanders to hear him. "What's going on here?"

"That's what I'd like to know," Nicola said to the new agents. "This is an OPA operation. No need to bring in the heavies."

The agent who'd taken Zachary's phone flashed his badge at Nicola. "Agent Acker, Investigations Division. We're taking over this case." He motioned us toward the white van. "Let's go."

Nicola's eyes narrowed. "I knew there was something about Aura. Headquarters never tells me anything."

"Is that why you were following us?" I asked her.

She ignored me as she pulled out her phone. "I'm calling my boss. There's nothing I hate more than interdepartmental pissing contests."

"Please leave now." Acker handed her a business card. "We're transporting them to 3A."

She stared at him, paling. "You can't do that, they're children. Let me at least call their families."

"Make one phone call and you're fired," Acker said as he waved us toward the van. We stayed put.

"I don't work for you." Nicola turned to us. "Aura, you don't have to go with them. Not without your parents."

"I won't ask again." Acker put his hands on his hips, pushing back the jacket of his uniform to reveal a holstered gun and Taser. "You two need to come with us."

Zachary stepped forward to shield me. "We'll go, all right?"

"Are we under arrest?" I asked Acker.

"Of course not. And I assure you, you'll come to no harm from us."

As I stepped toward the waiting van, I saw Acker's partner hand him my mother's journal. *Too late.*

Chapter Twenty-four

The back of the DMP van was like a box of nothing. No surveillance electronics, no at-risk-ghost-capturing equipment, not even a speck of lint on the black carpet. Just one long vinyl seat on each side, like in those planes that soldiers jump out of. Sadly, Zachary and I had no parachutes.

I sat on the right-hand seat, facing Agent Acker, who stayed within arm's reach—Taser's reach, to be exact—of Zachary beside him.

He watched the agent with cold calculation. The longer we rode, the more I worried about Zachary going all action-hero on Acker and trying to wrest his weapons from him. Last year he'd used his fists twice to defend my reputation. And then there were those football hooligan stories.

But even as I scrambled for a clever escape so Zachary wouldn't end up in jail or worse, my mind kept circling back to my mother's journal.

The words "My father was a ghost" scrolled through my head like the marquee menu in our school's cafeteria.

Was every bit of Shift weirdness connected to that one fact? Like Zachary being the ultimate red with the anti-ghost powers of the Last? Or me being the ultimate violet with the pro-ghost powers of the First?

And what about what happened when Zachary and I, um, mingled? We switched colors, or became something in between. (Magenta?) Our bodies, and maybe our souls, overcame the Shift itself.

The DMP would love to know all of this. And they probably *would* know it, once we arrived at this 3A place. Nicola had looked like she'd pass out when she found out they were taking me and Zachary there. What kind of place was it that they wouldn't even let us call our families? When would they let us go? What would they do to us? At the very least, they would read my mother's journal and know . . . everything.

I slumped forward, elbows on my knees, feeling vulnerable without a seat belt. The bench itself wasn't remotely contoured for a human butt, so my back was killing me.

To take my mind off the ache and anxiety, I tried to figure out our approximate location. It'd been at least two hours since the van had stopped, turned, or even slowed, so we were obviously on a long highway. Probably not I-95, or there would have been tolls. I-70 then, headed west, since east would have immediately taken us to the Baltimore Beltway. Judging by the steepening hills, we were headed into the middle of nowhere.

My attention kept returning to the envelope with my mother's journal pages in it, sitting in Agent Acker's lap. The mere thought of him reading them made me queasy, and not just because I wanted to keep Mom's secrets. Like I'd told Zachary, I always got carsick when reading anything longer than a text message in the car. Lots of people I knew were the same way.

A small but steady lightbulb began to glow in my brain. Crazy idea, but worth a try. It was better than Zachary having to assault a federal agent.

"Are you going to read those now?" I asked Acker, my voice deliberately shaky.

"I haven't been ordered not to, but procedure requires me to present it to my superiors first." His tone turned friendlier. "You'll get these back as soon as we've examined them. We understand they mean a great deal to you."

I wanted to tell him where to shove his understanding, but I needed his guard down. "Thank you. The journal is really personal. She didn't even want *me* to read it until I was old enough to understand."

"Understand what?"

"About sex."

His gaze dropped to the envelope in his lap. Then he turned it around and pressed the ragged adhesive seal tighter.

I stared at the toes of my scuffed creepers. "It's too dark in here to read, anyway."

Acker smoothed his fingertips over the corner of his jaw, right under his ear. Then he did the same on the other side.

I held my breath, hoping he would respond to the reverse psychology. Even in the dark, I could see Zachary's posture tense. He looked ready to pounce, probably wondering what the hell I was thinking.

Acker's foot started tapping, one heel against the floor of the van. I kept holding my breath.

Finally he reached into his inside uniform pocket and brought out a small flashlight. Glancing in the driver's direction, Acker opened the envelope. I made what I hoped sounded like a disappointed sigh.

Acker spent several minutes putting the journal pages in order. *Whew.* At least he wouldn't read the last part first.

Then he began reading, squinting at my mother's scrawl. The van made a turn onto what must have been an off-ramp. I had to clutch the edge of the seat to keep from slipping.

"Hmm." Acker turned to the second page, which was also crammed with barely legible handwriting. I was suddenly glad my mom was sort of long-winded.

He set the paper down and wiped his forehead.

Score. He was getting carsick. Gina always taught me to look out the side window into the distance to reset my equilibrium. But there were no windows in the back of the van, and from here only a tiny portion of the front windshield was visible, through a screen next to the driver.

Acker took a couple of deep breaths, shook his head, and began to read again. His eyes devoured the words—probably Mom's description of what happened at Newgrange, maybe her mention of Eowyn. I couldn't remember if she'd named Ian, and hoped not. The DMP had to see him as an ally or at least a friendly liaison.

Acker's forehead creased and he released a grunt. I wondered if he'd just read about the Shine. On its own, it meant nothing.

The road took us through a series of S-curves, the van jerking us back and forth. I was getting nauseated myself.

Acker called to the driver, "Jeffries, slow down! You're making me sick."

"We're running late. Just suck it up for ten more minutes."

Zachary sat up straighter at the news that we were almost there. I wanted to shout at him to chill. My plan might yet work.

Acker placed a hand over his forehead and the other on his stomach. Then he gave a loud belch. "Excuse me." He tried to resume reading, then rested his head back against the van's wall.

The road took a vicious right curve. I gripped the seat and planted my feet wide to keep my balance.

When we came out of the turn, Acker yelled, "Jeffries, pull over! I'm gonna be sick."

"Use a bag."

"There aren't any bags!"

"What about the kids?"

"We're deep in the heart of Pennsyl-nowhere. Where are they going to go?"

"Fine, but you get to explain why we're late. Wait until I secure the prisoners before you barf."

So we *were* prisoners after all. Acker had lied.

The van slowed, rumbling onto the shoulder. As Acker stood, my mom's papers spilled off his lap and across the floor. He shoved the back door open and lurched out before we'd come to a halt.

Zachary and I grabbed the scattered papers, then leaped out of the back of the van. We stumbled when our feet hit the road's sloping shoulder. Steadying each other, we dashed into the dark woods.

"Stop!" Jeffries shouted as Acker gagged and retched.

"Don't stop." Zachary took my arm with his free hand. "Keep running, no matter what."

I ran into the darkness, clutching my mother's words to my chest, hoping I wouldn't fall into a hole or trip over a root.

When the shots rang out, I ran even faster.

Chapter Twenty-five

I ran until my lungs couldn't hold my breath, until my legs were so numb, they felt like part of someone else's body.

Finally I pulled Zachary to a stop. "Rest. For. A sec."

As I collapsed to sit on a fallen tree, Zachary put a hand to his ear. He'd barely broken a sweat.

"Do you hear anything?" I pressed my lips together to quiet my breathing, but that just made it rattle in my nose.

"Not yet." He scanned the forest. "But they'll be sending out a search party, maybe with ATVs or dogs."

"Why did they take us?" I panted. "What do they want?"

"Probably these." He held up the journal pages he'd grabbed, then folded them and put them in his back jeans pocket.

"They were after Eowyn, so maybe they followed us from her office."

"And we led them right to what they wanted. Brilliant."

"But then why not just take the papers and let us go?" My throat tightened. "Why shoot at us?"

"It was just a warning shot. Probably." He helped me to my feet. "Let's keep moving until we cross a stream, cover our trail. Downhill should take us to water." Then he added, "Theoretically," to himself.

I looked at the sky through the trees. The leaves blocked most of the stars, but the waxing gibbous moon's yellow-white glow shone through. At just past midnight, it would be starting to set in the west. "If we keep the moon to our right, we'll head south, and if nothing else, we won't walk in circles."

"Good idea." He took my stack of journal pages, folded them, and put them in his other pocket. "Ready?"

I hurried after him on aching legs, grasping saplings and rocks to steady myself as I crab-walked down the steepening hill. My feet slid on the damp leaves, slippery as ice.

Eventually I got the hang of it, and as my confidence increased, so did my pace. I tried to catch up to Zachary so I could speak to him without yelling.

To my left, an animal dashed out of the underbrush. I turned my head, taking my eyes off the ground at my feet.

My toe snagged a root. I yelped as I pitched forward. I reached for anything to slow my fall, but I just rolled faster and faster. Rocks poked my gut and brambles slashed my arms and legs.

I hit something hard. "Ooufh!"

"Christ, that was close," said Zachary, who had broken my fall. Before I could ask what he meant, he pulled me tight against him. I turned my head to see, in the glow of filtered moonlight, the edge of a boulder six inches from where he'd stopped me. Beyond that edge was at least a twenty-foot plummet onto a pile of rocks.

"Aura, you could've been killed."

We held each other close as our breathing slowed. What if I'd died without telling Zachary how I felt? After a sudden accident I would've probably become a ghost he could never see.

And what good would it do Zachary to know I loved him, when I'd be gone forever?

I tried to pull back so I could look him in the eye. "Zach . . ."

"Shh." His grip tightened. "I hear something."

I listened over the pounding of my pulse. A distant rustling, as if the wind had stirred up a giant pile of leaves. But the night had turned heavy and breezeless.

"I think it's water," he said. My tongue ached at the mere sound of the word.

I only limped a little as we made our way down the rest of the hill—slower this time. The rustling grew more distinct, and soon we saw moonlight glisten off a small, slow river.

"Thank God." I ran forward, sank to my knees on the flat bank, and dipped my hands into the water.

"Don't drink it! It could be loaded with bacteria."

I sniffed the water in my cupped palms. "It smells clean."

"There's a bacteria that loves clear mountain streams best. Giardia, I think it's called."

"What could be worse than dying of thirst?"

"Dying of diarrhea."

"You win." I dropped the water and wiped my hands on my jeans.

"Let's hurry up and cross." He took off his shoes and socks. I started rolling up the cuffs of my jeans. "No need for that. Here, hold my shoes, and be quiet."

"Okay, but—whoa!" I flailed as he lifted me into his arms.

"Shh." He strode forward into the river. "No sense in us both getting hypothermia."

"You hear me complaining?"

"For once, no."

I resisted the urge to whap him with his shoe, and instead wrapped my other arm around his shoulders. I tried not to notice how little my weight seemed to sap his steady strength.

To distract myself, I blurted the first dorky question that came to mind. "What do you charge for your ferry service?"

"My fee's negotiable." He increased his pace, making the cold water splash around us.

"The song says not to pay you until you get me to the other side."

"What song?"

"From the eighties. 'Don't Pay the Ferryman.'"

"How old are you? Forty?"

"I like all kinds of music." I grimaced as a wave of frigid water seeped through the seat of my jeans. "The cool kinds."

"So what kinds aren't—ow!" Zachary lurched to the side. His arms tightened so hard I thought he'd crush me.

"Are you okay?"

"Aye." But his eyes were wide, and his breath came quick and shallow. "Let's keep going."

He limped faster, cursing quietly in Gaelic or maybe Glaswegian English.

When we reached the shore, he set me down carefully, then collapsed onto the smooth, sloped riverbank.

"What happened?" I knelt beside him.

"Stepped on some driftwood, I think. Turned my ankle. I'm fine, really."

"You're not fine, you're bleeding." I set down his shoes. "Give me your shirt or something so I can stop it."

"Let's use yours instead." His eyebrows popped up. "It could be my ferry fare."

My face warmed at the idea, and at the way his *r*'s rolled extra strong when he was trying to charm me. "Take it off or bleed to death."

"I won't bleed to death."

I put my hands on my hips, examining him. "Are you shy about taking off your clothes?"

"What, you'd rather I be an exhibitionist?"

"You wore a kilt to the prom." *Not to mention had countless bouts of fifteen-minute sex with Suzanne.* "You like people looking at you that way."

"Well." He looked toward the river, but a fallen tree blocked his view. "As a lad, I was quite, er, doughy."

"Doughy? Like bread?"

"Unbaked bread. Once when I was twelve, I lost a bet, and three of my so-called mates stole my shirt and made me walk a mile home, half-naked. The girl next door, the one I liked . . ." He paused. "She said I looked like a marshmallow. I hate marshmallows."

I winced. "That sucks."

"I was so crushed, I threatened to throw myself in the River Clyde."

"You poor thing." I glanced down at his bleeding foot. "But I'm still not taking off my shirt."

Zachary looked hurt. "That wasn't my point."

"But you wouldn't have stopped me."

"Well, no. I'm not a complete bampot." He paused, as if waiting for me to confirm that he *was* crazy, then pulled his black polo shirt over his head and tossed it to me. Zachary definitely wasn't a dough boy anymore.

Forcing my focus, I held what looked like the cleanest part of his shirt against the wound. He scrunched his eyes at the pressure, and his lips parted in a soft, halting gasp.

"Breathe." I was reminding myself as much as him. "Sorry about your shirt."

"No, you're not." He gave me a cocky grin as he leaned back on his hands. I pressed harder on the wound. "Ow." His grin vanished.

Once the bleeding stopped, I said, "Wiggle your foot and see if it hurts."

He did as I asked, his neck muscles tensing. "Doesn't hurt."

"Bullshit, you probably sprained your ankle." I pointed to a tilted log behind him. "Rest it on that overnight so it won't swell up like a balloon."

"We need to keep going." He reached for his shoes, but I snatched them away.

"Don't be an idiot. If you walk now, it'll get worse. And I can't carry you." I moved the log closer to him and adjusted the height. "Besides, I'm so tired I can't think in a straight line. And when I do, the line leads to us stuck out here for days, with me watching you die of tetanus or gangrene, or, I don't know." I smacked a mosquito on my arm. "Malaria."

"I promise I won't die," he said with a chuckle, which faded when he saw my face. "Sorry. I can't believe I said that." He shut up and propped his heel on the log.

I tied his shirt around his ankle as a makeshift compression bandage. Then I sat with my back to him and his bare chest, keeping an eye out for dumpers on the far shore—as much as I could, from our secluded spot.

Zachary let out a long breath, making a cheek-puffing noise. "So what do we do now?"

After a review of our inventory, we determined that we had, in total, jackshit and sod-all.

In other words, nothing. So we moved on to the much bigger version of "What do we do now?" "Now," as in, the rest of our lives. Knowing what we knew.

"What my mother did with my father—" The *F*-word felt strange in my mouth, connected to a real person. "You think the Shine made that possible?"

"Maybe. After all, my father and your mother couldn't have children, not before that light filled them up at the solstice."

"First him, then her. Making you the Last and me the First."

"Last, First, and only. No one else was born in our minutes."

"And we each have special powers to go with it."

"Right."

"So maybe it's destiny. We were put here to do ... something with ghosts."

"Maybe."

"So what if my mom had said no? What if she and my dad had hesitated, like Logan and I did, and there hadn't been enough time to make me?" I hugged my knees to my chest, despite the stiffness of my damp jeans. "I never would've been born. No Shift, no post-Shifters. The world would've stayed the same, with just a few people seeing ghosts."

"Maybe you did have to be born, or someone had to be born to your mother, to do whatever the First is supposed to do. But maybe your father didn't have to be a ghost." Zachary sat forward, almost touching me. "Maybe the Shift was only about ghosts because your father was one."

"So if he'd been a plumber, the Shift would've been about toilets?"

"I'm only saying, you can get all tangled up in talk of destiny. Anyone wouldn't have been born if their parents hadn't met. Or they would be born, but to other parents."

"But then they'd be different people."

"Genetically. Their soul would be them."

I'd never heard Zachary talk like this. "You believe in souls?"

"Sure." He gestured to the sky above us. "I think they're all queued up out there, waiting for the next person in the world to be born, and when that life begins, they hop into that body. Like a taxi stand at a railway station. They take the next available car."

"Seems pretty random."

"A lot less tragic than a person never existing because their parents never met or because they decided not to have children."

I remembered what Megan had said, after our four-way meeting with Logan, something about me and Zachary being like those VIPs who don't have to wait in line at a club, the ones the bouncers unhook the red velvet rope for.

Had we jumped the line when the club of life was temporarily closed?

"My mom said something about solstice meaning 'sun standing still.' And that at some exact moment, the sun stops leaving and starts returning."

"Which might have been when she and my father stood in that light."

"She wished that people did that, too, instead of just leaving. And then it happened—my dad came back so she could see him." I spoke faster, before the thoughts escaped me. "Maybe that's what the Shift is all about—giving people who died suddenly a chance to say good-bye."

I thought of Logan's twisty, turny road to peace and was filled with a sudden, aching sense of purpose—not just for me, but every post-Shifter.

I spun to face Zachary. "And *that's* why me and everyone younger can see ghosts."

He furrowed his brow. "Why?"

"It's hard for a pre-Shifter to understand."

"Then help me."

"Ghosts need to pass on. Some of them do it on their own, but others might never if not for us."

"Like your aunt's clients, the ones you translate for."

"Obviously," I said, "but lots of other ghosts don't need anything that drastic. They just need to talk, or be seen."

"But wouldn't it have been easier to let everyone else already *in* the world see and talk to ghosts? Why wait for all these children to be born?"

"Because we weren't afraid of them. Babies always smile or laugh at ghosts—they think they're pretty. They don't know yet that they're supposed to freak."

He gazed at me for a long moment. "I don't know if your theory is the least bit true, but it's pure beautiful."

I felt my eyes crinkle with joy. He might not understand what it meant to be a post-Shifter, but at least he appreciated it.

I twitched my shoulder in an attempt to shrug. "It just popped into my head. I'm still working out the kinks." I remembered that we now had access to more answers than ever. "Hey, let's reread my mom's notes. Maybe there's important stuff on one of the pages I skimmed."

Zachary got up on his knees and reached into his back pockets. "Oh, no."

My heart stopped. "Are they gone?"

"No." He struggled to pull out the pages, and for a second I thought his panic was a joke. Then he unfolded them.

The sheets were soaked through, the blue and black ink smeared beyond recognition.

"Aura . . . oh God, I'm sorry."

I grabbed the papers and pulled them apart, trying to find one entry that hadn't been destroyed. But the journal was now a giant wad of wet pulp.

A keening noise started at the back of my throat. I smothered my mouth with my hands to keep from screaming. If I released all the anguish I felt, the DMP would be able to hear it from Pittsburgh.

Zachary wrapped his arms around me. "Aura, I'm so sorry."

I pressed my face to his chest, the soggy pages clamped between us. My hands formed useless fists, opening and closing with the rhythm of my sobs. He stroked my hair, murmuring the word "sorry" again and again.

Finally my shudders eased into shivers. "It was all I had of my father."

"I know. I was so stupid."

"Not your fault. I didn't think of it either." My sob hitched into a hiccup as I clutched the papers, wringing out a cascade of water.

"Listen." Zachary touched the mass of white in my hand. "Now no one will ever know but us. Agent Acker only read a few pages."

"But we don't know how far he got." I turned away to wipe my face, wishing for a box of tissues. I didn't want to get snot on my sleeve, or use some random leaf that might end up being poi-son ivy.

"Here." Zachary started to unwrap the shirt from his ankle.

"No, you need it."

"And you can wrap it back up after you've used it. Unless your tears are made of acid."

"Feels like it." I sniffled and wiped my face with the shirt. "I was going to destroy the journal pages anyway. But not until after I memorized them." I blotted my eyes before they could overflow again. "Now they're gone forever."

"No. We'll re-create what we can remember."

"With what?" I started rewrapping his ankle. "We have no paper, no cell phones. We don't even have a pen to write on our arms."

"Come here." He lay on his back and patted his bare shoulder. "There's something you should see."

I eyed him warily. Just because we probably wouldn't destroy the world with a single kiss didn't mean I was ready to cuddle. Part of me still ached with humiliation at the memory of his voice sighing Becca's name.

"If you don't believe me," he said, "look up."

I lifted my chin, then gasped. The moon had disappeared behind the mountain, and a section of clear, dark sky stretched out above the riverbank. It held more stars than I'd ever seen, even in the field we used at home. The Milky Way was no longer a white blur, but rather a giant arm with sinews and veins.

For the first time, a sky full of stars didn't make me feel small. No longer a mere tapestry suspended above us, the universe felt close at hand. We were part of it.

"We'll talk about everything we read in the journal," Zachary said, "and write it in the stars."

I tightened his ankle wrap with one last tug. "You're so cheesy."

"Yes. Play along. We'll start from the beginning."

I gave in and lay down on my back beside him, resting my head on his shoulder. Maybe it was the change in position, or maybe it was the warm, rich scent of his skin, but my thirst- and tear-induced headache began to ease.

"No," I said. "Let's start from the end."

Chapter Twenty-six

I woke the next morning on my side facing the river, my head propped on Zachary's arm. My own arm was curled beneath me, still fast asleep.

One urgent part of me had woken up, and I wished ten times harder for that box of tissues.

I sat up, pins prickling my arm as blood rushed into it. Zachary lay in the same way as the night before—on his back, bare-chested, his wrapped ankle propped on the log.

"Where you going?" He blinked at me with sleep-heavy lids, surpassing previous levels of cute by several orders of magnitude.

"Nowhere you need to follow."

"Be careful."

"I'll try not to fall in." I stood, brushed the dirt from my butt, and stomped off, hating all guys for their ease in wilderness peeing.

I climbed the hill, weaving around the underbrush, trying to find the forest's least bug-ridden spot. If nothing else, I had to get out of Zachary's line of sight.

Finally I couldn't take it anymore and stopped by a nonmoldy tree so I at least had a handhold. I peeled down my pants, half wishing we'd never escaped the DMP. At least in federal custody I'd have running water and toilet paper.

A few seconds later, I didn't care about luxuries. I closed my eyes and exhaled in relief.

"Wouldn't you rather use the outhouse?"

I yelped at the sound of the woman's voice. By reflex I tried to stand up, but my feet slipped in the damp leaves. I was left clutching the tree trunk to keep from falling.

"Oh! I'm so sorry." A woman circled in front of me, her violet shimmer barely visible in the morning light. "Are you okay?"

It had been more than ten years since a ghost had caught me like this. Bathrooms were the first places to get BlackBoxed.

In the distance, Zachary called my name.

"No!" I shouted, yanking up my pants. "Don't come over here!" This ghost might be the only one who could help us. If he scared her away—

He hobbled over the ridge. "Are you all right?"

The ghost let out a shriek and vanished.

Zachary came closer, his steps more cautious, maybe now that he could see I hadn't been turned into bear breakfast.

"There was a ghost." I finished buttoning my jeans. "She said something about an outhouse."

His lips twitched. "Did she interrupt you?"

"Don't you dare laugh, Red Boy. You scared her off."

"But you didn't." He went full-on smirk. "Good thing I didn't wake you with a kiss, aye?"

"Shut up and help me find this house."

He studied the ground at his feet. "This looks like a trail leading from the water. Let's follow it."

We headed off, keeping the river within earshot so we wouldn't get completely lost.

"How's your ankle?" I asked him.

"Better. It's a bit of a sprain, no worse." He tugged on his shirttail. "And I can be fully dressed again."

"I hadn't noticed," I said with a straight face.

Soon the trees thinned into a clearing, where we saw a tiny house with an even tinier outhouse.

I didn't know whether to be relieved or more scared than ever. What if the ghost hadn't lived alone, and her shotgun-wielding husband was still around? Maybe he had killed her.

We entered the clearing and stopped in our tracks.

"What's that smell?" I whispered, though a deep instinct told me.

"Wait here." Zachary walked forward with barely a limp. I followed as he crept to the edge of the house, slid against the wall like a soldier, then peered around the corner.

"Aura, don't look." But it was too late.

Someone had died here. A long time ago, judging by what was left of her.

I reached out to steady myself against the corner of the building. Was this the body of the ghost I'd seen?

Zachary peered through the house's small side window. "It's empty. Let's go in."

I followed, my steps as heavy as my heart. Who was this woman, living in the middle of nowhere, with no one to miss her when she died?

Inside, the one-room house was dusty but tidy. The few furnishings—a wooden bed, dresser, kitchen table, and nightstand—looked hand built, but competently so. I was relieved that the back window's faded yellow curtain was drawn, so I couldn't see the body lying in the yard.

The wall above the twin-size bed held a small gallery of family photos. I moved closer to see. There were several of a middle-aged couple and a young woman who could've been their daughter. Flanking them were a pair of newspaper obituary notices. William Robinson had died of brain cancer at fifty-five, and leukemia had killed Dara when she was only twenty-eight. Father and daughter had died less than a year apart.

"How sad." I touched the central photo, of the parents dancing at their daughter's wedding. "They look so happy here."

Zachary read the obituaries over my shoulder. "Maybe the ghost is the mother? Fredericka?"

"I guess so."

"We should bury what's left of her."

Thirsty, I turned to the sink but saw only a basin. "No running water?" I picked up an overturned bucket—thankfully clean. "I'll get water from the river, and we can boil it. You should stay inside in case ex-Fredericka comes back to talk to me."

He frowned but didn't argue. "I'll look for food."

I hurried out of the house and downhill toward the river.

"There's a pump around back," said a woman's voice behind me.

I stopped and turned. A violet shimmer caught my eye, about ten feet away. The thick ceiling of trees gave me a decent view of the ghost's appearance, now that she was standing still. A long pale braid curled forward over her shoulder, dangling over the curved neckline of what looked like a graduation gown.

"Hi." I tried to smile. "Is that you behind the house?"

"What's left of me." She bent her head. "I think I had a heart attack."

"You lived out here alone?"

"Mm-hmm. Moved to this patch of heaven ten years ago, after I lost my family. Didn't see any more need for human company."

"I'm sorry."

"Why can't I go into my house?"

"It's my friend. He's kind of a walking BlackBox. But he wants to bury your body," I added, before she could get mad.

The woman's shoulders dropped. "That would be a blessing. I've been traveling the world, all the places I went during life, but I keep coming back to check on my—er, mortal coil. It's in pretty bad shape."

"I could say a few words when we bury you, if it would help you pass on."

"Oh, would you? I always wanted to attend my own funeral." She put a hand to her mouth. "My, that sounds egotistical. Go on and fetch your water. The well is safe to drink from, but the pump is near the . . . you know. It's near me."

"Thanks." I followed a path to an iron well pump. The handle squeaked as I pushed it down, then released it. Like an eighteenth-century miracle, water came out of the spout. I stuck my face under, lapping like a greedy dog.

The ghost had followed me. "Any special requests for your funeral?" I asked her, to break the silence and distract me from the corpse smell.

"Can you sing?"

"Not really." I started filling the bucket. "What song?"

"My favorite is 'The Rose,' by Bette Midler. Have you heard it?"

"Maybe once or twice, in the dentist's office. Hey, you could sing it yourself. That would be fun, wouldn't it?" It would be fun for Logan.

"I'll think about it."

I snuck one more gulp of water as it splashed into the bucket. "What's your name?" I already knew from the obituaries, but didn't want her to think I'd been snooping.

"It's Fredericka. You can call me Fred."

"Hi, Fred. I'm Aura."

"Aura," she whispered, almost lovingly. "You might be my salvation."

Back in the house, Zachary was leaning over the table, studying a topographical map. He'd put on a clean T-shirt, a yellow one with a snake coiled up under a sign that said DON'T TREAD ON ME. It fit well, so I assumed ex-Fred had kept some of her husband's clothes in her dresser.

"Any luck?"

"You could say that." I dipped a cup in the cold water and held it out to him.

"Boil it first," he said. "I didn't find purifying tablets. The stove is ready to light."

"The water came from a well pump in the back. Ex-Fred says it's safe."

"You met the ghost?"

"Yep, and they can't lie, so drink." I nudged the cup against his chest, glad (sort of) that it was no longer bare.

"Thanks," he said softly, and curled his fingers around the cup, brushing them against mine. Our eyes met, and I wondered if he was remembering us falling asleep under the stars together. How at one point I'd rolled to face him, looping my arm across his chest—purely for comfort, of course, since my body still insisted I sleep on my right side. How he'd pulled me closer, just a little.

I turned to the map. "How far are we from civilization?"

"Far. Look, here's the river we crossed. If we follow it . . ." He traced the waterway to the right, then unfolded the map's next panel.

And the next. And the next. And the next. The map ended with no towns in sight.

Zachary sighed. "We're up the arse of nowhere."

"We're better off going back the way we came."

"They'll be looking for us there." He unfolded the top panel. "If we go north, we'll hit a road." The two-lane Pennsylvania state highway went off the edge of the map. "But we can't tell how far it is to town."

"I'll ask ex-Fred. First, food."

We were too hungry to cook the pasta and canned goods, so we sat down to a breakfast of protein bars, crackers, and Cheez Whiz.

We'd barely started eating when Zachary said, "When we get home—if we get home—the DMP will be looking for us there, too."

I swallowed, my mouth suddenly dry. "Shit. They know I'm supposed to be at Logan's concert."

"Do you have to go?"

"I don't think he'll pass on if I don't."

"Then you have to go," he said flatly.

I ignored his comment. "The media will be watching to see if Logan shades again." I gasped, almost choking on a cracker crumb. "That's it! We head back to Baltimore tomorrow and go straight to the concert. We'll be safe in front of the cameras. The DMP won't dare pick us up with the whole world watching."

He gave me a skeptical look. "What about that Nicola woman? Won't she be there?"

"Yeah, since she's literally running the show."

"It seemed like she didn't expect them to take us away. You think she'll help us?"

"I wouldn't count on it." I tore the wrapper off a second protein bar. "And we still have to get there in time. Who can we call to pick us up once we find a phone?"

"Not my parents or your aunt. Their lines are probably tapped by now."

"Maybe one of our friends?"

"If the DMP is as thorough as MI-X, they'll go through our cell phones and monitor every contact."

"I guess we'll have to hitchhike."

"No, we'll call someone. Wouldn't want to meet the sort of person who would pick up a couple of manky teenage hitchhikers." He glanced at me. "Not that you're manky."

I chortled at his Scottish-ism, then touched my stringy hair. "I'm completely manky. I should heat up water for a sponge bath."

He licked a dab of Cheez Whiz off his thumb. "There's always the river."

"Yeah, right. The icebergs might get in the way."

Zachary wiped his hands and rested his arms on the table. "I'll keep you warm."

I ripped my eyes from his and stared at his long, strong fingers, imagining them on my bare wet skin, smoothing out the goose bumps. Everywhere.

But those fingers had touched Becca, too. How much of her, I didn't know, and hadn't worked up the nerve to ask. Maybe it didn't matter anymore. But I couldn't decide with him looking at me that way.

I stood and grabbed the topographical map. "Rest your ankle. I'm going to get directions from a ghost."

Chapter Twenty-seven

Ex-Fred not only showed me how to get to the nearest town (a five-mile walk once we reached the road, which was five miles from the shack), but also showed me where she preferred to be buried, under her favorite hickory tree. It was only several feet from her temporary resting place, so we wouldn't have far to drag the body.

Unfortunately, she was so adamant about having "The Rose" sung at her funeral—and not by her—she insisted on teaching it to me. Due to my total lack of musical talent, this took two hours.

So with lunch in our stomachs, gloves on our hands, and Vapo-Rub under our noses (I'd seen it used on a cop show, to cover the corpse smell), Zachary and I dug ex-Fred's grave late that afternoon. Then we wrapped the remains in the quilt from the bed and lowered her gently into the grave.

Zachary stood at ex-Fred's feet, gazing down at the deceptively small bundle. "I'll go inside so you can call her. You'll be all right?"

"I can handle ghosts. Most of them, anyway," I added, thinking of Logan.

Zachary slowly pulled off his gloves. "You know, grave digging gives a bloke time to think."

"About what?"

"Mistakes." He angled his chin at the hole in the ground. "Words I don't want to take to my own grave."

My stomach quivered. "Then we should talk."

He nodded.

"After the funeral," I added.

He stepped away from me. "Tell Fredericka I'm very sorry."

When he was gone, ex-Fred appeared instantly at my side. She glowed a brighter violet now that the sun had disappeared behind the mountain.

"I can't tell you how much this means to me. I always thought to myself, 'Fred, if you choose to live alone, then one day you'll die alone.' I didn't think I'd be only sixty-one." She raised her palms. "Ready for your big debut?"

I stepped back from the grave to avoid inhaling the scent of her remains. Then I unfolded the paper with the lyrics she'd dictated, took a deep breath, and began to sing.

She stopped me at the second note. "You're off-key. It goes like this, remember?" She hummed a bar. "Try again."

For the next twenty minutes, I sang "The Rose," stopping and starting again on ex-Fred's cues. If my ghost-translating profession gave out awards for valor, I would've earned the mother of all medals.

Finally, on the seventeenth try, I got it perfect.

Ex-Fred jumped and clapped her hands. "Wonderful!"

I gave a quick bow, then crouched down and scooped up a handful of damp dirt before she could ask for an encore. "Ashes to ashes, dust to dust." The soil fell over the shroud, making a soft patter. I brought up the only comforting words I could remember from Logan's funeral. "May eternal light shine on you, Fredericka, and may you rest in peace forever. Amen."

I was finally able to make out her features—a prominent chin, large eyes, and high cheekbones. She smiled at the grave, but didn't glow white-gold to indicate she was passing on.

"Amen," I repeated.

Ex-Fred looked at me. "That's it? No sermon?"

"Um . . ." I scratched the back of my head, suddenly craving a hot shower. "Fredericka was a woman of great—"

"Dignity."

"Dignity. Despite her rugged surroundings, she kept a, uh, a clean house." I peeked at her from the corner of my eye. No golden glow. "And she loved the two people who filled her life, William and Dara."

She shot me a sharp look. "How do you—"

"The photos and the obituaries." I was taking a risk. If I didn't mention them, she might not feel complete enough to pass on. Then again, if she was still bitter about their deaths, she could turn shade.

"Did you go through my drawers, too?" Her voice crackled. "Find all my secrets?"

"I swear I only read what was on the wall. I wanted to know more about you so I could give you a good funeral."

"Liar." Her outline shimmered as black lines stabbed her violet form.

"Soon you'll be with your husband and daughter," I said, though I had no clue if that was true. But most pre-Shifters believed that heaven was a giant after-party, so I hoped she'd find comfort in the idea.

Her fists relaxed, and the black brightened into violet. "You're right. I've been so busy reflecting on what's happened in this world, I'd forgotten about the next."

I stood and faced her. "They're waiting for you, Fred."

She blinked twice, then spoke in an almost childlike voice. "Are you sure?"

"It's not about what *I* know." I reached out to the place where her heart had been. "It's about what you know."

As she stared at me, she brightened. I looked up to see if the sky had grown cloudy. It shone as blue as ever through the treetops.

Ex-Fred was passing on.

In her stomach, a pale yellow light began to glow. She closed her eyes and gave a serene smile.

A wave of contentment flowed through my veins. In my job I'd helped countless ghosts prepare themselves to pass on, but this was the first time I'd seen it happen in person. I thought of Logan and his departure tomorrow night, and had the fiercest wish that he would follow this path. I only hoped he wanted it as much as I wanted it for him.

"Aura, you have a gift." The gold-white light spread in streams, then rivers, out to the ends of ex-Fred's legs and arms. "Never forget that."

Her form became a pulsing, woman-shaped star. Then, with no sound, she faded, leaving nothing but a dark afterimage on my eyes.

A gift, she'd said. For once, I had to agree.

Zachary and I filled the grave in silence, then placed the pick and shovel back in the small toolshed. Dusk had fallen, and the forest was loud with crickets.

I picked up the small bag I'd packed. "We've got food, cash, paper and pens, and the map. So we can go whenever."

"We should wait until later at night, when we can hide easier, and use the stars to navigate." Zachary picked up the solar-powered lantern at his feet, scattering the moths clustered around it. "Besides, I could use a swim."

I dropped the bag and faced him. "Are you serious?"

He unleashed a crooked, charming smile. "I promise I won't look at you if you don't look at me."

"Did you have sex with Becca?"

He startled, then looked at the grave, as if ex-Fred were listening. "We're beginning there? Really?"

I wouldn't back down. "Did you?"

He shifted his weight, like a boxer squaring off before a fight. "How can you ask me that? Especially after what you did with Dylan?"

"I kissed him. That's it."

"But he said—"

"Dylan said he was screwing me because he wanted to mess with you, and I let him. I wanted you to be as hurt as I was." I splayed my fingers at the sides of my head. "Hearing you with her—I wanted to rip my ears out."

His face crumpled. "I'm sorry. I never meant to hurt you."

"What *did* you mean to do?"

"I meant to take her home. Maybe a kiss good night. Maybe." He set down the lantern with a thud.

"So what happened?"

"After the dance the eight of us all got into the limo, and Becca told me we were going somewhere as a surprise. It turned out to be the Admiral Fell Inn. When the driver opened our door, he was holding an overnight bag for Becca. She said, 'I got a room for us. Is that okay?' At first I thought she meant all of us, a place to drink the rest of the champagne. But none of our friends moved. They were all watching. And she was looking at me like she was . . . almost terrified." He lifted his hands, then let them fall. "I was weak. I thought once we were in the room, I'd be strong."

My stomach curdled at the direction the story was headed.

"As soon as we walked in," he said, "I put my phone and wallet on the bedside table, then went to the loo."

"That's when she dialed me."

"My phone was under my wallet, so I didn't see what she'd done. And then . . ." He shoved a hand through his sweaty hair. "I dunno, Aura, things happened. I'd be a coward if I blamed her, and I'd be a liar if I said I didn't want it."

"What things happened?" I choked out. "Did you—"

"No. It never went that far."

My gut unclenched a fraction. "If Megan hadn't interrupted you . . . what would you have done?"

His eyes shut hard. "I can't say. All I can say is that what was going through my mind wasn't pure lust. It was a great lot of that, but also fear and doubt and guilt, and I kept thinking, 'This isn't happening, not with her.'"

"What about after you found out I was listening?"

"When I realized what Becca had done, I said, 'Get dressed, we're leaving.' First she said she was sorry, and then when I wouldn't grant instant forgiveness by sleeping with her, she got angry. We haven't spoken since. I even deleted her number from my phone."

I scrambled for a way to understand. "You said there was champagne. Were you drunk?"

"I was, but it's no excuse." He rubbed the back of his neck and stared at my feet. "I fucked up, Aura. I'm sorry."

My anger faded in the face of his full story—not to mention his lack of weaseling. I was ready to step off my own cliff of guilt. "I almost did it with Dylan."

Zachary raised his eyebrows. "Prom night?"

"No, a couple days later at his house."

"What stopped you?"

Zachary had been honest, so I owed him the same. "It felt like we weren't looking for each other. We were looking for Logan."

"It always comes back to him, doesn't it?" He gestured to my Keeley Brothers shirt, and I wished I'd replaced it with one of ex-Fred's. "He'll always be in your head."

"I'll never forget Logan as long as I live. But there's only one person in my head." I spoke clearly, though fear lumped in my throat. "Zach, I don't understand you and me. I don't know if we're a miracle or a disaster. I just know I want to be with you."

Zachary stared at me for less than a heartbeat. Then with one long stride, he was in front of me, grasping my shoulders. He pressed his forehead to mine as his words poured out. "Aura, I never wanted anything else. And when I thought we couldn't be together, not without maybe killing ourselves or ruining the world, I tried to lose myself in whatever I thought could make me forget. Schoolwork, soccer, even Becca. But nothing worked." His warm whisper brushed my cheek. "I can't forget you, any more than I can forget my own name."

He kissed me then, and the world, which no longer mattered, completely fell away.

Chapter Twenty-eight

We walked for almost half a mile along the river before we found a place that was deep enough to swim, yet sheltered by the overhanging trees. The river glowed a faint silver, the moonlight veiled by summer haze.

Zachary switched off the lantern and hid it under a bush, along with the bag I'd packed. Then he laid our towels on the riverbank. "I'll turn away while you undress and get in the water."

I shifted my feet. "We're not going to, uh—I mean, I don't have anything, like, protection-wise. Do you?"

"No, but maybe it's for the best. This wasn't how I imagined our first time, on the lam from federal agents and assaulted by a thousand mosquitoes."

"How did you imagine it?"

Zachary came to stand close in front of me. "You know that castle I showed you in the guidebook to Ireland?"

"Near Newgrange?"

"I've been to their website, seen photos of the rooms. There's a suite on the top floor where you can see the whole Boyne Valley from the balcony. It faces west, away from Dublin, so the light pollution doesn't fade the sky." He reached out and caressed my hair. "In my imagination, we drink brandy and watch the stars, until it gets too cold."

"And then what?"

"And then we go inside." His fingertips trickled over the curve of my shoulder. "You put on something a little less ... well, a little less."

"And then what?"

"And then we meet in bed, under the thickest, softest quilt." His touch rounded the angle of my elbow. "I kiss you and touch you all over, and you do the same to me, until we're both too warm for the quilt, and for whatever we were wearing when we crawled under it."

I didn't dare blink. "And then what?"

The tips of his fingers pressed against mine, firm and smooth. "And then ... and only then ... will you know how much I love you."

My mouth fell open. "You—what?"

"You wouldn't be so surprised to hear me say that, if you'd listened to my voice mail."

"You told me you—you told me you love me, back in—"

"May eleventh, nine-oh-one a.m. Approximately."

The last six weeks of misery flashed before my eyes. "Why didn't you tell me again?"

"I thought you knew and didn't care, and by the time I found out you'd never heard my message, I thought I'd lost you to Logan again. And I thought I deserved it."

I slipped my hand into his. "That's all in the past. I want to look forward now."

"Me too."

"But I don't like your castle vision."

His eyebrows pinched together. "Why not?"

"Because if we went to Newgrange, it would be for the winter solstice, right? That's six whole months from now."

His mouth relaxed into a smile. "Are you in a hurry?"

"Yes."

"Me too." He kissed me, hard and hungry. I kissed him back, harder and hungrier. As we filled our hands with each other's hair, I swore I could feel the earth rotate beneath our feet.

I gathered the strength to push him away, only because I wanted to continue with no clothes between us.

"Go on, hurry," he said, his breathing ragged. "I'll turn round."

"No." I caught his wrist before I could lose my nerve. "Don't turn around." I took a step back, almost to the water's edge, and slipped off my shoes. "I won't look away if you won't."

I tried to hold his astonished gaze while I undressed, but because I was sweaty, a couple things got stuck, like my socks, so all in all my stripping for Zachary was sort of lame.

Not that I could tell by the look on his face.

"Your turn," I said when I stood naked in front of him, resisting the urge to cross my arms or legs.

He discarded his embarrassment as fast as he discarded his clothes.

God, he was perfect.

So perfect he even remembered to wrap our clothes in the towels and hide them away. That, more than anything, told me that we would be okay. We'd always have each other's backs.

We held hands, fingers locked, as we walked into the water together.

The shock of cold stopped me after three steps. I covered my mouth to stifle a whimper.

Zachary looked back at me. "I said I'd keep you warm."

"Then why am I cold?" I said with a laugh.

"Because we're not there yet." He stepped closer to me. "Want me to carry you again?"

"No."

"Good, because I'd have to drop you sooner or later. You wouldn't like tha'."

"Let's go." I surged forward, the chill stealing my breath as it covered my legs and hips. Every nerve felt alive, down to my fingers, toes, and eyelashes.

We walked out as far as we could while staying hidden under the overhanging tree. Here the water came to my chest and his stomach.

"We forgot soap," Zachary said as we stopped and faced each other. "Shall I run back and get some?"

"Would you?" With a nervous laugh, I pulled my hair back. "Some shampoo and conditioner would be great, too."

"Straightaway. But first." He put his hands on my waist. "Do you trust me?"

"I trust you."

His eyes searched mine, then his lips parted, as if he wanted to say—or ask—something terribly important.

"I love you," I added, in case he wondered.

He sighed, then pulled me close, skin to skin. "Then go all the way with me."

"What? Wait—"

"Under the water." The corner of his mouth twitched up. "What did you think I meant?"

I laughed, then wrapped my arms around him, pressed my lips together, and squeezed my eyes shut to keep my contacts in.

"Hold on," he said. "And remember, don't drink it."

He took us down, and the water washed over my scalp in the coldest wave of all. I shuddered, but he just held me tighter.

With the rest of the world's sounds blotted out, the river seemed to be whispering to me, telling its million-year-old secrets. As my hair floated up, I felt weightless and free. I wished I never had to breathe air again.

Zachary brought us back to the surface, where the hazy moonlight suddenly seemed bright. He shook his head, and water dripped off his nose and eyelashes. I ran my hands through his thick, wet hair, letting it fall over his forehead.

The thought of his Sunday departure carved a hole inside that felt bigger than the rest of me. "Don't go home."

His eyes turned sad. "I haven't got a choice. If I did, I'd stay here." He cupped my jaw in one steady hand. "Until I could take you with me."

We kissed, full and deep. I clung to him, the cold water the only thing keeping my heart from exploding from the heat inside.

He broke away suddenly. "Did you hear that?"

With one arm around his neck, I rubbed the water from my ears to listen to the distant sound.

An engine.

"Bloody hell," he whispered.

I wanted to scream. The universe hated us.

We swam to the darkest spot we could find, under a fallen tree that reached out over the river. By the time we got there, where the water was only a few feet deep, we could see bright lights in the direction of ex-Fred's house.

"They'll know we were there," I whispered, crouching down in the water. "That grave is freshly dug."

"They'll know someone was there, not necessarily us." Zachary tugged me back against his chest, so that we drifted farther under the tree.

"Maybe they'll think we kept going. Why would we come back to the river instead of heading for the road right away?"

"That's a good question. Why did we?"

"Tell me you're joking."

"I am absolutely joking." He wrapped both arms around me, his light coating of stubble tickling my ear. "Does this remind you of anything?"

My obstinate mind flashed to the October afternoon eight days before Logan died. He'd held me like this, my bare back against his chest, after our aborted attempt at lovemaking. He'd whispered that he wasn't disappointed, that he understood, and that everything was going to be fine. Which of course it wasn't. I'd stared at my bedroom wall and wondered if I was about to lose him. Which of course I was.

"On the ship," Zachary prompted. "The other time we were pursued by DMP agents?"

I relaxed against him, relieved to think of better memories. "When we first kissed."

"But this is better."

I closed my eyes, letting myself live in the present. "Because we're naked?"

"Aye, that, too." He pressed his lips to my neck, grazing it with his teeth. I arched back against him, making him groan. "Careful," he said. "You don't want to do that."

"Don't tell me what I want." I reached behind me, trying not to fumble. "I know exactly."

I was pretty sure that every word Zachary whispered after "Ah . . ." was not in English.

Finally his hushed cries faded to a breathless silence.

"Check it out," I said. "The world completely failed to end."

He gave a soft laugh against the back of my shoulder. "Just you wait, lassie. Just you wait."

I waited, utterly still, while the DMP searchlights swept the forest, and while their ATVs crushed the night's natural silence. Though my limbs stiffened with cold, inside I felt warmer than ever.

Because I was good at waiting.

The invading noises retreated, heading north, away from us and the town we planned to reach. Five minutes after the last engine sound, we headed for shore.

While I dried myself, Zachary took the biggest towel and spread it on the ground. Then he looked up at me and tugged the edge of the towel. I took the hint and lay down, watching him watching me.

He knelt and slowly ran his hand down my arm, his lids heavy and his lips parted. "Aura . . . where can I touch you?"

"Anywhere."

His hand left my arm and drifted to the rise of my hip bone. "And where can I kiss you?"

I took a deep breath, long past ready for the future. "Everywhere."

Chapter Twenty-nine

I t was only the mosquitoes that made us get dressed. Eventually.

Zachary kept watch while I slept for a few hours, my head in his lap. I made him promise to trade off so he could sleep, too, but he conveniently "forgot" to wake me until it was time to go.

We headed northeast, not daring to stop at the house again, in case the DMP was waiting for us. I was glad I'd already packed for our departure before we went to the river.

When the trees thinned so we could see the stars, we realized that we'd gone too far west and needed to change course. Zachary began to favor his hurt ankle, though probably not as much as he wanted to. So it was well past dawn by the time we reached the two-lane road curving through the mountains.

Trudging along the shoulder, I noticed Zachary had grown quiet, occasionally muttering numbers to himself. Every few minutes he would take his hand out of mine and scribble something on a scrap of paper. Peeking over his shoulder, I figured out he was trying to remember a phone number, so I didn't interrupt.

Four hours after we found the road, it led us to a rickety general store with an off-brand gas station and a sign that read BORIS'S PIZZA.

The sight of the word "pizza" made my stomach growl. We hurried through the front door, jangling the cowbell attached to the handle.

The young man dozing with his feet on the counter jerked awake. Something thudded on the floor next to him.

"Morning!" He glanced at the Steelers clock over the door, which read 12:05. "I mean, afternoon." He bent over, then stood up, rubbing his dark brown eyes and clutching a tattered textbook. "Sorry. You need gas? Use pump two. Pump one's broken."

"We need a phone," I told him.

"Pay phone's on the back wall." He grabbed a phone card from the rack near the register. "Get one of these if you don't have enough change."

"I'll take two." Zachary set a twenty-dollar bill on the counter and picked up the cards. "Stay here," he told me.

Figuring he wanted me to keep lookout, I backed up a few steps so I could see through the glass door. The cashier shuffled his feet, probably wondering when he could get back to his nap.

I peered past the counter into the adjoining pizzeria, separated from the store by a glass door and wall. "Are you Boris?"

"That's my dad. I'm Alexei."

"You're Russian?"

"Not since I was two."

"Don't you dare!" Zachary's voice rose from the back of the shop. "You owe me, and you know it."

Alexei and I glanced toward Zachary, who lowered the volume when he spoke again.

"What are you reading?" I asked Alexei.

"Genetics textbook. I have summer school three days a week at Pitt. Trying to graduate early."

"You go to University of Pittsburgh?" I said in disbelief. I knew honor roll seniors who'd been rejected from there.

Alexei bristled. "You know, out here in the sticks they teach reading and writing. Sometimes it's not even from the Bible."

"Okay, okay. Sorry." I focused on the back of the store, but couldn't hear Zachary at all now. "Is your dad's pizza any good?"

"Pizza's okay. But we have the best stromboli in the state."

Family pride overcame my hunger. "Please. My grandmother's a baker in Philadelphia. Her dough is—"

"Spare me, okay?" He pulled a set of keys out of his jeans pocket and unlocked the glass door between the store and the pizzeria. "We don't open until one, but I make an exception for city skeptics."

As I followed, I peeked at Zachary, who stood at the far end of the aisle with his back to me, gripping the edge of the pay phone. He slammed down the receiver but didn't move.

In the pizzeria, Alexei flicked on the light, then the oven, then pulled two balls of dough from a stainless steel refrigerator. "I'll do one veggie, one meat, so yinz can appreciate the full spectrum."

I mentally translated the Pittsburghese "yinz" to "y'all," then sat at one of the tables near the window to keep an eye on the road. I wanted desperately to call Aunt Gina and Megan to let them know I was safe, but the act of calling could take away that safety—and maybe even endanger them.

But what would Logan do if I wasn't there in time? Could he turn solid without me? If not, he'd miss his last chance to play guitar in front of a crowd before he passed on.

Unless he decided to stay another three months, hoping for the chance to become human on the September equinox. I didn't even want to think about that.

Zachary came through the door from the shop. "Our ride will be here in six hours."

"Six hours?! It's noon. We need to be in Baltimore for Logan's concert by ten fifteen. It starts at ten thirty."

"It's not six hours each way. Our ride's not coming from Baltimore."

"Who'd you call? Was that the phone number you were trying to remember?"

"One of them. Come here."

I followed him through the outer door and into the parking lot. "Everything okay?"

"It's more than okay." He placed his hands on my shoulders. "Aura, I spoke to Eowyn. Remember she'd written her new number on the note with your mother's journal?"

"And you memorized it? Did you tell her what we found?" I would've bounced on my toes if he weren't holding me down.

"I didn't need to, because I'll see her next week when I'm home." His eyes sparked. "Where she'll give me her copy of your mum's journal pages."

I stared at him. "Wait—what copy?"

"Eowyn's not stupid. She wouldn't let something so important be so easily lost."

"But my mother sealed the envelope. She wrote across the opening."

"No, Eowyn did, faked the handwriting. She only promised your mum she wouldn't read them. She kept that promise."

I uttered the new truth in a trembling whisper, afraid to believe. "So it's not lost."

Zachary smoothed back my hair. "No' at all."

I gave a triumphant laugh and threw my arms around him. He lifted me off my feet, squeezing me tight.

By instinct I moved to kiss him. He jerked back just in time.

"Oops." I covered my mouth. "Don't want you turning me red before the concert."

"Right. Afterward, though . . ."

"Definitely afterward." I took his hands. "This is the last time Logan will ever come between us."

"I know." The heat in Zachary's gaze said that like me, he couldn't stop thinking about last night. About everything we'd done, in and by the river. About everything we had yet to do . . . somewhere, sometime.

The door swung open behind me, and Alexei called out, "Okay, people. Time to eat your words."

After six hours of fretting and eating (the best stromboli in the state), I was a complete stress mess by the time our ride arrived.

Zachary was stationed outside to flag down the driver. Through the glass front of the pizzeria, I saw his back stiffen at the sight of a black sedan speeding down the highway. I rose from my seat, waved good-bye to Alexei, and pushed open the door.

My fingers froze on the handle when I saw that the black car was a BMW. Convertible. Just like the one driven by . . .

You didn't.

Becca Goldman pulled up alongside us. With one long, French-manicured fingernail, she tilted down her sunglasses and looked at Zachary. "Now *you* owe *me*."

She switched off the engine, slid out of the car, and brushed her hand over Zachary's arm as she swept past us into the store.

Zachary gave me a sheepish look. "Sorry."

"What were you thinking? Becca hates me! She'd happily deliver me to the DMP."

"But she likes me slightly more than she hates you, so we come out ahead." When I didn't even crack a smile, he said, "Look, she's the last person anyone would expect us to call for help. The DMP has our phones, and her number isn't in mine anymore."

"But you remembered it."

"Eventually." He took my hand. "Aura, I'm not happy about this either, but I thought it was our best chance. She came all the way from Ocean City to help us."

"Why?"

"Because we need her."

I scowled at him. "Out of the goodness of her nonexistent heart?"

"Exactly." He tucked a lock of hair behind my ear. "Sometimes we help ourselves, and sometimes we get help from ghosts in the woods and bampots in BMWs."

The cowbell clanged as Becca swept out of the store. "Look at this!" She held out a small can of power drink. "I haven't seen Red Devil in four years. Apparently, the entire national supply is here in Where-the-Fucks-ville, Pennsylvania. I bought three—two for me, one for you." She pulled another can from a plastic bag and gave it to Zachary. "Let's go see this stupid concert."

"Two requests," he said. "One, stop pretending Aura isn't here. Two, put the top up on the car. We're hiding from the authorities, remember?"

Becca glanced at a spot above my shoulder, then hit the remote for the convertible top, which arced over the car's interior. "Let's go, Zachary and other person."

Though Zachary offered to let me sit up front next to Becca, I refused, preferring to huddle in the back and pretend that Becca's wish—that I wasn't here—was actually true.

Her energy drink took effect right away, and I wondered if it had disappeared from the mainstream market because it had been made from the pituitary glands of deposed dictators and executed serial killers.

After three and a half hours of crappy dance music and Becca's babbling about who was screwing who at Hailey's stepdad's beach house, we reached the Baltimore Beltway. Despite Becca redlining the Beemer's tachometer, we were running late.

She turned down the volume to near silence. "Here's the deal," she said. "Tyler has been texting his brother Eric, who's been texting his girlfriend, Alicia, who's been texting her best friend, Heather, the girl who plays bass in Logan's band. Logan knows you're coming, which means his brothers and sister and that bitch Megan know, too. They'll be looking for someone wearing that." She jutted her thumb behind her. "Zachary, tell your girlfriend to put it on."

I opened the plastic bag that had been shoved under the driver's seat. "You've got to be kidding me." I pulled out a wig with three-foot blond ringlets, along with a pair of plastic black-framed glasses. "How does this make me inconspicuous?"

"What about me?" Zachary asked Becca. "Won't I need a disguise?"

"No, silly. You're the diversion. You'll stay near the cameras, and if the DMP threatens you, you'll tell the whole story, adding the part where your girlfriend was tragically mauled by a pack of bears. It'll throw them off her trail."

"How official is this plan?" I pulled the wig over my head and began to tuck my dark waves underneath the elastic.

"I'll work on my story." Zachary turned to me. "Hmm."

I put on the glasses. "How do I look?"

"Gorgeous."

"Figures," Becca said. "I should've sprung for the fake warts."

"Becca," I said, trying to sound as sincere as I felt, "thank you for all you've done for us today."

"I did it for Zachary, not—"

"Bullshit. You're not even hot for Zach anymore since you got back with Tyler. You did it because you don't completely suck, and I appreciate that."

Glancing at the side mirrors, she switched lanes approaching the exit. Then she tapped her long nails on the steering wheel. "You're welcome."

Chapter Thirty

Six minutes before Logan's concert, Becca pulled up in front of his former high school in Hunt Valley. Camera crews from the local news stations were parked near the front entrance, and I saw a van with the logo of one of the big Hollywood media shows as well. I was glad Becca was going to drop me off around back, where no one would see me.

"Stay near the cameras," I told Zachary as he got out of the car, "in case the DMP tries to take you. But don't talk to the media if you don't have to. Remember, they are not your friend."

"Right." He grasped my hand through my open window and whispered, "I wish I could give you a good-luck kiss, but that would cause problems." He winked.

"It would also make me vomit," Becca said.

He gave Becca a brief salute. "Thanks."

She grunted, then slammed the car into drive. Zachary had to leap back to save his toes from being crushed.

"God, this place looks like a prison." Becca tore through the bus lane at thirty miles an hour, even though there were cars parked on both sides. "I always thought the Keeleys were cool," she said. "Sucks that they had to move to Hunt Valley and end up in public school. It would've been awesome to have a famous person from Ridgewood."

"Look, there's Megan." My friend was standing near one of the school's back doors, her foot propping it open.

Becca started to slow down. "About what happened prom night, with Zachary's phone? I'm really sorry."

I was too stunned to find the words. But as soon as I opened my mouth, she added, "I'm sorry it didn't work." She jerked to a stop and pointed at me. "You better be worthy of Zach, or I will fly home from UCLA and personally kick your ass. Now get out, and good luck."

I didn't bother with a retort. She had saved the day, after all, and besides, it was impossible to out-Becca Becca.

"Thank you." I opened the door and leaped out of the car.

Megan greeted me with a quick, hard hug, sweeping me inside the building. "Where have you been?" She led me down a dim hallway, past a door marked DRAMA, toward the backstage area. "We got the message you were on the way and you would look like a blond Little Orphan Annie. What happened?"

"Short version: The DMP picked up me and Zach. We escaped, so they're probably looking for us." We passed under a clock that read 10:25. "Long version later."

"Mickey's waiting for you offstage," she said as we rounded the last corner. "You should see his hair all bleached and spiked. He looks just like—"

We stopped. Standing in front of the door between the hallway and the backstage area was a uniformed DMP agent.

Watching us.

On reflex, I checked my wig, then realized that looked suspicious.

"Follow my lead." I took her arm and scurried up to the agent. "Um, hi? We're supposed to meet the singer backstage. You know, for after the show." I bit my lip and giggled.

He looked down his long, crooked nose at us. "I've heard about you ghost groupies. That's necrophilia, you know."

"Necro-what?" Megan piped, her eyes as wide as a manga heroine's.

"Never mind," he said. "Look, no one's allowed backstage but the band, and they're already there. The show starts in two minutes." He squared his stance in front of the door, to drive home his point.

Megan sidled forward, stroking her hair in front of her shoulder. "You know, if you let us in, we could find a way to thank you. Later."

"Miss, I am not some bouncer you can flirt your way past. I am a law enforcement official." He pointed to the hallway behind us, like he was banishing a pair of naughty dogs. "Out."

In the auditorium on the other side of the wall, the PA music faded out, and the crowd started to roar.

I'd have to find another way.

Megan and I squeezed through the mass of flesh to the front row. I hugged Siobhan and then Dylan, who tapped his watch and raised his eyebrows at me. Ten thirty. He didn't know that we had twenty-one minutes until the solstice—twenty-one minutes until his brother would be solid again.

The three human members of Tabloid Decoys came onstage, looking slightly terrified at the size of their audience. Logan's high school auditorium was the largest venue he'd ever played during his life, which was why he'd chosen it. Like most public schools, it wasn't BlackBoxed.

Corey, the drummer, sat behind his kit, while Heather and Josh picked up their bass and electric guitars. Logan's black Fender sat on a rack behind Josh. No one would think anything of it, since lots of guitarists switched out instruments mid-show.

The center of the stage went dark, like a reverse spotlight. The crowd screamed in anticipation, but my own throat trapped every sound. All I could do was stare.

And then, Logan appeared.

He glowed brighter than ever, as if the light inside him understood that this was the last night to burn.

Without taking my eyes off him, I slid my arms around the waists of Megan and Dylan. As we held tight to one another, I understood deep down that this was good-bye.

Onstage, Logan gave no fist pump, no cocky grin, not even a wave. When the crowd quieted, he stepped up to the microphone.

Clear and soft and sweet, he sang, a cappella, the first verse to the first song he'd written with the Keeley Brothers, "The Day I Sailed Away."

It was like he'd never left the stage. The post-Shifters in the crowd took a collective breath at the end of each line.

As he sang, his eyes searched the front row. With the stage in lights, the crowd in darkness, and his nerves on edge, it had always been hard for him to find me during a concert. Before each Keeley Brothers show, I'd tell him which top I'd be wearing so he could pick me out. No way he could recognize me now, in this ridiculous blond wig and glasses.

On the first chorus, the other band members joined with instruments and voices.

I shifted over next to Siobhan. "This song sounds empty without your fiddle."

Her eyes shone with tears. "It sounds empty without Logan."

I gave her another hug. Soon she and the other pre-Shifters would see and hear him one last time. I hoped.

At the end of the song, Logan remained at the microphone until the cheering subsided. He glanced nervously backstage, probably wondering where the hell I was.

"Thank you," he said. "Especially to you post-Shifters who came out to see a dead guy sing."

Beside me, Dylan translated for Siobhan in a low voice.

"As for the rest of you, who can't hear me," Logan said, "well—stick around."

With a nod of his head, he led Tabloid Decoys into one of their own songs. He screamed and crooned as the lyrics swung between tortured and seductive. During the interludes, he ran along the front of the stage, giving virtual high fives with his ethereal violet hands.

But the verses and chorus pulled him back to the center, like a dog on a chain too short. I closed my eyes, wanting only to hear him, not see him, trapped in front of a microphone he couldn't touch.

Megan squeezed my elbow. "I didn't think it would be so hard to watch him this way."

"They're loving it, all the people who never knew him alive. They think it's cool that he's a ghost."

She rubbed soothing circles on my back as the song reached its final chorus.

Logan introduced each of the Tabloid Decoys. As they bowed and waved, he said, "You gotta get their CD in the lobby after the show. They're freakishly talented." He grinned at his bandmates, then turned back to the microphone. "This next one's for my family, and all the children of the Emerald Isle."

With Corey's quick count-off, they launched into a Keeley Brothers classic, "Ghost in Green," bursting with Irish pride. The crowd sang along, and I finally let myself dance.

Afterward, as Logan conferred with Josh and Heather, I nudged Megan. "How close are we?"

"Ten forty-six. Five minutes."

"I need to get backstage." I craned my neck to see if I could sneak up the side stairs and behind the curtain. "Shit."

Two dumpers stood in front of the stairs, impassively looking out at the crowd like Secret Service agents. I checked the other side—same thing.

Panic spiked my pulse. If I wasn't backstage to help Logan turn solid, he would have to trade places with Mickey for real. After watching his big brother take the spotlight meant for himself, would Logan pass on? Or would he want another chance?

"This one's for Aura."

A hot shiver ran down my spine at the sound of my name from the speakers.

"You all know who that is by now. The only girl I've ever loved. I wrote her a song, but she's the only one who's ever heard it, or ever will."

The crowd gave off scattered boos.

"Oh, just deal with it," he said, smirking. "Anyway, this is by a band that used to be our favorite, Snow Patrol."

Josh strummed a series of soft chords, joined soon by Corey tapping on the drums. Heather played the melody on the bass, which gave it an even more somber tone than the original lead guitar version.

"Run" was a song about grasping for happiness just out of reach, about endless, temporary good-byes. A song only a ghost should sing.

Tears stung my eyes. How could his death hurt as much now as it did the night his heart seized and stopped? The loss was so much more than mine, and yet it felt like I bore the sorrow of the whole world.

As Josh played the swelling, hypnotic guitar solo, Logan swept his gaze over the front row, searching for me. His eyes held a lost, despairing look, magnified by the heartbreaking chords.

I reached up, knowing I was risking everything. With one hand, I pulled off my wig, and with the other, my glasses.

I wouldn't let fear come between us and our last good-bye.

Logan's gasp came through the microphone. He shifted as if to rush toward me, but the solo was ending. Time for the final chorus.

From the corner of my eye, I saw everyone looking, but I kept my gaze locked with his. He sang the last two lines strong and smooth, promising that he'd always be with me, even when I could no longer hear his voice. I whispered the lines with him, sending the promise right back.

The song ended, and I reached out my hand.

Logan gave me an amazed, grateful smile, then shouted into the microphone, "I'm about to do something that's never been done." As the crowd hushed, he lowered his voice. "I beg you, don't freak out, and don't try to understand. This might not work anyway, but if it does, please don't let them stop me. I need to play for as long as it lasts." He turned his gaze back to me. "Because after that, I'm gone forever."

Siobhan tugged my sleeve. "What's he saying?" she asked me, since Dylan was staring slack jawed at his brother and had stopped translating.

I kept my focus on the stage. "You'll see," I told Siobhan.

"I will? How?"

The members of Tabloid Decoys looked at one another, feigning confusion. They expected Logan to leave the stage and Mickey to walk on. Only Mickey, Megan, and I knew what was about to happen.

If it happened.

Logan stepped away from the microphone and slowly moved toward me. The auditorium silenced as he got down on one knee.

We were really doing this. It would be harder than ever to explain his transformation. But we both needed him to play.

He reached out his violet hand, palm up. "Thank you," he whispered.

I held my breath, slipped my hand over his, and believed.

The sudden warmth shot straight into my veins. Logan's hand closed around mine, and his eyes, now blue as sapphires, burned through me.

For a moment, we were all suspended in silence.

Then came the screams.

Dylan and Siobhan surged forward, elbowing me as they reached for Logan. Siobhan's voice pitched high and incoherent as she started to cry.

Logan hugged them both hard, his eyes squeezed shut. Then he shot offstage to where Mickey stood, disappearing long enough for a brothers' embrace before bouncing back onstage.

He grabbed the microphone in both hands, his face exploding into a smile at the sensation.

"Hey. Do not. I repeat. Do. Not. Panic. There's nothing to be scared of. This is just your average everyday fucking miracle."

Logan bounded over to his shiny black Fender, then knelt before it like an altar. He lifted the strap over his head. The instrument settled in his grasp, a part of his new, preciously temporary body.

Beside me, Siobhan was sobbing in Dylan's arms. "He looks so beautiful," she repeated again and again.

Logan conferred with his shell-shocked bandmates, caressing the curves of his guitar in a way that made my own skin tingle. As they reviewed the set list, he buttoned his shirt, open all these months.

Finally he patted Josh the guitarist's shoulder, then gave high fives to Heather and Corey, who stared at their hands afterward, stunned.

Logan adjusted the strap of his guitar, then hopped on his toes twice—just as he always did before starting a new set. The other band members retreated to their spots, and Logan went to the microphone.

"This song's for the ghosts." He raised the head of his guitar for a split second, then crashed into the four opening chords of "Shade." The band joined in, catching up by the second line.

Then they were off. Logan sawed away at the Fender like he'd never lost a minute of practice. All those weeks of air guitar had paid off.

The song drove forward relentlessly, fluidly, from the first movement to the second, changing tempo and key in a glorious rock opera fashion. Logan's face glowed like it never had as a ghost's, and I knew he had finally found, in his afterlife, one moment of perfect happiness.

When "Shade" crescendoed into the third movement, he nodded to Josh, who took over the lead guitar. Logan stripped off his own guitar and set it down, then grabbed the mic to carry with him. Punk rage spilled out of him as he pointed at the crowd and beyond, challenging the world to make sense of him and all the other lost souls.

Fury dissolved into charm as the song transitioned to the bouncy fourth movement. He moved to the other side of the stage and touched the hands of the crowd as he sang, just as he had before in his violet form.

They clutched at his arm and wrist, making him laugh and muff the lyrics. But the band caught up and caught on so he could run the verse again. Phones glowed all over the auditorium, people preserving and uploading the moment forever.

The final movement began with a cascade of noise. Logan picked up his guitar, but as he faced the front of the stage, he scanned the auditorium with alarm. I turned to see dozens of DMP agents swarming the aisles.

As a human or a ghost, he could be detained. They could trap him unless he passed on or turned shade.

His grip on the guitar's neck tightened, and with a wild wrath, he swung the instrument over his head, then smashed it against the stage.

Dylan clutched his head. "Holy shit, Dad's gonna freak."

I smiled. "Logan once told me, he always wanted to do that." And no one else would ever play that guitar.

Holding nothing but a scrap of fret board, Logan spoke to Josh, who continued the guitar solo, stretching and repeating it.

Then Logan shot across the stage, slid forward on his knees, and held out his hands to me. I shook my head, but he nodded and mouthed, *Now.*

I let him lift me onstage, then pull me to stand with him near the trapdoor, like we'd rehearsed. He bent low to my ear.

"I can't let them catch me," he shouted. "I have to pass on now."

"I thought to pass on, you had to be a ghost."

"I am a ghost. I may have a body, but I'll never be alive again." He pressed the fret board piece into my palm. "So this is it."

Logan took the microphone from its stand, then toed the trapdoor, testing it. The door dipped an inch and sprang back on its hinge, so I knew Mickey had unlocked it from below. Anyone investigating afterward would think Logan had disappeared through there. A foot in front of the door, the flash pot lay ready to burst into light and smoke, controlled remotely by a switch at Corey's feet.

I couldn't let Logan leave without his knowing the whole truth.

"My father was a ghost," I said, "when he made me. He was with my mom on the equinox, like you and I almost were."

The music seemed to fade with Logan's smile as he stared at me with full understanding. I wondered if knowing the truth would change his mind. If knowing the truth would change everything.

For a moment, his eyes grew inexplicably sad. Then his face relaxed back into a smile. "At least now you know."

"I'll always love you."

"I'll love you, too." He touched my face. "Forever."

He kissed me then, but not hard and full of longing as I'd expected. It was soft and sweet and chaste, his lips barely touching mine. Exactly like our first kiss.

Instead of a beginning, it was the end.

He took a step back and lifted the microphone to his full red lips. With our hands linked, he sang the last couplet with only a faint bass line for accompaniment.

Then Heather held the note on her bass as the crowd cheered, uncomprehending but knowing that this was one of the coolest things they'd ever seen.

Logan let go. I stepped back.

The climactic note approached. Corey raised his drumsticks, then slammed them down.

The stage erupted in sound and smoke and golden light. The glare made me shield my eyes, and as they closed, Logan's outline appeared behind my lids, in a pulsing violet afterimage. The band finished the song's last ten seconds in a giant, euphoric crescendo.

When I opened my eyes, Logan was gone.

Heather and Josh moved to center stage together and waved away the smoke, like a pair of magicians. Nothing remained. Corey came forward, and the three collapsed into an embrace.

The people in the first few rows clambered onto the stage, dodging security guards to grab pieces of Logan's shattered guitar.

I pushed my way toward the backstage area, hoping to escape the dumpers, who must have seen me with Logan. Besides, part of me still wondered: At the instant of the golden glow, had Logan gone through the trapdoor, or had he passed on?

Someone grabbed me. I yelped and turned, raising my fist.

Dylan put up a defensive hand. "Hey, it's just us." Megan and Siobhan were right behind him. "What the hell happened?" he demanded. "And why didn't anyone tell me?"

"Sorry," I said. "No one knew who didn't need to."

"Is Logan really gone?" Megan asked. "I thought he had to turn back into a ghost first."

"I thought so, too."

"I know where the trapdoor leads," Dylan said. "If he's still human and he went through it, maybe we'll catch him."

We rushed behind the curtain. Mickey stepped out, looking just like Logan.

"I saw him." Mickey released a beautiful smile, one I hadn't seen in months. He looked at Siobhan. "Did you see him?"

She nodded, then threw her arms around Mickey. The twins hugged and wept.

I spoke quietly to Megan. "Mickey should get onstage so people can start to believe it was really him." I cringed at the sound of Corey's drum kit falling over. "Soon."

"Yup," she said. "Definitely man-behind-the-curtain time."

Dylan nudged me. "Come on, before the dumpers get here and block everything off."

The two of us pushed past the remnants of sets left over from the last play, until we found the opening for the three-foot-high tunnel leading to the trapdoor. The tunnel itself was lined with blue running lights.

And it was empty.

Dylan and I stared at the darkness.

"You think Logan's really gone?" he said. "He did do the glowy thing. Or was that just the special effects?"

"I couldn't tell. I was so close, the light blinded me. Doesn't it seem like we should know?"

"You mean, feel his absence in our hearts or some shit like that?"

"Exactly." I held out the piece of broken fret board. "Here. I'm sorry we kept Logan's secret from you and Siobhan. It seemed safer this way."

"Yeah." Dylan took the shard of wood, cracked it in half, and handed me back the bigger piece. "I bet once the DMP gets ahold of us, the less we know, the better."

Chapter Thirty-one

A m I in major trouble?"

Gina tucked her bag tighter under her arm as she marched me down the hallway of Logan's high school. "If I weren't so grateful to see you alive, you'd be grounded until you collect Social Security."

"Sorry." We walked by the main entrance to the auditorium. Two hours after Logan's passing on, it was as empty as the rest of the school. The DMP and local police had cleared out the crowd, including the media, who by now had spread word of the "Miracle or Magic Trick?" to the world.

"This was not what we discussed," Gina said. "I thought the idea was for Logan to sing, and then pass on to celebrate the solstice. But then you bring Mickey onstage as a stand-in, and now people wonder if Logan really came back to life. It's chaos. Our clients won't want help passing on anymore—they'll want their lives back."

I stopped at a water fountain. "Only the crazy people will believe it actually happened."

"It's the crazy people I worry about." She came closer and spoke in a low voice. "How did you pull off that trick? When did Mickey and Logan switch places?"

I wiped my mouth on the sleeve of the clean shirt she'd brought me, gathering my thoughts. "Before the last song he did as a ghost. That was actually Mickey onstage, but we used special lights to make him look violet."

Her voice turned flat and angry. "Now it's my job to make sure the DMP believes that line of bull."

"It's not bull."

"Don't lie to me, Aura!" She shook her finger in my face. "I'm not only your godmother, I'm your lawyer. For your own protection, you need to tell me everything."

She was wrong. My silence would protect me much better than the truth ever could.

Even the DMP seemed to agree. The last thing they wanted was ghosts begging to be brought back to life, as Gina had suggested. So Nicola Hughes—who had spent the last two days trying to get me and Zachary released from a place we'd never arrived at—had helped us refine our story.

The debriefing after the concert had included me, Dylan, Megan, Mickey, Siobhan, and the members of Tabloid Decoys. The official story included the "magic trick" and ended with Logan passing on in the presence of close family. Family who were not yet available to speak to the media.

"All you need to know," I said, "is that Logan's gone for good, so he won't need legal protection anymore." My voice threatened to break as I thought of our last few moments, when our hands had touched for the final time. "He won't need anything anymore."

Gina put her arm around me as we continued down the hall, slower now. "I know it's not easy letting them go, even when they've stayed too long."

I frowned. To me, Logan had stayed just long enough. I now faced a true life-after-Logan, a life I was finally ready for. That didn't mean his departure didn't feel like having one of my limbs ripped off.

"Speaking of ghosts." I fidgeted with the comfortingly frayed belt loop of my jeans. "That guy you were in love with, the one who died and haunted you. What was his name?"

Her face pinched as she checked to make sure we were alone.

"Sorry if it's a bad time," I added.

"No, hon. With Logan leaving, I understand why you'd ask about him." She spoke in almost a whisper. "His name was Anthony."

My chest thrummed. "What was he like?"

She gave a little laugh. "He was kind and sensitive and smart. A little bookish, but also sort of a jock. Very stubborn. He never laughed at his own jokes, but he laughed at everyone else's." She rubbed her chin, showing a slight smile. "Let's see, what else? He ate, slept, and breathed the Eagles and Phillies. He preferred French pastries to Italian, much to your grandmother's disapproval."

I hesitated before asking for the answer I needed most. "You said my mom knew him."

Her smile widened on one side, making her look wistful. "That's when I fell in love with him. The first time she had cancer, before you were born, he drove her to all her appointments. He brought her food. He argued with the insurance companies for her. He was like her guardian angel."

"So he was a friend of the family before you, um, were with him."

"That's right." Her forehead creased, and I wondered if she was lingering on a memory, or trying to recall one just out of her mind's grasp.

Maybe my father hadn't been involved with my mom and aunt at the same time. Maybe when he was alive, he'd brought my mother nothing but comfort—though after his death, he'd brought her nothing but torment.

Thanks to what my mother had left behind, Zachary and I knew more truth than anyone alive, but we still didn't have all the answers. Yet.

We reached the front lobby, where a giant glass trophy case displayed the school's victories in everything from baseball to chess. Beside it was a smaller glass case built into the wall, of an entirely different sort.

"Oh my God." Gina put a hand to her long silver chain necklace. "That's beautiful."

Behind the glass lay a memorial for the students who'd never graduated. Not because they'd dropped out or started college a year early, but because they were dead.

Though he'd died eight months ago, Logan's wasn't even the most recent photo.

"I wonder how many of them are ghosts," Gina said. "Such a shame."

I remembered the idea I'd had by the river—that the Shine had reopened the world of the living to the suddenly dead. And that in response, the Shift had given the dead a way to find their peace. The Shift gave them us.

"It would've been more of a shame if Logan had never been a ghost," I told her. "This way he got a second chance."

"You mean a third chance." She patted my shoulder. "Are you trying to say being a ghost is a blessing?"

I thought of what Logan and I had shared last fall, and the way his face had looked tonight onstage, as a ghost and as a human. Some of the best days of his life were after his death.

I kissed my fingertip and pressed it to the glass in front of his photo. "For him it was."

I didn't have to go far to find Zachary. In the bus lane outside the school's front entrance, he stood with his parents next to a black sedan with tinted windows. Ian was off to one side, talking to one of the DMP agents who had debriefed me. Fiona spoke to Zachary as he leaned against the car, taking the weight off his hurt ankle. In the strobe of red-and-blue patrol car lights, I could see his jaw set in stubbornness.

When he caught sight of me, he set down his foot without a wince and moved in my direction.

His mother called his name, and Gina called mine. But we didn't stop until we were in each other's arms. For a long moment we barely breathed, much less spoke.

Finally he loosened his grasp to examine my face. "What did they do to you?"

"Asked questions. Mickey and I told them how the trick worked." Instead of winking, I squeezed his elbow. "I have to go to DMP headquarters on Monday for more grilling. But at least Gina'll be with me."

"What will you tell them?" He added in a whisper, "About your mother."

"Nothing. Hopefully, I'll bore the crap out of them and they'll let me go. For now." After all the trouble they'd gone to in capturing me, no way they'd give up on finding my secrets. "What about you?"

He dropped his arms but took my hands. "Not so lucky. The dumpers didn't like what I told the media about being illegally detained. They want me to leave the country."

I gasped. "You're being deported?"

"Not officially. By the time Immigration can draw up paperwork, I'll be gone anyway. But I'll be on a watch list, so it'll be harder to get a visa to come back."

I wrapped my arms around his waist. "Then I'll have to come to you."

"Promise?"

"Gina can only legally ground me until I'm eighteen."

Zachary stroked my hair. "Six months and a day."

"Besides," I said into his T-shirt so no one would hear, "I need to see Eowyn's copy of my mother's journal."

"True, it might not be safe for me to send it to you by post or e-mail." He put a hand to my chin, tilting it up. "But forgive me if it's not the first thing I show you when you arrive."

He kissed me then, because he could. I was free to be red, free to be his. Free to live, at last.

In a gesture of extreme mercy, Gina deferred my grounding until after Zachary left the country, so he and I spent Saturday catching up on everything we should've done sooner. Touristy stuff like the Air and Space Museum, and romantic stuff like a dinner cruise on the Inner Harbor.

We even went back to our sky-mapping field Saturday night, one last time. Without our sky maps.

Late Sunday afternoon, I drove the Moores down to BWI Airport, dropping them off to check in, then parking in the garage across from the terminal.

When I joined them at the end of the international terminal's long security line, I saw that the airline had loaned Ian a wheelchair so he wouldn't have to stand while they waited. His hair had thinned even more from the chemo, and his suit hung slightly loose on his once-muscular frame. But his green eyes still gleamed when he made a joke or gazed at Fiona.

Ian's renewed perkiness was partly due to his oncologist's rosier prognosis. The chemotherapy was buying him a few more months, and he was now expected to see the New Year. I hoped I would see him again, too, in this year and the next.

The security line moved way too fast, and before I knew it, the Moores stood a hundred feet from the boarding pass checkpoint. Time to say good-bye.

Zachary tugged me several feet away from the line. "I need to give you one thing before I go." He reached into the inside pocket of his blazer (his mother had insisted he dress up for the flight like a proper man), then withdrew a fat white envelope. "No, wait. Two things."

He kissed me as if we were the only two people in the airport, possibly the entire county. The terminal's noise faded as my mind heard nothing but our breath and the music stuck in my head—the music we'd listened to last night under the stars.

Zachary's face stayed near mine as he slipped the envelope into my hand. "Don't open this in front of me."

"Okay." I ran my finger along the seal, seriously tempted. "So we'll video-chat tomorrow after you get in?"

"Even if I'm completely shattered from the flight. But it'll be early for you, maybe five a.m."

"I don't care."

"Zachary, it's time!" his mother called.

He waved to her, then turned back to me. "We'll be together again soon, aye?"

"Aye," I whispered.

And with a sweet, fast kiss, he was gone.

Slowly I turned and headed down the long, polished hallway toward the main terminal. Halfway to the exit, I opened the envelope. Inside was a glossy brochure and three sheets of paper stapled together. My heartbeat surged.

Ballyrock Castle, County Meath, Ireland.

The first sheet was an e-mail printout addressed to Zachary.

> Re: Your reservation!
> This confirms your reservation and receipt
> of one night's deposit at Ballyrock Castle for
> the following dates:
> 20–24 December

The second sheet was a round-trip ticket in my name, from BWI to Dublin, departing December 19 and arriving the morning of December 20.

The third sheet was in Zachary's handwriting.

> Aura,
> Please say you'll come.
> Zachary
> P.S. Note the date I made the reservation.

I flipped back to the first page. March 30. Easter. The night I came to his apartment, the night we found out his dad had cancer. All along, he never gave up on us.

My new phone vibrated with a text message from Zachary. The DMP had returned the phones they'd taken from us, but we assumed they were bugged. So on Saturday we'd each bought a new one—red, of course—just for our own private communication.

I'M THROUGH SECURITY. SO YES OR NO?

I replied as I walked toward the exit: YES. 6 MONTHS = TOO LONG TO WAIT.

His reply: 6 MONTHS MINUS 1 DAY.

Me: OH. NO PROBLEM THEN.

Him: I LOVE YOU.

Me: SAVING THAT IN MY IN-BOX.

And then to follow up: I LOVE YOU.

Him: SAVED HERE. BYE.

"Aura."

I startled at the voice. Megan sat on a bench near the skywalk to the parking lot, drinking a bottle of iced tea. Her hair was pulled back into a long red braid, and she wore a blue cami with yellow capris.

I strolled over to her. "I didn't recognize you in color."

"Ha, ha." She stood and hugged me. "I figured you'd need a friendly face and a mocha fix right about now."

"I do. Where do you want to go?"

"Your choice. You're the one driving. I took the light rail down so we could ride home together. So you wouldn't be alone in the car missing Zach."

"Thanks. But what if your train had been late?"

"I would've called you and said to wait for me. Would've ruined the surprise, though." She slipped on her sunglasses as we entered the glass-enclosed skywalk. "Not that you seem surprised."

"I'm in shock." I handed her the papers Zachary had given me.

She started reading them. "Whoa." Her mouth rounded as she scanned his message on the last page. "How could you let that boy get on a plane?"

"It was two against one, and the two were his parents. I was legally doomed."

She folded the pages and gave them back to me as we entered the parking garage's stairwell. "Six months. My God, how will you last without your soul twin?"

"My what?"

"'Soul twin.' I came up with it a few nights ago." She shoved her sunglasses atop her head, fanning out her red bangs. "I was thinking about that VIP idea—you know, how you and Zachary got into the world when no one was supposed to?"

"I was thinking about it a few nights ago, too." I bumped my shoulder against hers. "Maybe you and I are soul twins, too."

"Nah, just soul sistahs." She offered me her iced tea. It wasn't the brand with the symbols under the lid, but I took a sip anyway.

"I thought you were going out with Mickey tonight."

"He's not here. Guess where he is?"

"A monastery?"

She laughed, harder than I'd heard in months. "He's at Shenandoah looking for an apartment."

I stopped. "He's going to college this year?"

"Yep. And since it's too late to get a dorm room, he has to find his own place." She grinned at me. "But that means when I visit him? No roommates."

"Sweet." I wondered if her mom would actually let Megan visit him, or if I would have to cover for her. "What changed Mickey's mind about school?"

"I think working with Logan the last few weeks, and especially seeing him last night, was really good for him. His parents seem happier, too, now that Logan's passed on, even though that scene Friday night was insane. Hey, speaking of Keeleys, call Siobhan and see if she wants to meet us for mochas."

I slowed down to pull out my original phone while Megan went ahead of me into the dark parking garage. Her head turned as she rounded the corner. I followed her, searching for Siobhan's number.

Megan halted. "Wow, I just saw your redness in action."

"Huh?"

She pointed to the garage elevator. "A ghost was standing next to that trash can, but she disappeared the second you walked through the door."

"Cool." I shrugged. "Won't last long."

My red "Zachary phone" buzzed.

I AM LOOKING AT A GHOST. RIGHT NOW. IN THE PUB. AMAZING . . .

I grinned and replied: ENJOY IT WHILE IT LASTS!

As we turned for my car, I looked back at the terminal, laughing at the image of Zachary spending the next hour or two pretending to his mom and dad that he didn't see ghosts. I'd opened up a whole new world of experience for him, even as he'd given me a whole new world of peace.

For a short time, we'd become each other, a little. Maybe that's what people do when they fall in love, mind, body, and soul. Or maybe we were just weird.

In any case, we belonged together, no matter what parents and governments had to say about it.

Soon enough, time and destiny would have their own say.

Chapter Thirty-two

After the marathon mocha session, which included profoundly delicious sandwiches—after my time in the woods I would never again take food for granted—I let Siobhan drive Megan home so I could make another stop alone. Somewhere I'd been only twice.

"Sorry I haven't visited much," I told Logan as I laid a bouquet of white roses on his grave. "It never seemed like you were here."

I stepped back, reading the scripture cut into the smooth stone: FOR WHAT IS SEEN IS TEMPORARY, BUT WHAT IS UNSEEN IS ETERNAL. Logan had told me he would've preferred something more contemporary, like, IT'S BETTER TO BURN OUT THAN TO FADE AWAY.

But eight months and three days after his death, I was starting to understand the quote his parents had chosen, and found it strangely comforting.

"I still don't know where you are. It seems like I should know, like there should be an empty space inside me." I swiped my hand over his full name, LOGAN PATRICK KEELEY, coming away with a thin layer of dirt. "But I still feel full. Maybe I always will. Maybe that's a good thing."

I rubbed my hands together, as if I could make the soil of his gravestone part of my skin. I hoped never to lose the part of Logan that dwelled within me. It would keep me from growing old, at least on the inside.

"You know what would be cool, next time?" said a voice behind me. "Black roses."

I lowered my hands slowly, then turned to face Logan. Standing beside his grandmother's grave two rows over, he shone violet in the fading evening light.

He tilted his head. "But my mom might think it's morbid."

I ran to him on shaky legs. "What are you doing here? I thought you passed on at the end of the show."

His face lit up. "Did you? Was it convincing?"

I could barely speak through my bewilderment. "It looked different from the other ghost I saw, but I thought maybe that was because you were going straight from human to gone."

"Turns out some things actually *are* impossible. You know, it hurt like hell falling through that trapdoor. They need a thicker cushion underneath." He beamed at me, literally. "Besides, I changed my mind."

My heart jumped and sank at the same time. "You're staying?"

"No, no. I'm definitely ready to pass on. But I decided I didn't want to do it in front of a crowd. I wanted it to just be us."

I gestured to the empty cemetery. "Here? Now?" My voice trembled with hope and fear.

"It's quiet. No music, no one screaming my name. Just you and me." He looked at the grave. "And Nana. Maybe I'll see her where I'm going."

I remembered Logan's grandmother weeping outside the funeral home during his viewing. "If she's still a ghost, maybe she'll follow you."

"That'd be cool. Can you help her pass on?"

"I'll try." When he frowned, I said, "All right, I'll make it my mission in life."

"Awesome. Oh, and there was a third reason why I wanted to do this here and now. I wanted you to know for sure that I was gone, that your secret was safe. No one'll ever know about your dad, not from me."

I knew then that he would have no trouble passing on, because he wasn't leaving only for himself. He was leaving to protect me. "Thank you."

"It's safe with Zachary, too," Logan said.

"How do you know he knows? I didn't tell you that."

Logan's eyes went round and innocent as he looked away. "I sort of talked to him. In the airport."

My jaw dropped. "You were the ghost he saw. When he was— when he had—"

"You, all over him? Yeah, I didn't see a bit of red on that dude. Must have been one hell of a good-bye kiss."

My cheeks heated. "Sorry."

"Don't be. I'm glad you have him." He touched his throat. "Wow, those words came out in one piece. They must be true."

I laughed, even as I wanted to cry. "Logan, why did you have to die to grow up?"

"Ha." He shoved his hands in the pockets of his baggy shorts. "You wouldn't have liked me as a grown-up. Just remember me like this. Or better yet, like I was when I was alive."

"Some of my favorite memories will be of you as a ghost. You had a good life, and a pretty good afterlife, too."

"One was too short and the other one, maybe too long."

We fell silent, staring at his headstone. The years on it were way too close together. Even the month and days gave me a pain under my ribs to see: October 18 and October 19—he'd died a few minutes after his birthday.

"So what happened with that kidnapping?" Logan said finally. "Did the dumpers hurt you?"

"Not directly. I almost fell off a cliff running away from them, though. I am so not the outdoorsy type." I looked up at the hazy orange-yellow sky. "But there were a lot of stars, more than I ever knew it was possible to see."

Logan followed my gaze. "I wonder if there'll be stars where I'm going."

"If there aren't now, there will be once you show up."

His eyes softened, and he lowered his chin to look at me. "I don't want to leave you."

"Don't worry." I stepped close enough to mingle with his violet glow. "You won't."

Logan wrapped his arms around me in an embrace as real as any that flesh could offer. "No good-byes this time. Been there, done that, right?"

I forced out the word, "Yes."

"Don't cry," he whispered. "I can't go if you cry."

It was too late, so I kept my face against his ethereal chest, my tears drenching the place where my name was forever inked.

But my next breath came slow and even, and the one after that was smooth as steam. The tears stopped flowing. Soon the last one dripped off my chin and fell at our feet.

"Ah, there," Logan said as a golden glow began to pulse at his core.

Part of me wanted to pull away, for fear of being engulfed in the light, maybe even dragged with him into that other realm.

But I was alive. No matter what forces had brought me into this world, I was here to stay for a long time. I could stand next to Logan, stand within him, while he walked that path without me.

Logan took his own deep, sweet breath, ready to sing a brand-new song.

"Close your eyes," he said. "It's gonna be bright."

Aura's search for truth—and love—
continues in

Shine

Don't miss the dramatic conclusion
to the Shade trilogy

COMING IN SUMMER 2012

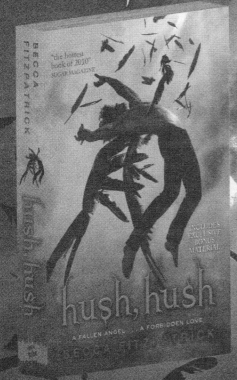